The Kelton Cases:
The Dead Priest

by K. A. Bledsoe

This book is a work of fiction. Names, characters and places are a product of the author's imagination. Any resemblance to actual events, places or people is purely coincidental.

Print ISBN 978-0-9815890-2-2

This title is also available as an Ebook.

Gardoyle Publishing
Cave Creek, Arizona
USA

Dedication

To all the authors that have come before, both recent and ancient.
Thank you for the stories that inspired our dreams and spurred us to
become writers ourselves.

And to all the future authors who I hope will continue to write,
keeping imagination and creativity alive in the human race.

Chapter One

"I have retrieved your heirloom brooch Miss Heldun, complete with its original box intact."

Lenore Kelton presented the trinket to the young lady. The box was open to display the exquisite diamond pin, the size of her palm but detailing a miniature garden with jewels, a truly unique, albeit a bit gaudy, piece of jewelry.

"Oh. Wonderful!" The twenty-year-old girl fluttered over, gathered and closed the box and tossed it to her makeup table, ignoring Lenore's intake of breath at this casual disregard of the million-credit brooch. Miss Heldun's eyes narrowed as she put her hands on her hips. "Did you also find the ruffian who stole it?"

Lenore sighed. These starry-eyed youngsters were all alike, thinking life was like a holonovel. She wouldn't even have taken the job without the fact that Dawn Heldun was the spoiled daughter of an extremely wealthy businessman who owned more than half of this planet and several moons. She'd given Lenore a contract promising a reward worth enough to refit the yacht with quality defensive systems. So, Lenore played along, trying not to roll her eyes.

"Of course I found the criminal. Couldn't pass up the offered bonus." She tapped on her wristcomp and her son Quinn came in, dragging a young man about the same age as Dawn. Cuffs bound his hands behind his back, he stumbled through the door, not fighting Quinn's grip even though he was the older one.

"Your thief, Miss Heldun," said Quinn, voice rough. Lenore approved of the disguised voice, slightly deeper and sounding like a tough enforcer or bodyguard. The helmet with an opening only for his eyes hid his true age of fifteen. Quinn gripped the other's shoulder to pull him forward and the boy fell to his knees, even though he had no reason for such weakness. Lenore hid a chuckle at Quinn's eye roll. Obviously, he felt the dramatics were as overdone as she did.

"Oh, Jack! Are you okay?" Dawn dashed to him and knelt to look him in the eyes, face scrunched into a frown. Lenore felt she hid her surprise better than Quinn when his eyebrows disappeared into his helmet as he looked at his mother.

"They didn't hurt you, did they?" Dawn said as her hands stroked Jack's face. "Poor baby. Why did you take Aunt Nikki's pin?"

"I needed something to remember you by, Dawny," he said. "If I couldn't be near you, at least I would have something that used to be close to your heart."

"Oh! If I'd known you cared so much…"

"I do, Dawny, of course I do."

She threw her arms around him despite his hands still bound behind his back.

Lenore groaned inwardly, tired of the display. She cleared her throat loudly, and the girl looked at her as if she had forgotten anyone else was in the room. She stood and raised her chin as she addressed Lenore.

"Thank you. You have done well. You may remove the cuffs as I am sure he poses no threat."

"I will do no such thing, Miss Heldun," Lenore said quickly to forestall Quinn's answer as she saw anger flare in his eyes. "He has committed a crime and will be turned over to the proper authorities. I only brought him here as proof that we captured him for the bonus you promised."

"Oh." Dawn shifted her feet and looked away. Lenore knew she wasn't going to like what came next. "I've heard the stories, about people who help innocents like me. I thought you were in it to do the right thing."

"We're in it for the money," growled Quinn before Lenore could respond. "Money you promised us."

"Oh," she took a few steps back from Quinn until she realized it put her closer to Lenore. Instead, she retreated to her table where she had thrown the brooch box. "Well, I don't have those kinds of credits on me or readily available."

Lenore reached into her jacket and, ignoring the girl's small squeak of fear, pulled out a data stick. "A credit transfer will do."

Now the girl retreated further until she was against the wall. "I...I can't do that. I...but my father can. He will take care of it, I'm sure. He always does." Now her chin came up again, but the slight tremble argued against the bravado. "Take the contract to him."

Lenore grumbled but pocketed the stick and jerked her head at Quinn to come. Quinn hauled Jack to his feet even though Lenore knew he would have guessed the girl's reaction.

"No, don't turn him in. I will drop the charges. Please, let him go. You heard him. He loves me, he wouldn't hurt me."

Lenore could see the anger in Quinn's eyes.

It's a good thing he's wearing that helmet. The girl might faint if she saw Quinn's whole face.

Quinn let Jack go with a small shove and tossed the electronic key for the binders to Dawn.

"So be it. What happens from here is on your head."

The girl winced at the comment and Quinn left, Lenore following her son.

As they were shown to the door by a servant, Lenore could feel the anger radiating from Quinn though she also felt a similar fire.

"That—"

"Shhhh!" she said and glanced back at Quinn and up at the ceiling to make her point. He followed her eyes and grimaced but didn't say anything until they were clear of any monitors.

Two blocks from the mansion, Lenore let Quinn vent.

"She had no intention of paying. What is it with the stupid holonovels and entertainment vids? I have seen enough of them to know that people get PAID for their services." He was pacing, throwing his hands up in emphasis, and looking around as if he wanted to hit something. Lenore watched, concerned about the volatile reaction from her normally even-tempered son. "Stupid stories ruining everything. Life is nothing like those shows."

Ah, thought Lenore, now slightly worried. He was still recovering from the previous case where he had been captured by slavers. His family had rescued him, but not before he had been tortured and put on the bidding block. His father, Diarmin, had told her Quinn's trauma would manifest in different ways and this was evidently one of them. *Maybe he isn't ready for missions yet.*

When he became aware of her scrutiny, Quinn stopped though he continued to smolder. Lenore decided to ignore the rant for now.

"Go back to the ship and inform your father of the situation. I will visit Mr. Heldun with the contract to get what we are owed." Quinn nodded, and she went on. "I will keep an open channel during the conversation and all of you, especially your sister, monitor and be ready for any possible situation."

"Dad, I can understand, but why do you need Allison listening?"

Again, she ignored the slight sulk in his voice. "I have a hunch that her excellent computer skills are going to be needed."

"Okay. See you back at the ship," he mumbled. As he turned to head the opposite direction, she stopped him.

"Quinn, despite the outcome, you did your job very well, although next time don't leave expensive binders behind." She held up the forgotten binders and grinned, hoping it would ease his anger.

His slight smile before he left did nothing to dispel her worry for him.

***

"What can I do for you?" Mr. Thom Heldun peered at a screen on his left as he sat behind a desk with many terminals in the desktop and on the sides. "Lenore Obar, is it?" The absence of any honorific and the fact he remained seated when she entered told Lenore that he considered her to be beneath him. As he probably did with most individuals not involved in his business affairs. In her experience, rich people were the same on every planet.

"Your daughter referred me and my business associates to you." She placed a pad on his desk with its display showing the contract signed by Dawn.

He laughed, not even bothering to look at the pad.

"Dawn? Referred you? Has she suddenly turned businesswoman?" He laughed again.

Taken aback by a father's complete lack of respect for his offspring, Lenore tapped the pad and pushed on. "She posted a reward for the recovery of a stolen piece of jewelry which we located. Before the search, we both signed a contract stipulating the amount to be paid as well as a bonus for also delivering the thief, which we did, well within the time allotted."

Heldun shook his head, continuing to chuckle. "You and your associates may be talented at locating people and things, but you failed to do your homework."

"Uh-oh," came Allison's voice through her subdermal audio implant. "Checking on it." Lenore could envision her daughter tapping away the instant she had picked up Heldun's comment.

"And what homework would that be, Mr. Heldun?" asked Lenore.

"Everybody knows that my daughter Dawn has no authority to enter into contracts with anyone."

"She is of legal age, with her own accounts."

"Ah, but they are only hers through me." He raised a finger and was obviously enjoying the 'lesson' he was about to impart. "When she turned eighteen, I knew that she was entirely capable of throwing away large sums on her imagination and idiotic, romantic notions. I had her declared incompetent to make any legal decisions without my approval. And," now he picked up the pad to peruse it, "as I do not see my signature on this document, this is not a binding contract." He let the pad clatter back onto the desk.

A groan coming through the implant did not bode good news. "I hate to say it but he's right. I found the document. Dad and I are looking for loopholes."

"You disagree with retrieving a precious heirloom?"

"Precious? Ha. She has a dozen of those which she has lost on a number of occasions. All her property as well as that item is insured. She only wanted to find her boyfriend of the week. Jeff, I think his name was."

Lenore didn't bother to correct him. "You feel no obligation to support your daughter in her decisions or life choices?"

"If I supported her or her mother's choices, I'd be completely broke."

Lenore picked up the pad and heard Diarmin's voice now. "Bad news. The only way we could get the money from her is if she wrote a new contract after she declared independence from her father, which would cut her off completely and thus would have no money."

5

"If there is nothing else," Heldun said as he pulled his side screen closer.

"I will be back for my payment, Mr. Heldun," she said, as she tucked the pad in her bag.

"I doubt it, unless you would like me to sue you for taking advantage of my daughter in her incompetency. Then it will be you who will pay." He didn't even bother to dismiss her, just turned his eyes to his work.

Knowing that was no idle threat, she turned and left without comment. She didn't need Diarmin's voice in her ear that echoed her own thoughts.

"Damn self-important rich asshole."

"Let it go," mumbled Lenore. "I'm heading back now. I need the walk."

"Understood."

It took more than half of the distance back to the spaceport for Lenore to get her emotions in check. The steady pace of her strides while dodging the crowds on the sidewalks helped settle her mind. *Time to look for another mission before all our money is gone.*

"Hello, Lenore."

Lenore froze at the voice behind her. It had been years since she heard it and could only mean one thing.

The Xa'ti'al had found her.

Chapter Two

"Careful."

That voice belonged to her former mentor. Slowly she turned to face him, his warning stopping her attempt to slip her hand under her jacket.

As he came into view, she could see the barrel of a weapon peeking out from under a harmless-looking bag carried over his shoulder. She dropped her arms at her side.

"Daviss. Four hundred Xa and you're the one who runs into me? What are the odds?"

He laughed and Lenore tried her best not to scowl. She hated that laugh. Not because it was annoying, but because it was perfect. She could never tell if he was truly amused or faking.

"The odds are, I'm sure, not worth figuring out." He sobered. "Let's go somewhere to chat."

"I'd rather stay here, if you don't mind," she replied.

"Come now," he tilted his head slightly as if chastising a youngster. Her blood pressure rose another notch as he continued. "You know very well if I wanted to drop you, I would have done so by now, and that crowds wouldn't cause me to hesitate one bit."

"Fine. Where?"

He shrugged. "You pick." The attempt to put her at ease only raised her anxiety. Using all her will, she turned her back on him, against instincts screaming at her not to, and led him to a place only two buildings down the street, an upscale restaurant, quite pricey for the area. If he was surprised at her choice, he didn't show it as they were ushered to a seat.

"You are buying, aren't you?" asked Lenore as she scanned the menu. "I am famished."

"By all means," he replied as he stowed the bag. Lenore should have felt relief at the vanishing of the barrel pointing at her, but her senses were on high alert. She entered her order on the table's console and he did as well. She leaned back, trying for nonchalance and debated with herself to keep quiet so he would speak first. Realizing this was a useless ploy against the person who taught her how to do that, she started the conversation.

"So, what brings you out to this part of the universe?" she said.

"I was on assignment and ran into an interesting tidbit that indicated where you were. You really should change your name, you know."

Lenore tried not to let him rattle her. He knew her name was the only thing she had that was hers. He knew she would be thrown by the idea that she had been sloppy. He knew her and how to push her buttons.

After all, he had programmed her.

But *she* knew that there were thousands of Lenores across the galaxy. And the fact that they had been on this planet for less than a day meant that the 'interesting tidbit' was nothing of the sort. She would figure out how he found her later. For now, she wanted information.

"Looking to cash in on the reward posted for me?" she asked, remembering her face on a pad, held by her interrogator in the stronghold of a high-up person in a prominent slave organization.

"Don't be ridiculous. You know I am not in this for the money. I couldn't collect that anyway since it was the Xa'ti'al who posted that."

"Why the bounty? Isn't it bad advertising suggesting that the Xa can't find someone?"

He shrugged again. "To keep you on your guard. Make others do the work of finding you. But most of all," he paused and narrowed his eyes slightly. "To keep your nose out of our affairs."

Fortunately, the server arrived with the food, giving Lenore time to rid herself of the chills produced by the menace in Daviss's voice.

"I want nothing to do with the Xa or its affairs. I'm keeping my distance." She took a bite.

"The Beryshie Corporation would say otherwise."

She swallowed, food competing with the sudden lump of fear in her throat as she recognized one of the fronts for the slave organization she had been investigating. Deliberately she took a few more bites as she tried to decide if she would feign ignorance. A glance at Daviss showed him eating as well, but his eyes were uncannily riveted on her, watching for her reaction. Though she was unnerved by the scrutiny, it also told her that he knew a lot about her recent actions. That decided it for her. She put her fork down.

"Let's stop this fencing, shall we? What exactly do the Xa'ti'al have to do with the Beryshie Corporation?"

His smile did not reassure her. "Only the Xa are privy to that information. If you want to know that, you should come back."

"Are you giving me a choice? I figured you were here to either force me to return or kill me."

He tilted his head again with that infuriating grin. "Well, I would like it to be your decision."

Lenore set her jaw and looked directly into Daviss's eyes, trying to convey her seriousness. "I will never work with people who work with slavers."

Daviss looked completely unruffled as he continued eating. "You knew nothing about Beryshie when you left and what you know now isn't what you think."

"Enlighten me." She pushed her plate away, appetite gone, and sat back in the chair, arms crossed.

"On the surface, yes, it looks like we are working with them. Despite our abilities, we have only managed to insert two agents and they are relatively low-level. They give us what information they can so we can eventually bring them down."

Lenore shook her head. "I don't buy that. By myself I managed to take down a significant portion across an entire planet. If the Xa truly were trying, the entire slave ring could be broken."

Daviss guffawed, turning the heads of other patrons. Lenore knew he was trying to rattle her, and his next words proved it. "Your ego is as large as ever. First, it wasn't 'by myself' at all. You had your talented family and the royalty of the planet helping you. And second," he paused to take a sip of water. "It was only a tiny portion, a nuisance, impacting the organization about as much as an insect bite. But." He put the glass down and leaned toward her slightly. "Even an insect bite can be irritating. You have been noticed and rumors of Xa'ti'al involvement are undermining our efforts."

"Efforts. Hah." Lenore shifted in her seat, uncomfortable at his detailed knowledge of the previous case. She stared back and attempted to steer the subject away from her family. "The Xa doesn't work for free. You won't take down the organization unless you are paid very well. The only reason you have undercover agents is probably for threats, leverage, or extortion."

His eyes narrowed slightly, and she felt a brief satisfaction at having elicited a reaction. But it was very brief and gone with his next words.

"Perhaps. But another job of the agents is to find recruits."

Lenore did her best to hide her surprise but knew she was unsuccessful when Daviss went back to eating, a tiny smug smile showing between bites. But she would play along with whatever game he was working at. All this open talk was unsettling.

"Oh?" She took a sip of her drink, waiting for his elaboration.

"Of course. The organization is excellent at finding a wide range of individuals and a select few are acceptable to join our elite ranks. After all, isn't life as a Xa'ti'al better than a slave?" He wiped his mouth with his napkin and pushed his own plate aside. "And yes, if the Xa really tried we could take them down but if we did, another would pop up in its place and we would have to start all over. So 'the enemy you know' as they say. This way, we can keep some of the worst atrocities at bay and save lives."

"Ah, I see," she replied, but she didn't believe this angelic act one bit. She knew too much.

"So, come back. If you want to take them on, who better with than us? We can also protect you from them. You know they will be coming after you, if they aren't already."

Lenore said nothing. He pressed on.

"You won't be punished, and your husband and children can become part of our family as well. I remember how talented Diarmin is and, from what I understand, your children are exceptional and perfect for the Order."

That did it. The thought of Quinn and Allison in the hands of these ruthless mercenaries sent an icy wash of fear through her entire being.

"You stay away from my family." Her voice was low, rough.

Daviss spread his hands. "If you come back voluntarily, I can guarantee their safety. If not, well..." He brought his hands together with one resounding clap. The threat was obvious, but Lenore knew it to be more. He knew her well, but she also knew him.

Before the echo of the clap faded, she had pulled out her blaster and held the barrel an inch from his nose.

"Call them off, Daviss," she said, ignoring the screams and scrambling of other diners.

"Call them off?" To his credit, he didn't flinch at the gun.

"You should get some new hand signs. I know that clap was a signal to whomever is waiting to take me in. Call them off or you will have only a millisecond to regret it."

"A public murder? It's not your style, Lenore. Besides, kill me and you will never be able to hide again."

"You threatened my family. You tell me if I am capable of killing to protect them."

Without his eyes leaving hers, he made a dismissing motion with his right hand. Had it been his left, it would mean to attack. She didn't remove the blaster.

"This is unnecessary. Everything would be solved if you simply returned."

"I won't go. I won't leave my family."

"The Xa'ti'al is your family. These others are just a distraction. You will come back. In one way or another, Lenore."

"We'll see."

Suddenly all the power in the restaurant cut out and darkness enveloped them. Lenore dove in the opposite direction she figured Daviss would and rolled to her feet, blaster stowed and night vision goggles in her hand. His curse as he hit the floor showed her guess to be right and she headed for the back door at a crouch, dodging between tables. She hit the door at a full run, hoping it was unlocked. It opened with a crash and she found herself staring down a different gun barrel.

Chapter Three

"What took you so long, Diarmin?"

Diarmin holstered the weapon and slammed the door shut, barring it from the outside with a large metal bar.

"I thought my timing perfect." A crash into the door and more loud curses indicated the Xa's attempts to follow. He grinned at her.

"I hope that hurt."

She couldn't help returning the grin. "Time to go." She started in the direction of the spaceport but stopped at her husband's whistle. She looked back to see him on a speedcycle.

"This is probably faster than on foot," he said, revving the engine.

Lenore wasted no time climbing on the cycle behind him.

"Hang on," he said.

She gripped tightly with her legs and clutched her arms around his waist as the cycle shot forward. In a heartbeat they were out of the alley. As he turned in the direction opposite of the spaceport where the ship was docked, Lenore shouted in his ear, hoping she would be heard above the rush of wind.

"Don't worry about misdirection. Go straight to the port."

Diarmin nodded and turned down a street, weaving expertly in and out of traffic. Another talent of his that she hadn't known. He lifted the cycle over another vehicle to avoid a collision.

It flies, too? Then she was too distracted merely holding on to think further.

In no time, Diarmin shouted, "Open the pod bay doors, Alli!"

Lenore didn't see a communicator but assumed Diarmin knew what he was doing as he brought the cycle over a wall. Directly in front of them was the shuttlepod with the cargo bay doors sliding open. He slipped in with inches above and below and braked hard to a stop before they became a smudge on the opposite wall.

"Close and prep for launch," he said.

"Already on it," came Allison's voice over the shuttlepod's speakers as the doors began to close. "Launching after you dock."

The ship was close by, queued up with other ships prepping for departure so Lenore and Diarmin were heading through the shuttle airlock in record time.

"Let's get to the bridge," said Diarmin. He headed across to the bridge with Lenore only a step behind. As they entered, Quinn got up from the navigator's seat with a pad to show his father. Without taking his eyes from the pad, Diarmin took his seat to handle take-off.

He swiped and tapped briefly then handed the pad back to Quinn.

"Good job. I only adjusted the first stop. The rest of the course will do fine. Strap in everyone. We aren't waiting for permission."

Long practice had them secured in their seats, Allison at her console, Quinn at navigation and Lenore in the chair at the science station. Diarmin maneuvered the yacht out of the line and to the proper distance as expertly as he had driven the bike. Quinn closed the communication channel on a protesting Flight Control.

"Here we go," he said, and everyone braced themselves as the ship jumped into quantum drive.

"Tracking program done," said Allison. "No devices detected."

"First course change in two minutes," added Quinn. "The next in two hours."

Lenore checked her wristcomp. Only fifteen minutes since they left the restaurant. Not bad for an ex-Xa'ti'al mom, mechanical genius father, fifteen-year-old son and eleven-year old daughter. Not bad at all. She smiled at her talented family. No way was she giving this up for anything.

After the course change, Diarmin tapped a few commands and pushed back his chair.

"What an adrenaline rush." His huge, infectious smile showed white teeth against his dark skin. "Anybody for some food?"

Chapter Four

"Aw, isn't there something other than this hoity-toity food?" Quinn's voice was muffled with his head in the cabinets. He yanked open the refrigerator, but Allison beat him to the prepacked pasta that was their favorite.

"Hey, that's the last one," he said.

"Gotta be faster," replied Allison. "There's some stew way in the back. I'm not a fan of this new stuff either." She pressed the heating switch and by the time she was at the table removing the lid, the pasta was steaming.

"Sorry, kids," said Diarmin as he began looking for his own food. "That's what happens when you get a free restock from a king's supply. People pay a lot for these delicacies."

His comment was met with groans, and he chuckled. Lenore moved up behind him after Quinn left for the table. The galley had barely enough room for two and couldn't hold three.

"To be honest," she said. "I am a bit tired of this fancy stuff. Not for me."

"Me either, but my grocery run was cut short. Good thing I purchased the speedcycle first."

"I was wondering if we skipped out with a rental," Lenore said as she fixed her own plate. Diarmin grabbed utensils since his food didn't need heating and sat across from his children.

"Nope. I figured the cycle would come in handy in traveling quickly around cities, but I didn't think I'd be proven right so soon." He took a bite, noting Lenore's grimace out of the corner of his eye.

"And you were right to keep the lines open, Dad," added Allison. "Though how did you know that guy wasn't friendly?"

Diarmin made a show of chewing and swallowing to give himself time to answer. A glance at his wife showed her eyes slightly widened as they flicked to both kids and back to him. He read that silent message loud and clear.

"I recognized the voice, that's all. And you know your mother has taught us to always have a back door."

"Which reminds me," said Lenore as she sat. "How did you hear me? And talk to Alli? I didn't see a communicator."

Quinn gave his mother a look that told Diarmin he knew very well she was changing the subject, but Diarmin followed Lenore's lead. He reached behind his ear and peeled off an oval the size of his thumbnail and colored to match his dark skin perfectly.

"My new microreceiver patch. And I have a transmitter, too." He peeled a similar diamond shaped patch off his throat. "We don't have the luxury of implants like you, so these are my solution. The transmitter reads signals from the vocal cords, and the receiver transmits directly to the aural receptor. Except if it is slightly off, it makes for horrible tooth pain." He rubbed his jaw at the memory.

"Quite clever," she said.

"Not quite up to subvocalization like yours, but I'll get there."

"What about lighter-colored ones for me and Alli?" asked Quinn.

Diarmin glanced at Lenore. She had her head down, appearing to be completely engrossed in eating, but he knew she was probably struggling not to say anything. She was still trying to accept the fact that their children wanted more active roles in their missions. "That's next on the list, but I didn't have time to acquire the proper materials. Or enough money." He winced inwardly at the slip, knowing the reaction Quinn would have to the mention of money.

"It always seems to come down to a lack of credits, doesn't it?" Quinn said, the bitterness obvious. "We simply aren't getting any jobs that pay."

"It's my fault," said Allison in a soft voice. "I should have found that declaration of incompetence."

All three reassured the girl, and Diarmin was glad to see contrition on his son's face. Allison was the most sensitive of the four, and Quinn was being oddly protective of her since the family had witnessed a brutal killing on a previous mission.

"Now, Alli. Both Dad and I agreed that the information about the contract was well hidden and very difficult for anyone unfamiliar with this planet to find."

"But hacking to find things is what I am good at."

"There was no reason for you to look," said Lenore. "That kind of control over a family member, especially an adult, is virtually unheard of. Not to mention, inhuman." The anger on Lenore's face surprised Diarmin and spoke of something personal about her that he was unaware of. "People like Thom Heldun enjoy watching people get roped into doing things like we did and not get anything out of it. It is why ruthlessness, lack of empathy, and even cruelty are common traits of the extremely wealthy." Her hands were clenched on either side of her plate, eyes glued to the rest of her uneaten dinner.

Both children were staring at their mother, obviously unsettled at her vehemence. Diarmin changed the subject.

"Why don't we try something different for our next job?" he asked, hoping his voice had the right balance of casual interest.

All heads turned to him, but only Quinn voiced the question that was in their eyes.

"What?"

"Something different. Instead of going to a planet to find something or fix something, why don't we try, oh, I don't know, say transporting something. We could haul cargo or even passengers."

Quinn blinked, Allison tipped her head thoughtfully, and Lenore's fists slowly uncurled. Diarmin hid a sigh of relief, glad his diversion was working.

"There are those three cabins on the other side of the galley that we never use. Or even go into, for that matter," said Allison.

"I sometimes forget they are there," said Quinn with a small smile. "Are they even usable? When was the last time we were in there?"

"I think it was the last time we played 'Hide and Seek' when Alli was seven and she hid in the middle one," said Diarmin.

Quinn laughed out loud. "I almost forgot about that. We were so scared we couldn't find her that we almost called Mom back from her job as the bodyguard."

Diarmin laughed too until he saw the look on Lenore's face. Since she lost her bio medplant that the Xa'ti'al had put in to regulate her

16

body's systems for missions, her emotions were much stronger and easier to read. Seeing those emotions was good in some instances, but not when he could easily see her regret for missing much of her children's younger years.

He pointed at the rarely used door on the other side of the lounge. "Good thing I noticed that door was slightly open." Everyone looked at that closed door. The port side was used all the time since it led to each of their cabins, but the starboard side had rarely been used.

"Wait, didn't Jonah use one when he was on board?" asked Quinn.

"No, he was going to stay in your room since you were in the lounge with the rescued slave children," said Allison, but her smile faded as Quinn's face went blank. It always did when he was reminded about when he was captured and nearly sold by the slavers. "But we finished quickly enough that he left before he needed to use the room."

"And since the grav plates were installed by the king's ship mechanics, we have plenty of room for cargo, if we don't find passengers," added Lenore.

"But if we get people, we can serve them the expensive food so that we appear upscale and also get rid of it at the same time," argued Allison.

"And we need to ask for money up front," said Quinn, emphasizing his opinion by tapping on the tabletop. "Some if not all."

Everyone began speaking all at once voices gradually getting louder in order to be heard. Diarmin put his fingers to his lips to give a piercing whistle. Silence was instant, and he was startled at the surprise on his children's faces. For a brief second, he thought he saw fear, then decided he imagined it.

"Enough," he said holding his hands up and grinning to soften their reaction. "I can see we are a family of thinkers, but let's not argue about it. There is plenty of room for both, so we will see who answers an ad first."

"I didn't know you could whistle like that, Dad," said Allison, eyes wide.

"I've whistled before," he said, confused.

"Yeah, when you are working, but that's like songs or tunes, soft," answered Quinn. "Not loud like that." He smiled slightly. "Can you teach me that?"

"Me too," Allison said.

Lenore laughed. "Later we can have a lesson on whistling. For now, Alli and Quinn, you go look at those cabins and see what we need to do to prep them for passengers. Your father and I will go create a message to see if we can find either people or cargo to transport. With luck, we might even get both. Now, scoot!"

Chapter Five

As the children scampered to the guest rooms, Lenore and Diarmin climbed to the bridge to fashion a message.

"Are you sure about passengers?" she asked. "You know I don't like strangers aboard the ship for any length of time. What if they figure out who we are?"

"I know your paranoia has kept us out of trouble more than once, but in this huge galaxy, chances are pretty low that we will run across someone who knows us." He winced and she knew he was thinking of the encounter with Daviss. "Well, someone *else* who knows us." He squeezed her arm gently as they sat behind the main console. "Passengers or cargo means we will spend a very short time anywhere, only long enough to load and unload. Also, we'll use one of our fake ID's and check anyone out."

"I'm cautious, not paranoid," said Lenore, trying not to sound petulant. "Especially after seeing Daviss."

"I understand," he said with a nod, and to her relief, seemed to let it go. She did want to talk about it, but not before she had time to process the event and consider everything about the conversation with Daviss. "So how do we advertise?"

"Let's start on the closest systems," she said. "Since we can only take a few, we need to indicate that we have limited space."

"Though if we get more, you and I can bed down in the cargo bay. Kids too, if necessary."

"Or if we have too much cargo, we can use the rooms to store it."

Half an hour later after discussion and some arguing, the message was ready.

"Shall I transmit?" asked Diarmin.

"No, wait until we see which fake ship ID Allison comes up with. We will need to tag the message with that."

"Of course." Diarmin punched a few keys to save the message.

Lenore stood to go check on the kids' progress.

"Wait," said Diarmin.

She sat back down, concern growing as she noticed the frown lines crossing Diarmin's brow. Experience told her he was contemplating a subject that was difficult to talk about.

He stared at the console for several heartbeats before speaking again, time enough for Lenore's stomach to knot itself fairly well.

"Have I really never whistled like that in front of the kids?"

Lenore knew the question sounded harmless, but the tone of his voice was low and slightly hoarse, so she knew he was holding back some emotion. But which emotion, she wasn't sure.

"I think I remember when Quinn was a baby it scared him, so you decided not to do it. Then you got out of the habit."

"Yes. I used to do it all the time." He still hadn't looked at her. "And now I just did it without thinking, like the old days."

She knew what he was trying to avoid saying, but she felt the topic shouldn't be buried anymore. "That reminds me. I noticed outside the restaurant you had a blaster."

Now his head came up and the look on his face made her regret bringing up the weapon, but it needed to be discussed. For his sanity as well as hers.

"It was set on stun." His gaze dropped again.

"Come on. I know that model has no stun setting." She reached out to cover his hand that was picking at a stray thread on his pants.

"I heard Daviss's voice and I was afraid for you. I had to be prepared for anything."

"Is that all?" She hated herself for pushing, but it was a pressure building. She also knew that he would have had the blaster long before Daviss arrived.

"Well, no." He launched out of his chair, and she thought he was going to leave but instead he leaned against the wall, breathing deeply. She waited.

"I … when I heard him. I was instantly transported to that time. To who I was. I…" he closed his eyes and shook his head. "I have been going there much easier since the…since Lord Timatay's estate."

"But you didn't kill anyone. We talked about this before. You did what was necessary to rescue me and protect the kids."

"But it has brought back all the memories. Nightmares. I'm even having…" he turned to face the wall, one arm against it as his head drooped. "Having violent impulses again. Quick flashes and easily suppressed, but the fact they are back scares me."

"That's why you shouldn't suppress them. You learn to control them, make them useful."

His head snapped around, eyes on fire. "Is that your Xa'ti'al training talking?"

"Well, yes. I know I hate the order, but they do know how to deal with those kinds of, um, issues."

"Issues? Or people? Am I one of 'those' people?"

"No, *I* am one of those people," she said, perhaps a little too savagely as she saw him recoil. "You *were* one but had to hide it in order to raise our children the right way. The way we never had as children." He was visibly relaxing now. Thinking about Allison and Quinn usually did that for him.

"That's true. I just hate being out of control." He straightened up. "I will manage. It's why I thought of passengers or cargo. No chasing lost princesses or dealing with slavers. A simple pick up and drop off. It will give me time to settle down. In fact, all of us need to have some down time. It's not just me. The kids are still showing the strain of our previous job. And you."

"I have noticed that every conversation seems to bring back unpleasant memories."

"It could have been a lot worse." Diarmin smiled. "We all came through with no permanent physical damage and the emotional wounds…we will help the kids get through all that."

"Yes, we will." Lenore smiled, but it disappeared as she took a deep breath. She hated herself for what she was about to say, knowing it would ruin the peace Diarmin was beginning to feel.

"Maybe you, or we, should consider telling our kids about our pasts."

"Never!" he said, arms scissoring downward in a cutting motion. "They know you were a Xa'ti'al, but I never want them to know what I was. Never." His head came up again. "Wait. Why did you suggest that?" His face turned thoughtful. "Did you already tell them?"

"No—" she began, but he ignored her.

"Is that why…the other day, Alli and Quinn had their heads together at her computer, but she blanked the screen when I walked in and their faces were guilty. I figured it was just kid games or some harmless site, but they have been acting strange." His face darkened. "The way they jumped when I whistled, almost as if they were scared. And they have been a little distant." Diarmin stalked over to Lenore and leaned in. "What did you say to them?" His voice was low, with a menace that unnerved her more than he ever had since they had met.

She lifted her chin. She'd regretted what had happened, but she wouldn't hide from her actions. "Quinn overheard you saying, 'Seventeen years, two months and three days' and he asked me about it." She kept talking, trying to ignore the thunderous look growing worse. "I could tell the two had discussed it and were very worried. I didn't tell them what you used to be, I only said it had been that long since you killed someone and that you were no longer that person. At all. Then I told them to drop it and that we would discuss it later."

Diarmin took a step back, crossing his arms. Somehow his silence was worse than his previous reactions. She wanted him to yell, argue. The angry disappointment was unbearable.

"I made sure they understood that was your past, you're a different man now." She stood and reached for him, wanting him to understand her reasons. He stepped out of her reach, and her arm fell to her side.

"You had no right," he said, softly.

"I know I was wrong. I'm sorry. Let's…" her voice trailed away at Diarmin's implacable expression.

"Okay, I've got a list and while there's a lot, we can do most of it ourselves, with only a few supplies." Allison breezed onto the bridge holding a pad, breaking the stare between husband and wife. Diarmin said nothing, just turned and disappeared down the ladder.

"Um, Mom?"

"It's okay, Alli. We just had an argument. Nothing to worry about." She held out her hand for the pad and plastered on a smile. "Let's see what we've got." She hoped Allison couldn't see how heavy her heart had become.

Chapter Six

"Hey, we got one."

"An answer to the ad?" Allison responded without looking up from her station on the bridge. Quinn had been in the navigator's seat idly charting courses for practice when the message pinged in.

"Yup. It's for cargo and one person from the planet Drenon to the Reese system." His fingers flew quickly through the program. "*Hm*, not bad. Trip will take roughly seven to ten days, depending on how straight a path we take. Go tell Mom and Dad while I figure a course."

"Oh, no. I'll do background checks and gather information about the planets while *you* go tell them. We need that before we need a course."

Quinn opened his mouth to argue, but he knew his sister was right. He also knew why he didn't want to deliver the message.

"I…it's just…I can't talk to either of them right now," said Allison in a whisper. Apparently, she felt the same as he did.

"They *are* being weird," he said.

"I know, right?" Allison glanced toward the ladder and then moved closer to Quinn to speak in a low voice. "Have they ever been like this before?"

Quinn shook his head. "No. I mean they've argued and had fights, but it's never been like this. I mean, not talking to each other? For three days? Are you sure you didn't overhear anything?"

It was Allison's turn to shake her head. "Like I said, when I came in, they were just staring at each other, but the tension… do you think it's something we did?"

"I don't think so. They're fine with us. It seems like Dad is angry, and Mom is letting him keep his distance."

"I don't like it," said Allison.

"Try being on the receiving end of a frustrated mother while training. I must have hit the floor a hundred times." He rubbed his shoulders and felt a little better at Allison's snort of amusement. Even though she was teased for only loving computers, she felt everything intensely. Quinn had worried for her when she had witnessed Lavan's death. Every little smile since then he counted as a win.

"I'll go tell Mom." He stood to head down the ladder. "You do the research so when they read the message, they will have information."

"Maybe with something to do, a mission to focus on, things will get better."

"I hope so." He patted his sister's shoulder awkwardly. "They probably will."

But as he climbed down the ladder to search for his mother, he wondered if the wall between his parents was already too strong to breach.

***

Lenore grabbed a pan and winced when she slammed it down too hard. She wasn't really hungry, but a training session with Quinn followed by her own strenuous workout hadn't gotten rid of her pent-up energies. She'd been through idle spells before and while it had only been three days since the advertisement was placed, her nerves were raw. She knew Diarmin needed his space, but he had never shut her out like this. Still, she felt he was overreacting since she really hadn't told the children anything about his past.

As she leaned down to find something to cook, light brown locks of hair obscured her vision. Roughly she shoved them back behind her ears, thinking she needed to cut her hair, or at least get something to hold it back. Rummaging around for some kind of comfort food, shoving aside expensive canapes and delicacies, her mind wouldn't give her peace.

And this was the worst time for Diarmin to not talk to her. She needed someone to bounce ideas off of about how Daviss had found them and even knew their activities down to the last detail. The planet of their previous mission was not a big intergalactic-known world, so any information about them would have to have been gleaned from someone with direct contact on the planet. And that was what worried her. She froze, crouched down, one hand in the cabinet as she realized the only way Daviss could have known about her was through the slave organization. He had as much admitted the Xa'ti'al's dealings with them, but he could be an insider, working on his own with them. For recruits? No, it was much more than that. She felt it instinctively but couldn't quite pin it down. She needed someone to talk to.

"Mom?"

Lenore straightened up, banging her head on the handle of the pan sticking out over the edge. She cursed inventively, stopping only when she noticed Quinn's eyebrows go up.

"Wow. Haven't heard that one before," he said, a grin tugging at the corner of his mouth.

"It's from a long time ago," she said, rubbing her head. "And that hurt far more than it should have."

"Maybe that will be my next research project, obscure curses. Maybe compare some that seem universal to only those locally sourced. Perhaps even going so far—"

"Did you need something Quinn?" she broke in, knowing Quinn was only trying to defuse the tension, but she didn't feel like being humored.

"Well." He exhaled slightly, his usual reaction when he was letting go of an annoyance such as being interrupted. "We received an answer to the ad. For cargo and a single passenger. Alli is doing research. I figure a couple days of travel to the planet to pick him up, maybe more."

His short answers showed him to still be annoyed by his mother's brusqueness. Lenore's hand moved from the top of her head to her forehead. She couldn't do anything right these days.

"Sorry, Quinn. Hard day. Thanks for telling me and for taking the initiative to estimate the time." She smiled and felt better when he returned it. The tension faded away but returned with her next words.

"Please tell your father so he can verify if we have enough space. I will meet you on the bridge for a discussion."

Quinn merely nodded and headed out the door, presumably to the cargo bay where Diarmin was spending all his time these past few days. Lenore grimaced as she put the offending pan away. This strain on her family needed to be resolved.

Chapter Seven

Lenore came onto the bridge and, as she seated herself at the command console, up the ladder came Quinn, then Diarmin.

Allison glanced back and forth between her parents. Her mother was reading the message and Dad moved to navigation. This was the first time they were all in the same room since she had interrupted the fight, and the atmosphere was thick. She cleared her throat, feeling odd to be speaking, but someone had to start.

"I've done some research on the planet where we are to pick up the cargo. Drenon is newly colonized, a mostly jungle planet and sparsely settled. The person requesting transfer is not a colonist, however. He is a researcher for a biotech company based on the third planet of the Reese system, where he wants to go."

"Newly colonized?" asked Diarmin. "Does it have spaceport facilities?"

Allison tapped some keys and checked her screen. "Looks like just a landing pad, but the tiny research station is nowhere near there. We'll have to ask if there is anywhere closer that we can put down."

"And the Reese system?" asked Lenore.

"That is heavily populated with people on the third and fourth planets as well as significant populations on three moons in the outer system."

"A straight course would put us at Drenon in only two days, three or more with our usual roundabout ways," Quinn added from the science station.

"Very well. Let's see if this," she consulted the console, "Ven Bondle answers a direct call." She tapped a key and within moments came a reply.

"Hello. Bondle here."

"Mr. Bondle. This is Nora Fleming of the ship L'Eponge Carre." Allison wondered at her father's brief sour look.

Later, Mom's still talking.

"Thank you for your response to our ad. We are less than a week away if you are still interested in cargo transport."

"Oh yes! As soon as you can. These samples must get back to the main facility quickly."

"A few questions before we commit. First, how much cargo space will be needed, and are there facilities for a small belly-down freighter to land?"

"Well, um, I don't need that much space. I have four six-all containers that are environmentally sealed which I will monitor for the trip." Lenore glanced at Diarmin. He nodded. Allison wasn't sure why Lenore looked to him to verify enough space. *Even I know that six by six by six-foot cases would fit easily.* But since it was more communicating than they had done in days, she was encouraged.

"As for the facilities," Bondle was continuing, "I am afraid there is only a pad and it is quite far from our facility. But there is a clearing large enough for a freighter near the laboratory as long as you have anti-grav. The lab wouldn't survive thrusters."

"We have anti-grav. I am sending a contract for you to sign along with our price. Please transmit your location with the signed contract as well as any needed permits. We will give you an estimate of our arrival when we have verified the information."

"Wonderful, thank you so much. This cargo is much needed on my home planet."

"Fleming out."

Lenore toggled the switch. Diarmin simply stood and left down the ladder without a word.

***

"Was that the ship?"

Ven Bondle had closed communications only a heartbeat ago, and his assistant's question startled him. He sighed heavily before answering.

"Yes. Are the containers prepared, Evan?"

"That's what I was coming to report. The internal temperatures are now ideal to begin the loading process and the regulation controls are working perfectly." Despite the positive report, Assistant Evan Mill began to wring his hands.

"Dismiss the engineer before you begin the transfer of product," Bondle said with a noisy clearing of the throat. "Nobody should know what we are transporting."

"Are you sure about this?" asked Mill. "Those are fragile specimens and we should wait for one of our own shi—"

"No!" Bondle took a deep breath. Despite his eager helpfulness and brilliance, Mill wasn't truly aware of the implications of their latest research. "Sorry, Evan but as I told you, these need to get home as soon as possible. I am just grateful that these people aren't asking too many questions." He made shooing motions. "Go. Start prepping the samples. They'll be here in less than a week."

"What are you going to do?" he asked, still wringing his hands.

"I'm going to forge some permits."

***

Diarmin sat on his workbench, staring at the mostly empty cargo bay. He had started to pace it off to be sure of the space available, but he didn't need to. He knew this cargo bay like the back of his hand as well as the rest of the entire ship. There wasn't a space he hadn't crawled into, worked on, or patched up. The measuring had only been an excuse to move, so he forced his feet toward his bench and sat, fighting against the urge to get up and do something.

"Daydreaming?"

He had known Lenore was coming down the ladder but didn't look at her.

"Trying to figure out which corner to put my worktables in so they aren't in the way of the cargo." He knew his tone was surly but didn't quite know how to fix it.

"Maybe you shouldn't have any projects down here since it appears someone will be monitoring the cargo." Lenore's tone was determinedly light, but it annoyed rather than reassured him.

"I won't have anything important, just the usual tinkering."

"Why don't you use one of the extra rooms? That way it can be locked and—"

"What do you want, Lenore?" Again, he hated himself for his churlishness but the longer they had gone without speaking, the harder it became to talk. He still couldn't bring himself to look her in the eye.

The fingertips of her left hand tapped continuously on the tabletop and he risked a glance. She was looking at the floor and what he could see of her face showed a complete lack of expression. That meant that she was holding all her emotions tightly in check, like she had been trained to do.

She was reverting to her old ways just like he was. *This isn't good. But how...?*

"Diarmin, this situation is, well, it's not good." She stopped tapping and lightly clasped both hands in front of her body. Taking a deep breath, she pulled her head up and their eyes met. He immediately felt his heart lift and regretted the distance that had grown between them.

"I was thinking the same thing," he said, feeling a slight smile. But his next words that slipped out stopped both it and the smile that had begun on Lenore's face. "I am not quite ready to forgive and forget, but I'm willing to try to put it aside for the mission."

"Okay," she said. "I suppose that is reasonable. But..." she looked down at her clasped hands and tapped her thumbs together. "How do we go from here? And more importantly, I have been thinking that we need to tell the kids more about our backgrounds. After all, their lives are going to be as much in danger now. Especially after Daviss."

"I've had similar thoughts. But where do we start?"

Lenore shrugged and they both stood quietly.

After only a few breaths of contemplation, both Allison and Quinn entered the cargo bay.

"Latest course change complete. We are out of transwarp and will be at the coordinates for the route to the planet in two hours," said Quinn as he handed the pad to his father.

"Good job. Thanks, Quinn," said Diarmin. But when Quinn and Allison remained unmoving, he felt his brow furrow. "Was there something else?"

The siblings looked at each other, and Quinn nodded for Allison to speak.

"We were wondering, Dad, Mom," she said, voice slightly hesitant. "Since we've got a couple of hours and can't do anything until we hear back from Bondle…how did you two meet?"

"We know you met while working but," Quinn gestured to his sister. "Alli and I were talking about it, and we realized we'd never heard the full story or any details for that matter."

Diarmin's head swiveled to Lenore whose head was doing the same. They smiled as their eyes met. Trust their brilliant children to find what they couldn't; a way to begin talking about the difficult past. His smile stayed as he looked back at his children.

"We met after your mother kicked my ass!"

Chapter Eight

The family arranged themselves on various seats in the lounge, a more comfortable setting for storytelling.

And maybe a discussion afterward, thought Lenore.

"Did you really kick Dad's butt?" asked Quinn.

"Sort of. But to be honest, that first time, I think he let me." Lenore looked at Diarmin who grinned and shrugged, neither confirming nor denying.

"That first time?" asked Allison. "How many times were there?"

"Too many to count over the years," said Diarmin. "But most did take place when we first met. Your mother didn't like me very much." Both kids' heads turned back to Lenore, mouths open, but she held up her hands.

"Enough. We can do question and answer all day, or I can tell you the story." Their mouths snapped shut and they settled in.

"Ok." Lenore gathered her thoughts, taking her time. She had to make sure nothing slipped out that the children weren't quite ready to know.

"I was still a Xa'ti'al and assigned to protect a prominent politician on Ortab. It was my first solo mission which is an important milestone for newly trained Xa. We had just finished an important voting session and our group, consisting of Senator Gregor, myself undercover as his aide, and two security guards, were walking toward his private transport. After a block, I noticed we were being followed, so I turned the group onto a different street to verify. Sure enough, the man following turned as well.

"I remember thinking that, whoever it was, was doing a poor job of tailing us, and I had no doubts I could take him. So, in order to avoid confrontation, I put my arm through the Senator's and steered him around another corner, leaning into him, pretending to flirt with him, whisper in his ear, that sort of thing. I placed a protection field on the Senator and ordered the guards to keep him going. They positioned themselves between the Senator and the follower and hurried along, which allowed me to await whomever came around the corner. In a matter of seconds, he appeared. I dropped him with a simple jab to the solar plexus and pulled out my hidden blaster.

"Flat on the pavement, the man held his hands out and spoke, his voice hoarse from my hit. 'Whoa, there. A simple 'hello' would have sufficed. No need for violence.' Then his fingers moved in a complicated signal that meant he had been sent by the Xa'ti'al. It wasn't quite right, but most who aren't actually Xa rarely get it exact."

Lenore grinned at Diarmin who wrinkled his nose and huffed, but she knew he wasn't really angry. She continued her story.

"'Let me see the other proof,' I told him before I would lower my gun. He nodded and slowly, which was also a sign he knew Xa, moved his left hand and flipped up his jacket collar to show a pin that identified someone as a messenger for the Xa'ti'al. I tucked my weapon away and held out a hand to help the man to his feet.

"He took my hand and pulled himself up, then just stood there grinning at me. 'Nora Soove? Though with that demonstration, I don't really have to ask.'

"Needless to say, I was irritated at this man's casual demeanor. 'You have a message for me?' I said, carefully keeping my tone neutral."

Diarmin snorted and Lenore looked at him. "Ok, maybe some irritation slipped out. Anyway…

"'Not that you asked, but I'm Kel,' he told me. He was dressed in loose, comfortable pants and a light shirt that I could barely see through his open jacket. The jacket was a deep blue, with pockets that were both obvious and, by the bulges around his body, hidden.

"I stood there silently with my arms crossed, waiting for the message. Kel sighed, rolled his eyes and spoke the line he had been paid to tell me.

"'The bird is to be set free.'

"I would have been less shocked had he pulled a blaster on me. That message was a code for me to abandon my guard duties immediately.

"'What? Why? Are you sure that was the message?' I asked.

"He looked annoyed as he answered, 'Of course.' He flicked his collar. 'You don't earn these by misquoting messages. So, let's go.'

"'Wait', I replied as I started back toward the Senator. 'I need to warn—' He stopped me by grabbing my arm and it was a sign how upset I was at his message that I didn't protest.

"'You are not supposed to. The message was to be for immediate response.'

"'You were told that?'

"'No, but I have done this often enough that I know the procedure.'

"I jerked my arm out of his grasp and went to warn my former charge anyway, feeling that I couldn't just leave him wide open to attackers. Yes, he had been kind of a slimeball, but it didn't feel right to simply abandon him. I strode to him and his guards to tell them I had been recalled and that he should be extra careful. I left with him screaming insults and threats of suing the Xa'ti'al. When I returned, Kel was nowhere to be seen. I went immediately to the spaceport as orders are specific with that particular message. I didn't bother to retrieve anything like clothes or personal items. As a Xa, I had all the important items with me and anything else was simply window dressing for the part."

Lenore suddenly looked up, aware she had been rambling with too much detail about the Xa and her personal life. The wide eyes of her children and inquisitive tilt of Diarmin's head told her of her error. As she tried to focus her thoughts, the com beeped with an incoming call.

"Awwwwww," said Allison. "Just when it was getting good."

"Let them leave a message," added Quinn, evidently also wanting to hear more.

"Now, that's probably our new client, Quinn," said Diarmin. "More stories later."

The children grumbled but didn't argue as Diarmin followed Lenore to the bridge to answer the call. The look he gave her was one of relief and she knew why. The story hadn't had a happy ending because shortly after Lenore left, the Senator had been killed.

And Diarmin had been the one to do it.

Chapter Nine

Diarmin watched Lenore as she opened communications. He remembered those days when they had met quite vividly. He didn't talk about it much, but he had an eidetic memory and Lenore's recitation had brought back all those experiences, including the ones he would like to forget.

"Ah, Mr. Bondle. Do you have what I asked for?"

"Of course. I am transmitting the permit and contract along with our exact location of the landing site."

"Very well. We will contact you when we are close."

"How soon do you think that will be? These samples are active for only a short amount of time once stored so timing needs to be as accurate as possible."

Lenore glanced at Diarmin but didn't wait for a comment. "I believe we can be there within forty-eight Standard hours. Again, I will contact you an hour out."

They were only about a day and a half away which caused Diarmin to wonder why Lenore had added a few hours to their arrival time.

"Wonderful, wonderful and thank you. I have already cleared your landing with the spaceport so you can land directly, no need to check in. The last line of the permit shows the needed authorization. Bondle out."

The line disconnected before Lenore could respond, and Diarmin saw her eyes narrow. She punched the toggle to the intercom, her finger a bit too forceful.

"Allison, come to the bridge please. We need to do some digging."

"Sure, Mom."

"I was right. Those narrow eyes mean you aren't happy about something," said Diarmin.

She looked directly at Diarmin. "Have you ever known a spaceport to give advance permission?"

"No," he answered. "Especially not one from a new colony. Any chance to slap fees on a visitor in order to help finance a building economy."

"Exactly. Ah, Alli," said Lenore as she tapped a few commands into her console. "I have transferred these documents to your station. First order of business, test the authenticity of the permit." She tucked her hair behind both ears like she always did when seriously getting down to business, then pulled up a chair to sit next to their daughter.

"I'm heading down to finish prepping the cargo bay," he said to the ladies. Both gave an absent wave without taking their eyes off the screen. Diarmin hid a grin. Like mother, like daughter. He was going to tell them he'd get Quinn to help, but he knew they wouldn't answer.

Shaking his head, he headed to find his son. He was relieved that his clever children had found a way to relieve the tension, but they would have to hear the entire story someday.

For now, they had a job to do.

***

"Well, it looks pretty clean to me," said Quinn as he jumped off the ladder onto the cargo bay floor, then gave an "oof" as he landed. "I keep forgetting that our gravity is back to normal." He flexed his knees and then walked toward his father who was standing next to his work bench.

"I always keep it clean, you know that," said Diarmin.

"Except this." Quinn spread his hands to indicate the area that his father referred to as his work bench even though there was no bench. It consisted of tables forming three sides of a square and a rolling chair that allowed him to push himself from pile to pile of his various projects.

"Hey, disorganization is a sign of an active mind and imagination," said Diarmin.

"Imagination is right," said Quinn as he lifted what appeared to be a ball with imbedded metal spikes. "What is this for?"

"I use that to test the personal protection fields."

"And this?" He reached for a jumble of circuits.

"Don't touch that!"

36

Quinn pulled back, startled at the near yell.

"Sorry, Quinn, it's just that it looks harmless but there's a charge running through that. You have to handle it with plastic only. Metal or flesh will set it off." He picked up the object with a pair of plastic tongs and transferred it to a plastic box on another table. "I called you down here not to clean but to help move these tables. Let's try the corner under the ladder. Keep my little projects out of the way."

"I don't think all the tables will fit in that space, Dad, unless you cover the hatch to the engine room."

"Not all, just one tucked between the wall and hatch. As far from the cargo bay doors as possible to keep away prying eyes. The rest of the tables we can fold up and stack in one of the extra bedrooms along with most of my projects."

As Quinn helped him box up whatever his father allowed him to handle, he noticed that Diarmin seemed less tense.

Good, Allison's idea worked. But Quinn still felt guilty.

"Dad?"

"Hmmm?" he answered absently as he lovingly wrapped what looked like an old-fashioned mace sprouting wires.

"I'm sorry."

"For what?" He looked at Quinn, a slight frown on his face.

"For overhearing what you said about, you know, about years, months and days." Quinn looked down, guilt weighing on him. His father said nothing for a long moment so he continued. "And for kind of making Mom tell me about it."

"Quinn, there is no reason for you to apologize."

"But I caused the fight between you and Mom."

Diarmin chuckled softly, but when Quinn looked at him, he still looked sad and the stress lines around his eyes hadn't gone away.

"You didn't cause that fight. And you know your mother can't be made to do anything she doesn't want to do."

"But I—" Quinn stopped himself short before he admitted that he knew of a few ways to emotionally influence his mother, and incidentally his father as well.

"We should have discussed how to tell you and Alli about our backgrounds years ago. I was angry because we were supposed to tell you together but she..." Now it was Diarmin's turn to interrupt himself.

"Anyway, we have worked things out and decided that you two are old enough to know most of our stories. But later," he said. "We need to get this done before our guest comes aboard."

Quinn closed his mouth on his many questions and the fact that his father had said 'most' instead of 'all' of their stories.

Chapter Ten

The ship was an hour away from the planet, but Lenore had ordered it to a stop when Allison told her the latest findings.

"You're sure?" she asked from the command seat.

Allison tried very hard not to roll her eyes. She knew her mother wasn't questioning her abilities, merely needing to be absolutely certain of the information, especially for something of this magnitude. And that took multiple explanations and confirmations.

"I am positive. The permits have the correct names signed, but when they are placed next to authentic signatures," she tapped a button, putting up both on the display screen. "You can tell that they don't match. It's not even close, definitely an amateur job. And," she continued as Lenore made a sound in her throat that couldn't quite be a growl. "And there are no official applications filed with the authorities as you can see by this list I managed to pull." She put a different display on the screen. "This is from the spaceport and this from the planetary government. Nothing to show that a request has been made for a ship to land away from the port *or* to haul anything off the planet."

"They could just be slow in filing official documents," Diarmin suggested.

"No, look. This shows that they have processed several in the last few hours, and the permit was from two days ago." She looked directly at her mother who was deep in thought. Allison's eyes flicked to her father who was sitting in the navigator's seat, but his attention was also on Lenore. Quinn was at the research console, back to everyone else.

Lenore pulled at her lower lip as she mused aloud. "Should we refuse this job? Not a good sign when official documents are fake."

"It wouldn't be the first time we did something that wasn't exactly legal," said Diarmin. Allison's mouth dropped open at her father's comment, and her mother gave him a sour look. Quinn had also turned with a surprised expression, but when his eyes caught his father's, they matched grins.

They've been talking. I'll get it out of Quinn later.

"I think we should ask him," said Allison, the words slipping out. As all heads swiveled to her, she stammered somewhat. "Bondle, that is. I mean we don't know why he lied about the permits. Everything else he has said seems to be the truth."

"Like what?" asked Quinn.

"Well, he kept talking about samples and with the information I pulled, he works at the biolab on the planet. Now, the system he wants to go to, Reese, let me show you..." Allison pulled up the information on her screen. "It's a closed system with a warning to outsiders not to land on any of the planets without express permission due to code four-five-eight. Now that code means—"

"That there is a plague," said her mother.

"Yeah. How did you know that? I had to hack several sites to find out what that code meant."

Lenore just shrugged and gestured at Allison to continue.

"See, a biolab... samples... plague..." she ticked off each with her fingers. "Put them all together and he has medicine of some sort. Maybe even a cure. We gotta help him, even if it isn't 'exactly legal'. The planetary government could be the bad guys here."

Now her father grinned at her, winking at her paraphrasing his own words.

"Diarmin, what have you been teaching our children?" asked Lenore, her exasperated tone belying the smile tugging at the left corner of her mouth.

"That sometimes you have to go with your instincts. I think we should talk to Bondle," said Diarmin.

"After all," Quinn piped in, "we have come all this way. Be a shame to give up a paying job. Especially when our accounts are so low."

Lenore threw up her hands. "If my family is ganging up on me, might as well go along with it." She sent a message asking to speak with Ven

Bondle. The speed with which he answered meant he was waiting for the call.

"Yes. You are an hour away, Captain Fleming? My cargo is prepared for immediate loading when you arrive."

"First things first, Mr. Bondle. It appears there might be a problem with these permits."

"Oh, um, okay. I can, um, will show you the originals after you land. Remember here and not, um, not at the spaceport and then you can verify—" his stammering was interrupted by Lenore.

"The landing seems to be another issue, Mr. Bondle. I assure you that we do not ship illegal cargo."

Diarmin coughed into his hand and Lenore threw him an irritated look.

A large sigh from the intercom made Lenore's eyes narrow. "Please, Captain. I will explain everything when you arrive. My cargo is not illegal. It is medicine sorely needed back on my planet, but I am avoiding the spaceport because they will slap such a high export tax on it that I won't even be able to afford to keep the lab. Please. Once the crates are delivered to the planet, my government will pay double our agreed-upon fee."

Now her mother's eyes widened, and Allison's eyebrows shot up, probably just like her father's.

"Very well. We shall speak further upon our arrival in one standard hour. Fleming out."

"Double," said Quinn. "That would be one hell of a payout."

"Yes," she mused. "And that is what worries me."

***

"Approaching Drenon," said Diarmin from the navigation console. Quinn was sitting next to him to learn how to avoid detection.

"Two satellites are transmitting back to the spaceport," said Allison from her console. "Sending their coordinates and scanning vectors to your display, Dad."

"Thank you, Allison." His fingers tapped on his board, some simultaneously. "Wow. This is a pretty tight system, ah wait. There it is. See that, Quinn?"

"That overlap of the satellite scanners?"

"Yep. That usually means there will be some free space on the other side." More tapping. "And there it is," he said and nodded as Quinn pointed. "Yes. Now we slide in undetected between scans, and then fly low enough to be under the satellite sensors. The landing site is very close, so hold on everyone."

Lenore gripped the arms of the command chair, oddly enjoying this side of Diarmin. Usually she was on a planet or away from the bridge when he did his fancy flying, and she tended to forget his proficiency. Quinn appeared eager to learn and, already talented at flying the shuttle, he would most likely become as capable a yacht pilot as Diarmin.

"Good job, Keltons." She tapped a few buttons on her own console then stood. "From here until I say, we are on Level Three Alert."

"Really? Level Three?" asked Allison.

"Absolutely. Monitor all communications and I will carry hidden weapons when I meet Ven Bondle. The ship will be prepped for launch in case I give the emergency signal, and everyone will be on the lookout for anything out of the ordinary."

"Yes, yes, and don't let anyone in we don't recognize and never give in to any kind of threat. I know what Level Three Alert means, Mom." Allison gave a toss of her curls. "I was just thinking do we need that high of an alert?"

"We are landing illegally to pick up an unknown cargo that may or may not be dangerous. We already know this person has lied to us and furthermore…"

"Okay, okay. Just making sure we aren't being paranoid," said Allison, then she winced in anticipation.

"Better paranoid than hurt or dead," said Lenore.

"Landing struts extended," said Quinn. Another tap of the command console activated the external cameras. Lenore brought up the belly cam which showed nearly all greenery except one clear area that grew in size as the ship descended. She switched to the rear camera that was in line with the buildings on the other side of the clearing. Zooming in detailed one large building with smaller ones attached and one separate building that appeared to be housing. Four containers were stacked relatively close to the building with two men on either side.

"Scanners show no weapons," said Allison. "On either the people or anywhere in the compound."

Lenore merely nodded; the scan was expected with a Level Three Alert. The two men standing there, despite the fact that if the ship fired up the engines they would be instantly killed, showed either ignorance or trust.

No matter. "I'm heading to my room to prep," she said. All three nodded. They knew she would be arming herself to the hilt. Once again, she felt a stab of pride for her talented and quite competent family.

Lenore descended the ladder in her usual reckless fashion, confident in Diarmin's smooth landing. Within minutes, she was geared up and left her room as she heard the antigrav engines shut off. At the same time, she felt the pull of a slightly heavier gravity kick in as the ship's grid went offline. Diarmin clattered down the ladder to meet her.

"Open the cargo bay? Or through the hatch?" he asked.

"Go ahead with the cargo bay. No weapons detected and speed seems to be important. I will meet them. You stay in the bay, observing." She handed him an earpiece after they descended the ladder to the cargo bay. "If you hear anything suspicious, you know what to do."

"The kids?"

Lenore grimaced. She knew what he was asking and felt now wasn't the time, but he had a point. "They can listen as well, but from the bridge. There they will be secure enough, and it will give them experience with confrontations without being in danger themselves." She put a hand on his arm. "I truly don't think there is anything underhanded but better to be prepared."

"Be safe." Diarmin hit the button to open the large bay doors, and she watched him put the piece in his ear as the doors creaked open. With a nod to her husband, she squeezed between the doors as soon as there was space enough. Not waiting for the ramp to extend, she lightly jumped to the ground and headed for the buildings, pressing her vocal implant to activate it.

The two men were already maneuvering two of the four six-all crates, each on antigrav platforms, toward the ship. Lenore hurried her pace to intercept them.

"Hold it," she said, planting herself squarely in front of the crates. The man on the right peered around the crate and yelled at the other to stop. Both hit a button on the handles and the platforms slowly ground to a halt only two feet away from Lenore.

The man who gave the order dropped the handle and came to speak with her. He was rather short, his dark brown hair slicked back and looked young, perhaps in his late twenties. He wore an unbuttoned white lab coat over a blue shirt with black pants and peered at Lenore as if he needed glasses. The other man seemed to be similarly attired but with a closed coat.

"Captain Fleming, I am Ven Bondle." He held out a hand and she took it in a brief, strong grip. "What's the delay? As I told you, time is of the essence."

She released his hand and then held hers out, palm up. "I believe you said you would show me the original permits?"

Bondle sighed. "I am sorry for the deception, Captain Fleming. I must admit that the permits I sent you were not official." He cleared his throat and tugged on his lab coat in a nervous gesture. "I simply do not have enough cash to get the proper permits through quickly enough before the active cultures go inert."

Lenore felt her lips twist. It happened often enough, needing an extra 'rush' fee that everyone knew was actually a bribe. But another word caught her ear. "Cultures? Do they pose a danger to my crew?"

"No, no. Not at all. Please, I am desperate." Bondle's hand came up as if to grab her arm but obviously thought better of the idea. "My planet, Reesling, third planet of the Reese system, has been subjected to a variety of plagues for over three generations. We have labs on many planets trying to find a cure. I believe what I came up with will not only cure the most recent strain, but there is an organism in these jungles that is adaptable and can be altered to cure any future diseases. Please. Millions are dying and the plague is beginning to spread to the other planets. The Reese system has few ships, and none are close or fast enough to get the cargo home before the half-life of the altered DNA becomes inert. If this cure is successful, the entire system will commit significant resources on this planet, but that won't happen unless I get these samples there as soon as possible."

Lenore took in the rushed speech with her arms crossed. That certainly matched with Allison's findings. She peered closely at Bondle, looking for any of the telltale signs that would indicate deception.

"Reese is a closed system," she said. "I don't know if I should risk my crew landing on a plague-ridden planet."

"I can get us permission to enter the system and we have safety measures to insure protection to outsiders. If we didn't, we couldn't import or export anything. Please, Captain." His face took on a look close to pleading. "Oh, and here..." He fished around in one of his lab coat pockets and pulled out a credit flimsy. "This is everything I could scrape together for the advance payment." He pressed it into her hand, his eyes intent on her face. "Please."

He seemed very sincere and Lenore could find no tells that anything he said was less than the absolute truth. Her teeth clenched briefly, and she made a decision, hoping she wouldn't regret it. She shoved the flimsy into her own pocket and nodded.

"Very well. Let's get these loaded."

Bondle's face broke into a huge smile and he grabbed her hand and shook it vigorously. "Thank you, thank you, thank you." He dashed back to the control handle and activated the platform. The other man had already started as soon as Lenore assented, so he was already moving. Lenore paced alongside the man in front.

"I'm Fleming. You are?"

"Assistant Researcher Mill," he answered, not taking his eyes off the terrain in front of his load.

"Did you help develop this cure?"

"Yes."

"Do you agree that they pose no danger to me and my crew?" Mill gave her an odd sidelong glance but didn't stop moving forward as he answered.

"The crates are very secure and the cultures within are triple sealed." He reached the ramp, stopped, and for the first time, looked directly at Lenore. "Even if all those layers were somehow breached, the cultures have not been purposed yet and so would not affect a living organism. You are safe from these samples." He turned away to guide the crate up the ramp, Diarmin at the top ready to help guide the six-all to the correct place in the cargo bay.

Lenore wondered at Mill's specific word choice but filed it away in the back of her mind to think about later and went to help Bondle.

Chapter Eleven

After the cargo was stored to Bondle's satisfaction, Lenore had Quinn show him to the first guest room. As soon as they disappeared up the ladder, Diarmin scanned the six-alls for anything that might pose a danger.

"No electronics except those that control the climate in the crates," he said to Lenore. He tucked away the scanner in one of the drawers along the back wall that held a variety of tools and instruments needed to maintain a ship. "I could only do a passive scan. Bondle said any penetrating scans will damage the cargo, but it looks like exactly what he says it is."

Lenore's arms remained crossed. "Huh. Then why do I feel nervous about all this?"

"Because it's a tad illegal? Avoiding the shipping taxes and fees?" said Diarmin with a small smile.

Lenore stared at the crates. "That's not it. Like you said we've done that before." She looked back at her husband, noticed the grin, and realized he was teasing her. "Stop that. There is absolutely no reason to suspect Bondle, but it's one of my gut instincts that I hope will prove to be wrong."

"Then let's get this ship and cargo on the way to the Reese system as soon as possible," he said, gesturing for her to precede him up the ladder.

As they climbed the second ladder to the bridge, Quinn joined them. Allison vacated the command chair and Diarmin took it.

"Thank you for starting the launch prep, Alli," he said as he continued the process.

Quinn took the navigator's seat while announcing that Bondle was settled in his cabin.

"I told him we would announce lift-off in time for him to strap in safely," said Quinn as he logged into the nav console. "Here's the course I came up with, Dad."

Diarmin pulled the course up on his screen. Lenore sat at the science console at the back of the bridge and accessed the file as well.

"Why are we stopping at Sultra?" Diarmin asked his son.

"It's the best place for refueling," replied Quinn. He tapped on his console and a map of star systems came up with a red circle around the Sultra system. "We will still have about a fourth of our fuel, but there is a large station on the edges of the system that is a huge hub for traders and transports." He grinned at his parents. "Maybe we can even pick up another passenger or two."

Lenore nodded to Quinn, pleased at his suggestion.

"Good idea, Quinn," said Diarmin. "Everything else seems in order. Plug it in and let's go."

Quinn's grin widened, obviously pleased at the first time a course he had plotted was accepted without any changes.

Lenore pressed the command to activate the speaker in the cabins. "Please strap in, Mr. Bondle. Anti-grav engines online."

"Ready, Captain," said Bondle.

Lenore closed communications and nodded to her husband. Diarmin expertly lifted the ship, and Allison put the satellite courses back on the viewscreen like when they landed.

"Thanks, Alli, but we don't need to be as careful this time."

"Huh?" Both kids said simultaneously.

Diarmin grinned, and Lenore shook her head. *What's he up to now? At least he's in a better mood.*

He did avoid most of the low-orbit detection satellites, but just as he exited the atmosphere and fired the main engines, one of the tracking lines on the screen turned red. A loud alert warning was quickly cut off by a transmission.

"Attention unidentified spacecraft. You are in orbit around Drenon. Please identify yourself and proceed to the primary colony landing pad."

Diarmin pressed a button on the console and gave his kids a wink. "Drenon? I thought this was Cirspin."

"Negative. Identification please."

"Sorry, wrong planet. My bad." Diarmin turned the yacht's nose toward space and accelerated. Lenore felt the pressure pushing her into the chair and shook her head again. *Showoff.*

A red light began to flash on every console. Quinn was the first to identify it.

"They are sending a ship." He put up blips on the viewscreen to show both their yacht and the pursuer.

"Ha. Too little, too late," said Diarmin.

"Ten minutes to intercept," said Allison.

"Five minutes to the transspace point," said Diarmin. He pushed the engines to maximum. "Make that three minutes."

Before the three minutes had passed, the red blip that was the planet's ship slowed and began to turn back toward the planet. Diarmin continued at maximum to the transspace point and with a few taps, they were on the first leg of the trip.

"See?" he said as he secured the command console. "That's why we didn't need to be so careful." Lenore cleared her throat and gave Diarmin a *look.*

"But don't try that yourself," he said then lowered his voice to a whisper though Lenore could still hear him just fine.

"At least until you have a lot of experience."

Chapter Twelve

"What are you working on?"

Diarmin started at the strange voice and nearly dropped the microtool he was using to adjust the tiny sensors in the receiver patch he was working on. Instead he gripped the tool in a fist and whirled around to see Ven Bondle staring at him, eyes widening at Diarmin's reaction.

"Nothing important," he replied, trying to slow his pulse. He dropped the tool on the workbench and covered up the work surface with a heavy cloth so none of the little pieces would shift. As he struggled to calm down from his overreaction, he thought that maybe a stranger on the ship hadn't been such a good idea. He had nearly gotten his violent emotions under control after they were reawakened in the rescue attempt. But, then again, he was used to his family, and they were careful not to disturb his concentration while he was deep in a project.

"I didn't mean to interrupt," said Bondle as he took a step back. Diarmin wondered what his own face must look like because Bondle's had fear plastered on it. He deliberately smiled and relaxed his shoulders, body falling into the easy charm he had always been able to project. It's why he was so good at his job.

Former job. He put the memories out of his mind.

"You startled me that's all." Diarmin grinned. "Surely a scientist knows what it's like when you are completely focused on a problem."

"Of course," said Bondle and his return grin told Diarmin that the affable demeanor was working to calm the passenger. "I should have known better than to disturb a fellow tinkerer. I was just checking on the containers and really have nothing else to do so…" He lifted his hands briefly and sighed.

"Bored?"

"A little." He shoved his hands back into the pockets of the lab coat he never took off and chuckled. "The only other time I was on a ship was to go to Drenon, and then I was doing research the entire time."

"Ah, I understand. We have some entertainment vids you can watch or even some games we can put on the screen in the lounge."

"Not really my thing, but I suppose it's better than nothing."

"If you prefer exercise, there's some equipment in—" A beep from the intercom interrupted him.

"Dad?"

"Yes, Quinn?"

"Course change in two minutes."

"On my way," he replied. Diarmin wiped his hands on a towel and turned to Bondle. "After the change I will show you how to access the entertainments."

"May I come watch? I've never been on a bridge before."

Diarmin hesitated. Technically the bridge was off limits but as long as he watched the passenger closely it would be fine. And it was only a course change, nothing vital.

"Of course. Follow me."

They went up the two levels to the bridge and as Bondle stepped off the ladder, his head swiveled madly to take in all he could. The look of interest on his face was almost amusing.

"It's smaller than I thought it would be," he mused.

Diarmin told him to stay by the ladder and took his own seat at the command console.

Quinn, seated at the navigator's station, answered. "It's only a yacht, not a large cruise vessel or freighter."

"No, I don't mean that. I meant I thought it would be as large across as the lower level. This is only about half the size."

"Two-thirds to be exact," explained Quinn. "Behind that wall is the life support systems for the ship. Gotta breathe, you know."

"I see. Fascinating."

Diarmin cleared his throat as he punched in the commands for the course change. Quinn glanced at him and turned red at Diarmin's slight shake of his head. It was one thing to let a stranger on the bridge. Quite another to explain the layout of vital systems. Bondle noticed the subtle exchange and colored slightly.

"Sorry. I like to know the answers to things. Thank you for indulging my curiosity." He gave a slight bow to Quinn.

Quinn merely nodded and turned back to his console.

"Dropping out of transspace in three… two…one…" said Quinn.

A very slight tremor shuddered through the ship. Diarmin checked the space around the yacht. All clear, no other ships in the area. He didn't say this aloud because of Bondle but continued with the process.

"Thirty minutes to the next point."

"Acknowledged," said Quinn in a neutral voice.

Diarmin hid a smile. He was trying to be professional again, his way of apologizing for his earlier slip.

"Why thirty minutes?" asked Bondle. "I thought transspace shifts only took a minute or two to reorient then off again."

Diarmin noticed Quinn's shoulders tense but he wisely said nothing. Diarmin took the pressure off by answering himself. This wasn't information about the ship, simply basic knowledge that anyone could look up if they were so inclined.

"This is a small, private yacht, Mr. Bondle, so we have to drive in the cheap lanes, so to speak." He kept his fingers active on the command board while he explained. "Some of the private yachts can afford the fast routes but we take the ones less traveled. Freighters on regular routes have the courses charted beforehand. Sometimes only the computer handles the changes and they are quick indeed, but that takes money."

"Is that why it costs more to travel commercially?"

"One of the reasons. Those fees are built into the fare."

"But space is so large, why are routes needed? And who monitors them?"

"It may seem like there is a lot of room out here but things like stars, planets, black holes, nebulas, dark matter, and other things get in the way of straight courses so there are fewer available routes than you think. Didn't you take basic astrophysics in school?"

"I suppose I did but I really wasn't interested in anything but biochemistry so…" Bondle shrugged.

"Another reason we cruise for a short distance out of transspace is to pick up any messages that may have been sent while we were out of communication. And speaking of which, it appears we have a message."

He looked pointedly at Bondle. Bondle stared back for a few moments then took the hint.

"Oh, you probably want to have privacy for that. I, um, will go see what vids you have in the lounge." He hastily descended the ladder. Quinn stood and quietly walked over to look down the ladder.

"He's gone. Do we really have a message or were you trying to get rid of him and his questions?"

"Both actually."

"I noticed when explaining about the cheap lanes, you didn't mention that we purposely take the out-of-the-way routes." He grinned. "To avoid pursuers."

"Not something he needed to know. Now let's listen to the message."

"Do you want me to get Mom?"

"Do you know what she's doing?"

"I think she and Alli are decoding more of the information we got from either the slave organization or Lord Timatay."

"Let's not bother them until we know what the message is. Could be simply an advertisement." He winked at his son who snorted at that answer. Diarmin hit the playback command.

"Hello. My name is Kurla Plaad. I am responding to your message for passenger transport. I know that was several days ago, but I am hoping you will be in the area of Sultra Station. I need to transport myself and my deceased mentor, High Priest Phylian. Please contact me as soon as you are able so we may discuss terms." Three different contact codes followed the message.

"Interesting. What a coincidence that our refueling stop is Sultra," said Quinn as he cocked his head at his father. "Too much of a coincidence?"

"Quinn, you are becoming as paranoid as your mother," said Diarmin, though he was thinking the same thing. "Weren't you the one to say it was a large hub?"

"Yes, I did." But his face didn't shed its suspicion.

"Keep on our course. I will take the message to your mother."

Quinn nodded, his expression going blank. Diarmin cursed at himself as he downloaded the message onto a pad. Quinn went emotionless like that when he was remembering his capture.

And I was stupid enough to remind him of it with my comment about paranoia.

***

"Try that section, Alli," said Lenore, pointing to the relevant text. Even though they had the Chanis cypher for the data, not all the blocks needed the cypher. Some of the data was also incomplete because they didn't get everything in their raid to rescue Quinn. Figuring which was which was only the first step.

"Knock, knock," said Diarmin, rapping on the door frame.

"Hey, Dad," said Allison without turning her head.

Lenore leaned back from Allison's terminal and stretched, her popping spine telling her she had spent too long at this.

"What's up, Diarmin?" she asked.

"Executing a course change and received a message."

Lenore took the pad he handed to her and listened to the message.

"A woman and a dead priest?" she asked.

Diarmin nodded and Allison snorted.

"At least the priest won't eat much."

"Very funny, Alli. Do we have room for both, Diarmin? I don't know if we should put a body down in the cargo bay with the six-alls."

"Hey, the priest could be cremated and in a tiny urn for all we know," said Diarmin.

"You're right. I guess I am still envisioning the last body we had on the ship."

"I know," he said. "I did too. But I figured the woman can have the bedroom next to Bondle and if there is a coffin, we can put it in the third room. We won't be accepting any more passengers anyway."

"Good idea, though we will have to move the exercise equipment. Again."

"I'll see what I can find about Kurla Plaad," volunteered Allison.

Lenore chuckled. "You just don't want to help move all the stuff."

"Of course I don't," she said in the tone she used when trying not to sound too pompous. "But you can store some in my room. I don't use that corner." She pointed to the corner at the end of her bed.

Lenore sighed. "Let's go do some heavy lifting, Diarmin." But her grin belied her suffering tone.

They walked out the door and heard sounds coming out of the lounge. Diarmin pointed at the ladder to the cargo bay and headed that way. Lenore followed.

"What did you want to talk about away from anybody's hearing?" she asked her husband as they reached the far side of the bay, the point farthest from the ladder opening.

"What are the chances this is merely a coincidence, happening to be at the exact place where we plan to refuel?"

Lenore stopped herself short of laughing because of the seriousness of her husband's face. *He is really worried. Odd, I'm usually the paranoid one but I didn't go there.*

"Maybe we should trust in luck for once. Not every job will be dangerous." She lowered her voice. "I am more worried about those containers than a random passenger." She waved a hand in the direction of the six-alls. "The assistant who helped load indicated the possibility of danger but wasn't very specific."

Diarmin rubbed his chin. "Bondle is asking a lot of questions but he doesn't seem to be the shady type."

Lenore noticed her husband's wrinkling forehead and tried to put him at ease. "We will be vigilant. It's our ship after all and nobody knows it like we do."

"Right."

But his flat tone told Lenore that his worry was still there. And now, unfortunately, he had awakened her paranoia again, just when she thought she might be relaxing for the first time in a very long time.

Chapter Thirteen

"Full disguise? Really? After all you said yesterday?" asked Diarmin as Lenore exited their cabin and headed for the hatch that connected the ship to Sultra Station. The black wig had very long tresses that occasionally obscured her face, but the nose putty and eye-color lenses showed she wasn't taking any chances.

"Look," she said, pulling on her gloves. "You got me thinking. There are several unknowns and I was wrong for letting my guard down. We don't know how Daviss found us in the first place and since we haven't heard from them at all yet, I need to be on full alert whenever I leave the ship." She settled her belt pack then cinched her belt a little tighter which accented her waist, her outfit showing off her breasts and hips. This outfit was what she called 'Look at everything but my face.' *Was she wearing lifts too*?

"You mean 'we' need to be on alert," he said, his worry growing at Lenore's mission attitude.

"Yes, that's what I meant," Lenore said absently as she stuffed her holdout blaster in her boot.

"A blaster, too? You know what happens if you get caught with that? They're illegal for citizens on this station."

"I figure it's worth the risk. Okay, I'm ready." She held out a hand and Diarmin deposited a credit flimsy in her palm.

"This is nearly all what Bondle paid us up front, minus the cost of fuel. It's not much."

"It should get us enough food to last for this mission." She peered up at Diarmin through the long bangs of her wig. "Don't worry. I will take every precaution and be back within the hour." She gave him a peck on the cheek and opened the hatch.

Diarmin knew she was trying to play it cool but the way she peered carefully through the hatch to the private lounge before she entered told him she was at full vigilance. He watched her go with that fear he always had whenever she left on a mission.

But this was a simple resupply and passenger pick up. He tried to convince himself she would be fine. He failed miserably.

***

Lenore paced along the station corridors, keeping her face down as if looking at the pad she was carrying, but eyes roving all around, hidden behind her bangs. She had tried to ease her husband's worry, but her heart was pounding and senses on high alert.

As the corridor opened up into the large central area where most of the shops were, she paused at the entrance and scanned the plaza. The area was roughly oblong with a fountain in the middle surrounded by shops of all sizes. It was relatively early so there weren't many people and the shops were just beginning to open for the station's day.

There! That man by the fountain. He looked at his pad and then around. Is he trying to match a face? Maybe mine?

The man's eyes lit upon a clothing shop. He smiled, pocketed the pad and headed for the entrance to the store.

Oh. Just looking for a certain place. Lenore took a few more steps, eyes now scanning for a store that sold food packaged for small private ships. An elderly woman with a cane was approaching and Lenore paused. She saw the woman's cane hit a slightly raised deck plate, causing her to stumble. By reflex, Lenore reached out a hand to help.

"Thank you, young lady," said the gray-haired woman with a smile. She went on without a backward glance, but Lenore chided herself for being so reckless. She patted her pockets and belt pack, but all her possessions were still there. A quick swipe of her sleeves showed she hadn't been planted with any tracker. For her own peace of mind, Lenore pulled out her mini device scanner, but it showed nothing. Just a harmless encounter.

As she pocketed the scanner, a piercing shout made Lenore turn around in a crouch, hands up to prepare for anything. When three children ran by, laughing and obviously playing a tagging game, she grew angry at herself.

Stupid, stupid me. My overreactions make me stand out more than anything else. I need to relax and seem like a normal customer. Though her eyes never stopped sweeping the other shoppers, she took a deep breath, lifted her shoulders and kept on until she found the food mart.

Ten minutes later, she had bought enough staples to see her family through the next couple of weeks. Plain food but that would be a welcome change.

"Shall I deliver these to your berth?" asked the clerk after he scanned the credit flimsy Lenore held out for him. Squashing her suspicions at what was a common question, she pulled out another device from the small pack at her belt.

"No, thank you. I brought a portable grav lift." She placed it on top of the waist-high pile of boxes and a field extended around them, raising the entire load about two inches off the ground. She attached a cord and tugged the load. It pulled easily and she headed toward the door.

As the clear doors began to slide open at her approach, Lenore noticed a familiar face on the other side of the plaza. She immediately dashed to the side of the opening, the load of boxes jerking with her to bang lightly against her legs. Lenore ignored this as she identified the face.

Daviss.

A man and a woman were flanking him, and his head turned from side to side.

How did he find the station so quickly? We have been here for less than an hour and there have been no opportunities to place a tracker since we last checked. Daviss and his cronies were heading out of sight of the store she was in. Lenore made a snap decision.

She maneuvered the load to the back of the store. The clerk's head came up as she startled him heading for the back room.

"I forgot there is something I have to do. Shouldn't take long." She thrust one of her few credit notes at the young man. "There is another of these for you if this is untouched when I return."

"Of... of course," he said. He appeared about to refuse the money, but Lenore pressed it on him. She didn't have time to argue. Taking out her pad and going into full acting mode, she exited the store, peering again through hanging hair. Daviss was at the far end, disappearing into a corridor nearly directly opposite of the one she had entered the plaza.

Quickly she headed to follow, eyes looking at stores and then the pad as if she was searching for an address. As she approached the area where Daviss had gone, she quickly walked past, letting her peripheral vision tell her if he was there. He and the two others had paused about three meters in and were talking. She stood on the other side and activated her hearing implant.

"...the main shopping area though there is another on the very uppermost level."

Lenore didn't recognize the voice so it must be the other man.

"But that is for high-paying customers," said a voice that held a touch of superiority. *That's Daviss, all right.* "She would never go there."

"The source indicated this station would be the next stop." That was the woman. "Do we have any reason to suspect it is incorrect?"

"No, she's here. But won't be for long." Daviss made a sound like a growl. "We need to split up. But don't confront her alone. She's mine." The menace in his voice made Lenore shudder and she didn't wait around for an answer from either of the others.

She made a wide detour back to the shop with her supplies, keeping an eye on the corridor but nobody exited back into the plaza.

They must be checking the docking ports first.

Anxiety hastening her steps, she dashed into the store, tossed her last credit note to the clerk and headed out the door, ignoring his "Thank you, come again."

She started back toward the ship, forcing herself to not hurry, knowing that would be exactly what they were looking for. She debated calling Diarmin but decided she shouldn't risk it since she would be there soon enough. As she rounded the final corner to the docking bay, one of a dozen on the station, she noticed a young woman peering intently at the numbers of each berth.

Our new passenger, perhaps? Good, that means we can leave right away. But bad in that Lenore was in disguise and didn't want to wear it the entire time on board.

She glanced for cameras and saw only one right past the entrance that she had just come through. She activated the gravitic grapple at her left wrist and shot at the camera. A slight tug pulled it off the wall with a few sparks indicating its failure.

Lenore ducked back into the corridor, leaned down behind the boxes and quickly removed her wig. A rag in another pocket swiped off her nose putty and makeup in one pass. She stuffed everything as well as she could into the bag and hurried to catch up to the girl.

"You wouldn't be looking for Berth twenty-four, would you?" she said as she came up behind.

The young blond woman jumped at Lenore's voice. Her simple brown dress swirled as she turned to Lenore. "Oh, you startled me. Yes, I am. I think that must be it." She pointed in the correct direction.

"That's the one. I am Captain Fleming. Are you ready to board?" Lenore glanced around. "No baggage?"

"I am Kurla Plaad. And no baggage, just what I have on me." The girl slightly lifted the cloth bag she was carrying.

"Very well, Ms. Plaad. Let's go. The sooner we board, the sooner we can be on our way."

Chapter Fourteen

Quinn waited with his father at the hatch that led to the ship. The recently refueled ship was connected to the spaceport by the latest adaptable docking collar, so they could walk straight from the midhatch into a waiting lounge, a small but well-appointed room with several comfortable seats and small table. It had been a little expensive, but his mother had argued that the small upgrade was worth the investment to appear more reputable to their newest passenger. Lenore was due back anytime and the passenger as well.

"Where's Alli?" he asked his father.

"Still on the computer," replied Diarmin, a slight frown pulling his mouth down. "She and I aren't happy at the lack of information about Kurla Plaad. All we found are the basics that are in any public records, birthdate, planet of origin, things like that."

"But isn't that good? She hasn't done anything illegal or is famous in some way." Quinn shrugged. "Perfect for us to stay out of sight."

"Well, yes and no." Diarmin crossed his arms. "Yes, it is good there is nothing negative about her, but the facts read like a made-up background."

Quinn bit his lip on all the questions that brought up. *How does Dad know what a fake background looks like? Had he been in law enforcement? Was that why he had killed?* He glanced over, noticing the deep worry lines as he constantly watched the port.

Now isn't the time to ask, thought Quinn. *Not when he is that tense and nervous about mere passengers.*

The door on the other side of the lounge opened to show a young woman being followed by his mother hauling a load of boxes. The stranger looked to be in her mid-twenties, a little shorter than Lenore, and had wavy, yellow-blond hair that reached just below her ears. Dressed in a simple brown dress that swirled around her ankles, she carried nothing but a large duffel bag over her shoulder. Her eyes were bright with intelligence and the smile on her face appeared to be genuine. Quinn was embarrassed to admit to himself that his heart gave a little leap when she turned that smile on him.

They approached the hatch and Lenore introduced them. "This is my first officer, Kel Eckert," she said, indicating Diarmin, "and Navigator Sean Mikin."

Diarmin held his hand out. "Pleased to meet you Ms. Plaad."

Instead of taking the hand, the woman clasped hers together to bow over them. "Kurla, please." She also bowed to Quinn, so he didn't offer his hand but inclined his head slightly.

"Should we expect more luggage? Surely that satchel isn't all you have?" asked Diarmin.

Kurla gave a slight chuckle. "Which is a polite way of asking where my deceased mentor's body might be."

Quinn was impressed with her correct read of the question and he could tell, by the slight tugging at the corners of her mouth, his mother was impressed as well.

Lenore answered. "Diplomacy and courtesy are emphasized on my ship."

"Ah, very wise, Captain." She held her bag out. "You may inspect this if you wish, but it only contains my personal items. You won't find High Priest Phylian's body in there. In accordance to our ways, it was cremated, and the ashes scattered on the planet we were visiting when he passed."

Diarmin took the bag, placed it on the table and inspected the contents. Quinn couldn't hold back his curiosity.

"Pardon me for asking, Ms. Plaad," he said.

"No Ms. Please. Makes me feel ancient. Just Kurla." She grinned at Quinn and lifted her chin slightly. "At least until I pass apprenticeship and become an Honored Priest. But I interrupted your question, young man." Her gaze rested on Quinn.

"Kurla," he began again after glancing at his mother. The slight nod indicated he could dispense with the Ms. "You indicated in your message that you needed transport for you and the priest. We expected more than one person."

"Of course, but the explanation is a long one, too complicated to explain in a short message." She took the bag back from Diarmin and handed him a credit flimsy, presumably with half the fee they had agreed upon.

Diarmin accepted it graciously and waved her toward the hatch. She stepped through and beckoned to Quinn to walk beside her.

"Allow me to explain," said Kurla, looking directly at Quinn. "My order is the Order of Continuing Clarity. When a High Priest passes, his body is required to return to the earth and his spirit must return to the Holy Temple on New Drea."

"His spirit?" asked Quinn. He was vaguely aware of his parents following closely and listening, but he focused on Kurla.

"Yes. Spirit, soul, whatever you may call it." She smiled again, this time with a little wonder. "I am extremely fortunate to have been far enough along in my studies to serve as his vessel when he died."

"Vessel?" asked Lenore.

"Of course." Kurla paused outside the ship's lounge and turned to face Lenore and Diarmin. "High Priest Phylian's spirit resides in me now and will be given to the Holy Temple and other High Priests when we return so his spirit will continue to enrich all the future acolytes."

"I see," said Lenore.

"Perhaps I should let him tell you." She briefly closed her eyes and her face blanked of all emotion. When her eyes opened again, her demeanor changed. She appeared to stand a little taller and instead of a smile, a seriousness suffused her face.

"Pleased to meet you," she said, but her voice had deepened and was more sonorous, almost resonant. "I am High Priest Lor Phylian and appreciate your quick response to accept us as passengers. I can only exist in this form for a short time."

"Our pleasure," said Lenore.

"Will we be talking to you or to Kurla on the trip?" asked Quinn, not sure if this was real.

"Worry not, youngster. It will be mostly Kurla from this point on. It is difficult for me to take control like this, so I will be in the background, hoarding my energies for the final transfer. I did wish to meet you and now I will return my apprentice to you." Bowing with hands clasped, her eyes closed again as her head drooped and soon the smile was back.

"I am getting better at that," she said. "But it does make me tired."

"Let me show you to your cabin," said Quinn, trying to keep his face from turning red when he saw his mother's eyebrows raise slightly.

They entered the lounge and, as they crossed to the opposite door, Quinn pointed out the galley and entertainment vids.

In the other hallway, he indicated the room in the middle. "This one is prepared for you, but if you prefer to be farther from our other passenger, we can prepare the other one. He is in that cabin," he added with a wave at Bondle's room.

"Why wouldn't I want to be next to him?" She leaned toward Quinn, eyes twinkling. Her voice was lower and held amusement. "Is he a noisy neighbor?"

Quinn felt his stomach swoop slightly as he caught a light scent from her hair, not exactly flowery but very pleasant. "Um, well, no just thought you may wish privacy."

Her laughter rang out and now he knew his face was red. "I have been sharing accommodations with an elderly priest for three years. From small rooms to my own mind. Privacy is a long-forgotten luxury." She appeared to notice his discomfort and put a hand on his arm. "But I appreciate the offer. I will take the one you have prepared. It's closer to the lounge anyway."

He nodded. "I will let you get settled then." He turned back to the lounge but spun around just before she closed the cabin door. "Oh, I nearly forgot to tell you. The cargo bay and bridge are restricted areas."

"Very well. Thank you, young navigator Sean."

"You're welcome, Kurla."

As her door closed, Quinn retreated to his own cabin, wondering to himself why it did indeed feel like a retreat.

***

As soon as Quinn was out of earshot, Lenore's hand closed over Diarmin's wrist to get his attention. She leaned toward him so her voice wouldn't carry.

"We need to leave as soon as possible. Are we done fueling?"

Diarmin nodded. "Completed about ten minutes ago. What's the hurry?"

"Daviss is here on the station."

"What?" Diarmin's eyes were wide but he managed to keep his voice at a whisper. "Impossible."

"Maybe, but we can figure out how when we are safely in space." She pulled the load of food inside the ship and closed the hatch to the lounge. "How long before we can leave?"

"I have to restart the engines from scratch since they have to be completely off when fueling. Then undocking and permission to leave."

"How long?"

"The lounge is paid for so I will undock and let the ship sit free of the station. While the engines warm up, I'll request an immediate spot in the exit queue. About ten minutes if they aren't too busy."

"Do it. I will stow the food."

Lenore pushed the pile into the galley and deactivated the grav lift. The boxes would be fine during takeoff and could be put away later. She returned to the corridor as Diarmin was securing the hatch and inputting the codes that would allow them to undock.

"Not a word to the kids," she hissed in his ear and started for the ladder to the bridge.

Diarmin nodded and then gently caught her wrist. His lips scrunched in a grim line. "You were right to be in disguise."

Though Lenore agreed with him, being right didn't make her feel any better.

Chapter Fifteen

Allison heard low voices and treads on the ladder. Without taking her eyes from the screen she identified the two as her mother and father. She caught a few words like "Priest" and "cargo" but turned her attention back to her work.

"Here you are," said her mother. *Strange, she seems more tense than usual. Her eyes are kind of wide.*

"Of course. Still researching like usual." She grabbed a pad off the console and handed it to her father. "I only found a little bit more on Kurla, mostly just a couple passenger manifests with her name."

Diarmin took the pad and scrolled down the short list as he took the command chair. "What are you working on now?"

"Looking up The Order of Continuing Clarity and that High Priest guy," she replied, tapping away and scrolling through screens.

"How do you know about those?" asked her mother. Vaguely she could hear her father requesting a departure time as soon as possible. *Always in a hurry.*

"Come on, mom," she stopped herself short from rolling her eyes. "I know how to use the intercom system on the ship."

Lenore put her hands on her hips. "But that conversation started in the spaceport lounge." Her mother and father exchanged glances and she thought they looked worried.

"Yes, while both hatches were open. I just turned up the gain and caught nearly everything." She turned back to the computer and waved her hand at the command console. "It's recorded if you want to listen to it again."

"Allison!" Both her parents together.

She was startled as her father spun her chair around to face them.

"Why would you eavesdrop like that?" he asked at the same time her mother said, "What did you hear?"

Her eyes flicked to her mother whose arms were now crossed.

"I wanted to get a head start on researching our newest passenger, so I listened. After she talked about it, I started researching so I turned off the intercom." She couldn't quite understand why they seemed angry. "It is a public part of the ship, she was talking freely to you, and I wanted to make sure we didn't miss any details. It's not like I am listening to them in their rooms, or on private messages, not that they've made any but if they did—"

"Okay, enough," said her mother. "I understand why you did that, but no more snooping unless specifically ordered to."

"All right," she said but wisely said nothing about how she had wanted to help alleviate any suspicions since both of them had been nervous about strangers on board. They were even more jumpy now so it obviously hadn't helped.

"Have you found anything yet?" asked Diarmin.

"Only that such an order does exist on New Drea, but it is a very small and relatively unknown group. What is written about them matches what Kurla has said. What she didn't say, but I have pieced together, is that a High Priest and apprentice often travel together to broaden their education and search for other people who might be worthy to join. That's all I have so far. I was just beginning to look under the surface, local rumors, ship manifests, that sort of thing."

"Very well, keep at that but no more listening in," said her father as her mother went toward the ladder.

Allison nodded and turned back to her computer.

Now I'm glad I didn't tell them about the video in the corridor outside the guest cabins. I'd probably get in more trouble if I mentioned Quinn's red face and stammering around Kurla.

***

Lenore descended the ladder quickly and headed down the hall. After a few steps, she noticed she was a hair away from 'stomping' so she altered her aggressive strides, berating herself for her lack of control. *Why am I so upset at a little eavesdropping? Or is it because of Daviss on the station?* She crossed her arms then uncrossed them, chiding herself again.

As she entered the lounge, she nearly ran headfirst into Quinn. Lenore didn't quite jump because she had her body under control now. But she hadn't noticed he was there and thus was angry at herself for that.

"Hey, where are you going?" asked Quinn. His face also showed that he hadn't known she was there either, which, oddly enough, made Lenore feel slightly better.

"I am going to check on the passengers and let them know we will be taking off shortly."

"Already? I can tell them if you want," he said.

"No, you get to the bridge. The Captain should be the one to see to the passengers whenever possible."

Quinn nodded and she continued to the cabins. Politely she knocked on Bondle's door and opened it when she heard a "Come in."

She took one step into the room. The scientist was sitting at the tiny desk with several pads scattered around him, and two more pads on the bed. He was scrawling, however, on a tablet of paper. A quick glance showed what looked like chemical formulae. Lenore wondered why the paper when most pads had the capabilities to do scientific designs or calculations, whatever he was doing. She shrugged. *Everyone has their own way of doing things.*

"Mr. Bondle," she said, and he looked up at her, his eyes blinking as if to focus better. "We have finished our business here and are preparing to leave as soon as we have obtained permission."

"Thank you for letting me know, Captain," he said. Bondle grabbed the straps on the chair, belted himself in and returned to his papers.

Shaking her head, Lenore closed the door and headed for the middle cabin. Since this door was closed, she assumed the woman was in here. She rapped lightly and the door slid quickly open.

"Captain. Come in, please." Kurla backed away from the narrow door and swept her arm in a welcoming gesture.

Lenore only took the single step inside as she had with Bondle. "I wanted to inform you that we will be departing shortly."

"Ah, then I guess I should make sure all my belongings are stowed safely," she answered with a grin. She grabbed her small bag and placed it in the closet next to the lavatory. "There, all done!" She winked at Lenore, the grin turning mischievous.

Lenore couldn't help but smile back. The girl's charm was undeniable. "An announcement will be made when departure is imminent."

"Thank you, Captain."

Lenore nodded and left, closing the door behind her. She debated returning to the bridge but didn't want to face the questioning glances of her family. She saw the packages of food strapped in the corner and decided to stow them before take-off.

As the last box slid into place, Diarmin announced departure in sixty seconds. Lenore secured the galley and headed to her cabin. She was unpacking her bag and stowing the wig and rest of her disguise when she felt the ship accelerate. By now she was experienced enough to brace herself, not needing to strap in. The cabin was neat as a pin within the ten minutes needed to go to transwarp. The physical activity helped to calm Lenore and she was ready to face everyone else without losing her emotional control.

She had just left the cabin when she ran into Diarmin.

"We need to talk," he said, pointing toward their cabin.

"Don't you need to be on the bridge?"

"The kids will call us if there is anything unusual."

Lenore suppressed a flare of irritation but entered the cabin and stood there as he shut the door.

"Well?"

As Diarmin flushed slightly at her question, she realized she had let her annoyance show, which started the cycle of negative emotions again.

"When did our daughter become so paranoid and sneaky?"

I guess he's not beating around the bush. Fine. I won't either.

"She's always been sneaky, you know that." She ignored Diarmin as he opened his mouth to say something. "And you know what I always say, 'Better paranoid—'"

"'Than hurt or dead.' Yeah, we've heard that enough. She's been sneaky with her computers, not with people. Now she's spying on our passengers. What's next? Invasive sensor sweeps?" Diarmin began his nervous pacing, but in their tiny cabin, he could only get three strides in.

"She was the most trusting of all of us. What happened? Quinn has been more distrustful but that's to be expected with all he has gone through."

"You raised them; you tell me." Lenore crossed her arms again, letting her irritation show.

He stopped his pacing, eyes snapping with an anger she rarely saw.

"That's why I am worried. Alli is not like she used to be." He stepped toward Lenore. "She's picking up all that paranoia from you. Do you want her to be like a Xa?"

Lenore ground her teeth to keep from yelling. "Don't put all the blame on me. You have been exhibiting more than your fair share of suspicion and dangerous emotions ever since you fired a hand weapon for the first time in years. You're the one who has changed. And in retrospect, it's a good thing I was so paranoid, or I might have been caught by Daviss."

"That was a coincidence. Also, I am dealing with my issues, but you didn't answer my question."

It was like a splash of cold water in her face as the realization hit her that she hadn't answered. *Is it even slightly possible I want Allison to be like me?* Icy fear rippled down her spine and the look on Diarmin's face calmed her instantly.

"You are right, I didn't, and I am sorry." She relaxed further as Diarmin's eyes lost some of their anger. "Obviously I don't want her, or Quinn, to be like the Xa. I have always said that and will continue to say it. I think we can both agree, however, that recent events have changed all of us, especially the kids." Lenore uncrossed her arms and Diarmin's shoulders slumped as he nodded.

"How..." he trailed off as he sat heavily on the edge of their bed. "How can we teach them to protect themselves without becoming mistrustful of everyone?"

Lenore sat next to him.

"I don't know. Maybe we should explain to them that a little paranoia is good, but it can go too far. Maybe," she patted his knee. "Maybe start showing a little more trust ourselves so our kids won't become so jaded. Starting with this assignment. After all, I think a single young woman and scrawny scientist hardly pose a threat. It's off the ship where we can allow suspicion, not here in a safe environment."

Diarmin's smile made her heart lift for the first time in days.

Chapter Sixteen

"What is this fabulous dish?"

Everyone was in the lounge for the evening meal. The extender to the table had been pulled out of storage and couches pushed to the corners to make room for the family and passengers. Even though it had been Diarmin's idea, he was still worried it was the wrong one, but he couldn't say exactly why. Awkwardness prevailed, but Kurla Plaad was doing her best to break the ice.

"That, Ms. Plaad, is called foie gras with Morellian wafers and the main dish is, I believe, Keyon legumes, a rare delicacy said to adjust itself to the eater's preference," he replied.

"Well," Kurla took another small bite and chewed thoughtfully. "It does appear to do that, and it is absolutely delicious." She pointed with her fork at Diarmin's food. "How come I get the good stuff and you all are eating stew? Well, except for Mr. Bondle."

"We save the best for our passengers, Ms. Plaad," said Lenore quickly, glancing at Quinn and Allison. Diarmin figured she spoke up hoping they wouldn't mention that the family was tired of eating the outlandish food that had been given to them from a king's larder. But since they had hardly spoken two words since everyone sat down, Diarmin wasn't worried too much about that.

"Oh, please, call me Kurla."

Silence descended again on the table.

"So, um, Kurla," said Lenore. "How did you become a member of your Order? Sounds like an interesting group."

"That's a long story, but I will try to make it short." She put down her fork, leaned forward with her elbows on the table and made sure to look at everyone in turn as she spoke.

Interesting, thought Diarmin. *Tricks to engage and create trust. Must have learned it in her training as a priest.* He took another bite of stew and listened.

"My parents were farmers on the agricultural planet Omiem, which means 'Home' in the native language." She sighed. "Quite unoriginal, I know, but most of the population are like that, my parents especially. My older brother and sister were quite content with their life, working the farm and digging in the dirt coming as natural as breathing. I found happiness in other things, like books."

"Books?" asked Allison. "Not holonovels or vids?"

"Actual paper books, if you can believe that. The only place to find those 'luxuries' as my family called them, was in the city's public libraries and I wasn't allowed to go there alone as a youngster."

"Not even games?" Allison's eyes grew huge as her voice dropped to a whisper. "No computers?"

Kurla laughed. "I know. It seems so primitive and I never realized how sheltered I was. When I was sixteen, I went on a trip with my school into the only large city on the planet. I was overwhelmed at all the technology and experiences that I had never seen growing up. Don't get me wrong." She held a palm up, probably in reaction to the look of horror on Allison's face. "My parents loved me, and I never felt neglected, only that I didn't fit in. When the class visited the history museum, it changed my life. Most of the students listened to how our ancestors came to the planet to 'get back to the land' and lead simpler life. But all I could think about was that there were other planets and different cultures and I craved to see them all!"

"So that's why you joined the Order? Because they travel?" asked Quinn, his first words at the table. Diarmin was pleased at his children's participation.

"Well, not exactly. That was a coincidence." Kurla picked up a legume daintily on the tip of her fork, popped it in her mouth and chewed slowly with a slight smile on her face. The entire time looking directly at Quinn which disconcerted Diarmin. From the slight blush, Quinn was a little flustered as well. *Probably not for the same reason I am though.*

"So? How did that happen?" It was Bondle's turn to ask.

Very interesting. She has managed to engage everyone at the table.

71

"When I turned eighteen, I informed my parents that I was leaving the planet. They were disappointed that I didn't want to be in the family business, but they had figured that would be my choice. I had saved up some money, and my parents surprised me with a small account that they had started for me when it became apparent that I might want more. 'For schooling or whatever else you may need,' they said. I was very grateful and booked the cheapest flight out. All that I owned was contained in one bag and amid tears from parents and siblings and the few friends I had, I left. The strange thing is I wasn't sad at all, only excited about the huge universe and all its wonders that awaited me.

"However..."

Here she stopped and looked around the table again and Diarmin realized everyone's attention was riveted on Kurla. He could have sworn the slight smile on her face showed she was aware of the attention and reveled in it. He vowed to be less mesmerized, but it was difficult, especially when he reminded himself that he was trying to be less suspicious and paranoid. To set a good example for his kids.

Right.

"However, as you know, it takes money to travel and with my naive upbringing, I thought I was rich when I left, but I ran out of credits quickly. I had only been to two planets and was now stuck in a spaceport, no place to live, no job and no money. I had fallen asleep at a cafe table after wandering for over a day. The manager shook me roughly awake and asked me to leave if I wasn't going to order anything. I staggered out the door, still exhausted, and didn't notice an older gentleman following me until he gently touched my elbow. So tired was I that I didn't even react.

"'Excuse me,' he said. 'But haven't you anywhere to go?'

"I shook my head. 'Was the transient hotel filled?' he asked. I stared at him dumbfoundedly. 'What's a transient hotel?' I asked. The man smiled and took me to the place he was speaking of, explaining that in most spaceports, there was a space provided for those that couldn't afford a place to sleep or just wanted a place to take a nap before the next flight. He dropped me off there, helped me secure my belongings in a locker and left me in a large room with dozens of beds and beings from all places sleeping here and there. He assured me he would return after I get a good rest, and I passed out. When I awoke, the man was sitting on the bed next to mine and I professed my gratitude. I looked around the room and vaguely realized that, though there were as many people as when I fell asleep, they weren't the same ones. But so fascinating. There was a blue-skinned woman, several very large people with huge muscles. I even saw a being with scales and flippers wearing some sort of breathing apparatus."

Kurla paused. Diarmin noticed that everyone had stopped eating to listen. "I'm sorry, I am going on and on. I don't need to describe that hotel, I am sure you all have been to one at some point, well-traveled as you appear to be."

Allison opened her mouth to say something but stopped at a slight nudge from her mother. Lenore probably didn't want to let Kurla know that the children had never been to a transient hotel.

"Well, speeding by the details, the man turned out to be a priest of the Order of Continuing Clarity. They traveled around, looking for people in need and offering help wherever possible. I was fascinated and returned with him to New Drea to learn more about it. A few months later I joined."

"You gave up everything to belong to a strange priesthood?" asked Quinn.

"Well, I wanted to travel, and this seemed the best way to learn, from a group who knew about traveling." She grinned at Quinn. "Not to mention I had no money and no idea how to survive in the great big galaxy and these people were kind enough to help." She lifted her gaze to the ceiling and her eyes took on a distant look. "And now I feel obligated to return that help wherever I can. Well, after I return High Priest Phylian of course."

Silence descended at the table and Kurla blinked a few times and looked around. She cleared her throat and applied herself to the rest of her food, her gaze now firmly on her plate. Others began eating as well and Diarmin wondered at the girl's apparent embarrassment. He tried to start another conversation.

"That's a good story, Kurla." He glanced at Ven Bondle who hadn't said much the entire meal. "Mr. Bondle. How did you come to be a scientist?"

A palpable feeling of relief swept across the table as Bondle looked absently at Diarmin.

"Oh, um, well. It's not as interesting a story as hers but I'll try.

"As I have said, my planet has been threatened by various plagues for over a hundred years. My father died of one when I was seven so my mother returned to work to support us. My older brother worked as well. Since she couldn't pay for advanced schooling for me, I set my sights on bioresearch since that was the only field supported by the government. My decision was solidified when I was fifteen, after my younger sister died."

Diarmin glanced around the table. His story was full of loss, deeper and more intriguing than Kurla's but his dry, emotionless recitation did not engage the listeners.

"That year I submitted a paper concerning a possible interpretation of the plagues as one continuously adapting disease, not several different plagues. It won a national award so I came to the attention of the government. They enrolled me into a special, advanced program that let me focus specifically on finding a cure using my methods I had outlined in the paper. I graduated in three years and was instantly put on one of the ships that traveled to a variety of planets to search for a cure. I was fortunate enough to be among the group looking at new colonies and at the third stop, I found the organism I needed to create the cure. The ship dropped off supplies for the lab and two years later, here we are."

Bondle immediately returned to his food, obviously finished talking even though his story left way too much unsaid. He was either uneasy with attention on him or simply didn't want to talk about it. It left another uncomfortable lull.

"On the contrary, that was an interesting story, Mr. Bondle," said Lenore. "And it leaves me with a lot of questions."

"Which, unfortunately, will have to wait," said Diarmin. "Perhaps at the next meal."

Lenore shot him an annoyed look but stood at the same time and helped clear the dishes. The kids were eying both parents but said nothing.

"Thank you for the stories but it's time to return to work." Diarmin placed his dishes in the recycler and left for the bridge, hoping his family would get the hint and leave the passengers alone.

Chapter Seventeen

Since it was Allison's turn to clean the galley, she was the last one to the bridge. But since everyone was staring at screens not saying a word, she knew she hadn't missed any discussions. As she sat at her console, she wondered exactly what had caused the tension. All the passengers did was tell their stories. When she heard her mother clear her throat, she knew she'd find out now.

"Alli, where are our passengers?" she asked, keeping her voice low.

"When I left the galley, Kurla was scrolling through the entertainment selections and Mr. Bondle had returned to his cabin," Allison answered.

"Did you see him go into the cabin?"

"Well, not exactly but he said to thank everyone for the meal and that he was going back to his cabin." Allison shrugged. "He left through that doorway, so I assumed that's where he went. Shall I pull up the video to his cabin and check?" She was joking since she had been given the lecture not to snoop but her parents' answers surprised her.

"Yes."

"No."

Lenore looked at Diarmin, annoyance clear on her face. Her father looked a little angry.

"I can't believe you said 'yes', Lenore. Why would you invade his privacy like that?"

"I don't trust Bondle. Haven't since he came on board. Especially after his made-up story."

"Why do you think it was made up?"

"Come on. Didn't it sound rehearsed?"

"Not really, but even if it was, it's probably because he wants to tell that story with as few words as possible because it's distressing to him."

"You don't think he was trying to play on our sympathies?"

"Not at all. If anyone was working the table, it was Kurla."

"What?" Lenore uncrossed her arms and leaned back in her chair.

"Now it's my turn to say, 'come on.' You should have caught all the little tricks of the trade used to engage an audience and seem sincere."

"Or she could simply *be* sincere. And who says I didn't catch them? Sometimes people are naturally gifted storytellers, and it seemed to me that those 'tricks', as you call them, were used unconsciously."

Privately Allison agreed with her father but wisely kept her mouth shut and fiddled with her control board. Quinn had no such compunction.

"I agree with Mom," he said. "There is something off about Bondle. He had zero emotion as he told us about his sister dying. Nobody does that."

You do, thought Allison. *Especially when you talk about your experience as a captive.* But again, she said nothing.

"Quinn," said Diarmin. "Sometimes people hide their emotions when talking about a painful subject." His eyes slid to Lenore and returned quickly.

"But Bondle was asking all those questions when he first came aboard, then suddenly stopped and instead hides out in his room when he's not eating or checking his cargo," said Quinn.

"We were very hesitant in answering a lot of his questions. Maybe he got the hint that we weren't just going to tell him everything."

"Enough," said Lenore, her hand lightly slapping the console. "We can guess all we want, but there is really no way of knowing what is in his mind. Ah," she said, holding up a finger when Diarmin opened his mouth. "Same thing with Kurla. Bottom line is, they haven't done anything to make us truly suspicious so we will simply be watchful."

"And trust them unless they show they can't be trusted for some reason," Diarmin added with a pointed look at Lenore.

Her mother nodded, but it seemed a little reluctant. Allison finally chimed in.

"Well, we can't read their minds, but they are where they're supposed to be."

"You didn't spy on them, did you?" asked Quinn.

"Of course not. I just ran a general scan of the ship." She slid in her chair to the side so everyone could see her screen. "See?" She pointed at the relevant section. "Four blips on the bridge, one in the lounge and one in Bondle's quarters. Six blips, six people where they are supposed to be."

Her father had stood and approached while she was recounting her actions. He laughed and ruffled her hair.

"Trust our clever daughter to be the practical one. Good job, Alli."

Allison looked at her mother and brother. The small smiles of approval were all she needed.

***

"Transition complete," said Quinn.

Diarmin tapped a few more keys then locked the board. "Good job. Another one in eighteen hours. Maybe I should let you handle it?" He smiled as Quinn threw him an eager look from his seat at navigation. Allison and Lenore had gone back to the cabin to continue decoding.

"If you think I am ready," he said.

"I believe you are, but," he held up a hand briefly as Quinn's eyes lit up. "Let's wait until we have no passengers or fragile cargo, deal?"

"Okay, Dad." Quinn turned back to his board. "Can I ask you a question?" he asked, not looking up.

"Sure." Diarmin braced himself. Every time his kids were hesitant to ask something, it meant they wanted to know something that he might not want to tell. He knew the kids might start asking about his past but wasn't sure if he was ready to discuss it at all, much less the details.

"When we were all talking about trusting the passengers, you and Mom were exchanging some significant looks." Now he locked down his own board and looked at Diarmin. "Can I ask what those were all about?"

Diarmin breathed an inner sigh of relief. He knew that someday soon he would have to tell them, but it wasn't this moment and that was good enough for now.

"It's complicated but I suppose I can tell you. Your mother and I have been worried that you and Alli are learning to be overly suspicious of people." Diarmin held his hands out. "Not that you haven't had good cause lately, but we don't want you both to become mistrusting of everyone. There are a lot of very good people out there in the galaxy, despite recent experiences telling you otherwise."

"So that's why she went from trying to convince you that Bondle is up to something to saying we should trust until there is reason not to."

"Yes." He shook a finger at Quinn. "You are getting entirely too good at reading us, young man."

"I have learned from the best," he replied with another grin.

"That is true." Diarmin pushed the board away and stood. "It is nearly time for Bondle to make his nightly check on the cargo. I should be there."

"You could set the ship's chronometer to him," said Quinn.

"That's a scientist for you, very methodical. Can you watch the bridge until he is done?" He headed for the ladder.

"Of course. And if you want, I will take first watch. I'm not tired at all and I wanted to practice some more course charting."

Diarmin paused at the ladder and glanced at Quinn as he took the command seat and swung the control board in front of him. "Since I am a little sleepy, I will take you up on that. Have a good night and wake me if anything happens."

Quinn gave an absent half salute and Diarmin descended to the hall, then headed toward the cargo bay. *He is growing up fast and ready for more adult responsibilities. In fact, his sixteenth birthday is next month.* Diarmin shook his head. *It seems he was just a toddler last year. Such is a parent's life I suppose.*

He descended the ladder and a glance at the timepiece on the wall showed he was a few minutes early for Bondle's inspection. He wandered over to his workbench, trying not to feel melancholy at the passage of time. He barely had time to scan his work to decide on which project to work on when he heard steps on the ladder. He recovered the table with the cloth, thinking he would start tomorrow, and turned to face Bondle.

"Hello, Mr. Bondle. Come for the nightly inspection?"

Bondle started then gave a weak chuckle. "Don't know why I jumped. You have been here for every inspection in the last three days."

"Sometimes being introspective can make a person unaware of their surroundings and so are startled easily," said Diarmin, realizing that even though Bondle gave the impression of an absent-minded old professor, he really was quite young. If his story was accurate, he would be in his mid-to-late-twenties.

"Introspective?"

"You did tell the story about your past at dinner," said Diarmin. "I know I tend to have my thoughts inward when reflecting on my life."

Bondle stared at Diarmin. "Huh. That's probably it. To be honest, I have been too focused on my work to give my past any thought. In fact, these last few days are the first I can remember with having time on my hands. My life up to this point has been in pursuit of this." He lightly patted the nearest six-all. "I only hope it is worth it."

"You have these elaborate cargo containers. Are you sure the cargo isn't dangerous?" Even as he said it, Diarmin winced inwardly. He didn't want to suspect Bondle, but Lenore's suspicions hovered in his forebrain.

"Even if the container was damaged or breached accidentally, which is only about, maybe…" He drifted off in thought for a couple moments. "About only a point-five percent chance per layer so very slim. However, if that did happen, the anti-viral agents would not pose a threat to us. Each is also self-contained, but the real danger is outside contamination of the specimens. If any toxins or bacteria or foreign substance is introduced, it will activate the enzymes and purpose the drug for something unknown." Bondle gave a tug of his lab coat. "That is why I believe this medicine will work against the plague. It is designed to go after whatever virus is mixed with it. It won't matter if the plague mutates thereafter, the medicine will too."

"That sounds like a breakthrough for any planet that may go through something similar." Diarmin admitted he felt a bit of awe if this medicine did what Bondle said.

"I hope so. Once our planet is rid of the plague, we will continue to manufacture this medication so no other has to suffer through such a nightmare." He turned thoughtful again and Diarmin left him to the inspection of the containers, retreating back to his worktable under the ladder to do some of his own reflecting.

I believe Bondle is exactly what he says he is. I don't know why Lenore is suspicious. Maybe it's because I recognize a kindred spirit, so focused on work that the past gets buried.

"Good night," said Bondle as he went back up the ladder. Diarmin returned the slight wave and followed after a few moments, figuring he'd better get some sleep since he would take over for Quinn at mid-shift. And sleep would put off having to face the fact that maybe it might be time to stop burying his past.

Chapter Eighteen

Quinn was glad that his father had let him work the first shift. He did want to practice charting courses, but he also wanted some time alone to think. He saw his father tense up when he wanted to ask a question and he knew it was because he didn't want to discuss his past. Allison didn't seem to care that they knew very little about their parents. But Quinn had sensed the underlying threat in the voice of the man who stopped his mother back on the planet of the rich guy. He regretted closing the link when his father told him to. He might have found out something important about his mother's past. Maybe Allison didn't want to know, but it was becoming an obsession with him.

What was so bad about the Xa'ti'al that his mother had left? Why were there always ships chasing them? What did his father do in his previous life before Quinn was born, and why did he tense up whenever he thought about it? Not just tense but wired so tight, like he was afraid he would let something slip. His parents always told him and Allison that honesty was the best policy within the family. *Well, it's time they live up to that assertion.*

Quinn pushed the command board away irritably, then stood and began to pace. They wouldn't tell him anything if he asked directly, he was sure of it. Slowly and with continuing the story of when they first met would be the best. He noticed how his mother let slip a few details. A few well thought out questions would divulge more.

The bridge wasn't big enough to allow him to walk off his frustrations, so he locked down the bridge and climbed down the ladder. He strode down the hall but before he turned into the lounge, he thought he heard a noise coming from the cargo bay. He knew Bondle wouldn't change his inspection schedule if his life depended on it so he figured it must be his father. *Now might be a good time for some harmless questions.* Quinn climbed down the ladder, debating which subject to ask about and nearly ran into Kurla.

They both bounced back from each other and said "Oh" at the same time. Kurla giggled at the simultaneous exchange and Quinn grinned, feeling his face heat up.

"I'm sorry," she said as her face colored prettily. "I wasn't watching where my feet were taking me." She ducked her head and looked back at him through her lashes. Quinn felt a little bit taller and older so he thought perhaps he should behave so.

"You're really not supposed to be down here, Ms., um Kurla."

She looked around as if she hadn't realized where she was. "Oh, I am sorry. When I get in these moods, I usually don't pay enough attention to my surroundings. The High Priest often said it was my biggest failing."

Quinn stood away from the ladder and motioned for her to climb. She started up the ladder as he asked, "What mood is that?"

At the top, she let him come alongside her and walked down the hall slowly.

"I know I always wanted to travel, and I am very grateful for the opportunity, but I can't get used to spaceships, especially one this small. I needed to stretch my legs."

"We have a treadmill in the third bedroom. You can get a lot of exercising on that."

She smiled at him and his breath caught in his throat. "Thanks, but that's not quite what I mean. I grew up on a farm, lots of land to run around on and open skies overhead." She held her hands up. "Don't get me wrong, this is a very nice ship, but I guess I am feeling a little confined."

"I understand. I was feeling something similar which was why I was wandering too."

"What planet did you grow up on?"

"Oh, um, well, I didn't. I grew up on... um... on a ship." Quinn was flustered and he wasn't sure why.

"Really? I don't think I have ever met anyone who was raised on a ship." They were in the lounge now and she turned to him, wide-eyed. "What was that like?"

"I don't know, good I guess." How could he explain when he didn't know what growing up on a planet was like?

"I expect it would be lonely. I always liked going to school, hanging out with my friends. I still talk to them once in a while, see how they are doing." She sighed. "I hope after the High Priest is returned that I can go visit. Would be nice to see my home again."

"I did go to schools on a few different planets," he said, not mentioning the fact that he had gone only for missions, a week or two at the most. But their conversation was raising a lot of questions in his mind. Was his upbringing that different? He had never really thought about it. Living on the ship was simply how life was. He fell silent as they walked the corridor outside her cabin.

Kurla lightly grasped his forearm as they kept walking. "I am sorry. I didn't mean to upset you."

"You didn't." He managed a smile but wondered himself if there was any real emotion in it.

"And I didn't mean to wander into the cargo bay." Now she gave him a teasing grin, and he returned it.

"That's okay. At least it wasn't the bridge. Speaking of which, I need to get back. I am on watch, after all."

"Oooh can I come? I haven't seen the bridge yet."

Quinn was quite aware that she was still touching his arm and could hear a little voice inside reminding him of the family's conversation earlier. But he also remembered that his father let Bondle on the bridge so he went with that memory.

"Okay, but not for long and you have to stay by the stairs."

"Sure, thanks." And her smile lit her eyes and warmed his heart.

Chapter Nineteen

Lenore entered the bridge, noticing the frown lines on Diarmin's face. He appeared to be concentrating but she knew that when he was working, the frown lines were limited to a couple of wrinkles between the eyebrows. These radiated down the sides and even around his mouth and she guessed he was probably clenching his teeth as well.

"Got a minute?" she asked as softly as she could, but he still looked surprised.

"Sure," he said as she sat in the navigator's seat and spun it to face him. "I wanted to talk to you too."

"About what?" she asked.

"About Quinn." Diarmin shifted in his seat. "Last night when I left him on the bridge for the first watch, he seemed fine but when I relieved him for second watch, he was very surly. Hardly said two words to me and I think one of those words was just a grunt."

"Maybe he was tired."

"No, I know him when he is tired, this was more than regular grumpiness. Do you know if there is anything wrong?" His fingers idly flicked at the control board.

"He's almost sixteen. Isn't moodiness normal for teenagers?" Lenore was trying to hide her concern. As far as she could remember, this was the first time Diarmin had ever asked her about one of the kids. He had raised them and was usually the one to explain their behavior to her.

"I guess, but I can't be sure. You know neither one of us had a normal childhood or adolescence, so we have no frame of reference, no experience ourselves to draw on." Diarmin shook his head. "I think there is more to it than simple mood swings." He looked up from the board. "I just thought maybe you noticed something in the training. That maybe it was still his recent trauma making things difficult."

"No, he appears to be putting that behind him. Well, as much as he can."

"So, what did you want to talk to me about?"

Lenore blinked at the sudden change in topic but let it go. "How much did you overhear of the conversation with Daviss? And did the kids hear anything?"

"When I recognized the voice, I told them to close down the line with you and just communicate with me. They protested at first, wanting to help, but I convinced them that this was an emergency and an open line would distract you. They heard nothing from the restaurant." Now the frown lines were back. "I, however, heard everything. It was not a pleasant meal."

"No, it wasn't, and you and I need to talk about the entire discussion at some point. However, one part stands out." She took a slow breath, trying to figure the best way to say it but when she looked at her husband, she decided to just start talking. "Daviss knew all the details about our previous mission, and that meeting was well planned. It's like he knew exactly where we have been for the past year."

"How?"

"I'm not sure but my best guess is he has contacts in the slave organization watching us. Maybe others. The woman with him on the station said that a source told them we would be on Sultra."

"I do remember you asking Daviss what his connections to the slavers were. I thought you were reacting to what he said about Beryshie Corporation. Now it sounds like you already suspected it."

Lenore licked her lips before responding. "In the information I have been decoding, the stuff I don't let Alli see, I have found a connection between the Xa'ti'al and the slave organization. I don't know if Daviss is directly involved with them, but it would be one explanation on how he knew so much of the previous mission."

Diarmin crossed his arms. "You have never mentioned that to me."

Lenore felt her emotions bubbling again and struggled to identify them so she could control them. Embarrassment? Doubt? She eyed Diarmin and saw him watching her just as closely. Nothing but honesty would do here, so she fought the emotions down.

"I didn't tell you because I didn't want to worry you." He snorted and she knew she was beating around the bush. "Okay, not just that but I wanted solid evidence and for you to have deniability and… and, I think I am too used to keeping secrets."

He snorted again and this time she knew her emotion was anger.

"Hey, you are keeping your fair share of secrets as well," she said, trying hard not to cross her arms like Diarmin. "The bottom line is…I don't think we can afford to keep secrets anymore. We need to be completely open and honest with each other *and* the kids."

"Between us, yes. But the kids…I don't think so." He tightened his crossed arms and looked down.

"But—"

"I don't want them knowing what I was!" Diarmin's eyes flashed as he glared at her. She didn't react other than to stare back, trying to project calm. He needed to face his past so he could get beyond those violent feelings the memories were bringing out.

"Look. If one little thing had gone wrong, I would now be in the hands of the Xa'ti'al and maybe you would too. Where would they be? How would they know what to do? They simply don't know enough about our past and would probably try to rescue us, ending up caught themselves."

Diarmin was silent for several moments and Lenore let him work it through. She'd had plenty of time to think about all this.

"We need to talk further but not while we have passengers," he said, and she could see him struggling to cool down.

Lenore nodded and he stood. "I am already overdue for Bondle's morning inspection." He headed toward the stairwell then paused to look back at Lenore. "I think we can start by continuing the story of when we met. Then you and I will decide in what way and how much to tell them."

"I agree," said Lenore. He left down the ladder and she took the command seat. Her teeth began to hurt from clenching down on the argument she had wanted to make. She knew he didn't want to reveal his past, but she also knew that that was one of the most important things that needed to be told.

For all their sakes.

***

Diarmin trudged toward the cargo bay, head down and silently fuming. He wasn't exactly sure if he was angry at Lenore for holding back information or for suggesting they tell the children everything. He stomped down the ladder and saw Bondle already by the six-alls.

"I heard you that time, no surprise this morning," said Bondle but his smile faded as he looked at Diarmin.

Diarmin did his best to show a polite demeanor but wasn't sure if he was successful.

"I, um, I did wait for you but decided I should go ahead and inspect. Safety first, after all." Bondle looked like he wanted to back up, but the large container was at his back.

"That's fine. Go ahead." Diarmin angled toward his workbench behind the ladder.

Bondle nodded and continued with his scans. Diarmin had barely sat when Bondle announced he was finished and headed out of the bay. Diarmin let his shoulders slump as he thought about the conversation with his wife. Lenore had always kept information close so he could understand why she kept the connection between the Xa and slavers a secret. When they were first married, Diarmin had to charm, coax and wheedle information out of her and still only had bits and pieces of her life before they met. Reluctantly, he admitted he did the same, but she knew what he was when they met and surely she didn't want to tell their kids that he had been an assassin.

They are too young, he told himself. *They won't understand.* Diarmin forced himself to admit his worst fear. *What if...what if they look at me differently? They were already wary when they knew I killed in my past. What if they knew that I didn't just kill once or twice or in self-defense? That there are over two dozen contracts I have carried out and that is above and beyond those I have hurt or killed while doing my job.*

He sighed deeply and flipped up the cloth covering his worktable. But would being older help them adjust? *Maybe we should tell them, while they still remember me as a good father who turned his back on that life and swore to never kill again.*

He had no idea how long he had been brooding when he came back to awareness. He stared down at the table, longing to work at a project.

It was the best time for introspection. But he had to go prepare breakfast for the passengers and his family.

Chapter Twenty

After breakfast, Lenore suggested that the family take their posts on the bridge. They took their places, Allison still blinking sleep out of her eyes. She yawned as she reported two heat signatures, one in the lounge and one in a cabin.

"I assume since one person is in Kurla's cabin that's her. And since the vid being watched on the monitor in the lounge is one about single-cell organisms, I am guessing the person watching that is Bondle," she said.

Quinn gave her a quick chuckle which Lenore was happy to hear. Maybe he was feeling better today, less moody. That notion was dispelled, however, when Diarmin asked for a navigation update and his smile disappeared. Since he turned his head away, she couldn't see his expression, but the tightening of his shoulders indicated some negative emotions. Maybe now was time for another story about their past, especially since they had nothing to do until the transition.

After all systems were checked and reported, she decided on which to tell and spoke quickly as Allison was already getting out of her chair.

"So, anyone ready to hear about another time your father and I worked together?"

"The second time you met?" asked Allison, already sliding back into her chair and turning eagerly to her parents. Lenore noted that Quinn angled his head to hear but didn't look back. She also noted the look that her husband gave her, slightly widened eyes and tight lips.

"Not the second time," she said and was glad to see Diarmin relax, though she knew he wouldn't stay that way with her next words. "That is his story to tell. I will tell of the third time." Now Quinn turned and she was glad to see his interest. Somewhat aloof, but it was a step in the right direction.

As Lenore opened her mouth to tell the story, a red light came on her console. "Wait a moment. Red light," she said as she accessed the correct system. Before she could make out what the ship was telling her, she heard a 'ping' from Quinn's console.

"I have a red light, too," he said.

"Mine is showing an increase in the power consumption, going toward the environmental systems," said Lenore.

"There is also a power increase going to, well, it looks like... navigation?"

Diarmin strode toward Quinn's station. Bending down and reaching around Quinn to tap a few keys, he found the problem.

"Yes, navigation, but more precisely to the maneuvering thrusters. The ones designed to keep us on course. Odd, for a ship in transspace."

"As far as I can tell, the environmental systems are working fine but the power has increased from a slight drop in the oxygen levels on the ship." Lenore pulled up more details. "The increase in power has compensated for now." The warning light went off.

"Same here," said Diarmin. He straightened up, a slight wrinkle between his eyebrows. "I don't like it. Two systems needing extra power simultaneously? There must be a problem."

"With environmental or thrusters?" asked Quinn.

"It could be with the power grid," suggested Allison.

Lenore agreed as Diarmin nodded absently. "We just ran a systems check that didn't show anything, so we need to do a more in-depth scrutiny of all three systems." He headed for the door that accessed the environmental systems on the side of the bridge opposite of the ladder.

"I will do a physical inspection. Lenore, you check the navigation controls and Quinn and Alli run diagnostics on the power grid." He grabbed the oxygen mask on the side of the door as he opened the sealed compartment that kept them all warm, breathing and alive. The mask was only for emergencies, but oxygenators could be dangerous if ruptured.

Lenore held her breath, but the sealed door showed no pressure changes or gas leaks, so she went back to the thruster system.

In ten minutes, Diarmin was headed out and resealing the door.

"All looks good in there. No leaks and the scrubbers are working fine."

"Power grid seems stable," said Quinn.

"Although we have burned a little more fuel than usual," Allison said. "Looks like the increases have been steadily rising for over a day."

"Same with the nav thrusters." Lenore saw a grim look settle on Diarmin's face and knew what he was thinking.

"Looks like we may have a leak outside somewhere," he said with a grimace.

"Can't tell from here," she said. "We need to go out there to check."

"I keep saying we need cameras that cover the entire hull," Allison said.

"Too expensive," Lenore said as she stood to face Diarmin. "Who goes out?"

"Me, of course," he said. "I'm the mechanic." He sat in the chair as Lenore tried not to appear too relieved. He knew that she did not like going extra-vehicular at all.

"Quinn," he said. "We need to drop out of transwarp to do this."

"Aye, Dad." Quinn's fingers danced in harmony with Diarmin's as they brought the ship back into normal space.

"All stop," ordered Diarmin.

The ship slowed and stopped with only a slight pull that they could barely feel.

"Scan the vicinity, Alli," said Lenore.

"No ships, no planets, no nearby systems. Nothing." Allison bit her lip. "We are literally in the middle of nowhere."

Diarmin stood and looked at Lenore.

"Well, let's get this over with."

***

Lenore headed down the ladder behind Diarmin. Her heart was pounding though it shouldn't be for a simple EVA. *I am in mission mode so my adrenaline is pumping, that's all.*

"If we are going to that side, we should turn off the gravity so that it won't mess up your magnetic boots," she said, trying to think ahead to what was needed.

"Good idea." He paused before going down to the cargo bay. "Why don't you go warn the passengers while I get the suit out." He grinned. "And then you can help me squirm into it." He disappeared down the ladder and Lenore tried to suppress a shudder, glad he was the one going out there.

She reached into the medical nook, right off the corridor before the cargo ladder. The nook contained an old medbed with drawers below holding various first aid supplies, but it had saved both of their lives on several occasions. Grabbing a couple of strips of anti-nausea pills, she went through the lounge to the passenger cabins since Bondle was no longer watching a vid.

Bondle first. She knocked but there was no answer. She knocked again a little louder and was about to simply enter when the door slid open.

"Sorry, Captain," he said, blinking. "I had an earpiece in and didn't hear you."

"We are temporarily turning off the gravity so I suggest you strap in." She held out a strip of pills. "Here is something in case you get queasy from weightlessness."

"Is everything all right?" he asked, taking the strip.

"Of course," she said. "Merely a maintenance check."

"Okay." His eyebrows scrunched up. "What about my cargo?"

"I am heading down there now to make sure it is secured. We will give you warning when gravity will be restored."

"I appreciate that, Captain." He gave a small smile. "I will probably just strap myself in the bed." He slid the door closed and Lenore headed to Kurla's cabin.

Unlike Bondle, Kurla's door opened only a breath after Lenore's knock.

"Yes?"

Lenore repeated her message, holding out the pills.

"Are we stopped?" asked the girl. She started wringing her hands. "Is that what I felt?"

"Yes. A minor repair issue." She reached out to pat the girl awkwardly on the arm. "We should be on our way shortly."

"Thank you," she said, smiling shyly. "Sorry for my behavior, but I don't usually feel any stopping motion on the big ships so I got worried."

"Perfectly normal reaction. Please strap in and we will keep you informed."

Kurla nodded and went to strap into the secured chair in her room.

"Here." Lenore tossed her the strip of medicine. "Shall I close the door?"

"Please don't. I feel claustrophobic enough as it is."

Lenore nodded and left her buckling up to head down to the cargo bay.

Diarmin had the door to the engine room open, where the suits were stored, and was struggling to put on his skin-tight inner pressure/cooling suit.

"Unh! These damn ancient suits," he said between tugs. "Why don't we get those new ones that are one entire unit. Oof."

Lenore went to help. "Priorities, Diarmin. Fuel for the ship is a little more important." She tugged the suit up over his hips as he wiggled his body to stuff his arms in the full sleeves. "Besides, we hardly ever use them. Why are you putting this on anyway? You won't be out there for very long, and your portable life support will maintain all your suit's systems."

"Since this is not an emergency and we have the time, might as well be thorough." One last grunt and he sealed the garment. "We also need to set a good example for the children. Now, unh." He grunted as he lifted the bulky suit. "How about this monster."

The rest was a little easier and Lenore made sure the helmet was secure. "PLSS working?"

Diarmin breathed in and out slowly and looked at the dials on his arm. "All systems working great. These old suits were built to last." He dropped his arms to his sides. "Ready to go."

"Not without these." Lenore handed her husband two coils of metal cable.

"Aw. I've got magboots. Do I need tethers?" His grin as he took the safety lines showed he was teasing.

"And I am attaching a third to your tool belt since the airlock is nearly completely opposite where you need to go," she said, making sure it was secure.

"Well, add 'Put airlock on starboard side' to our list of upgrades." He checked the airlock then opened the inner hatch. "See you shortly."

Lenore nodded and sealed the hatch behind him. As she watched Diarmin depressurize the airlock, she grabbed onto a bar and activated the intercom next to the hatch. "Quinn, you and Alli strap in and shut off the gravity."

"Already strapped," came the response. Then the ship speakers crackled to life to show Quinn activating the ship-wide com system. "Gravity going null in five...four..."

Three seconds later, Lenore felt the gravity shut off at the same time Diarmin opened the outer hatch. He turned and looked at her, then deliberately made a big show of attaching the first cable to the hull. With a smile and wave, he was out and closing the hatch.

Lenore took several deep breaths and hauled herself hand over hand to the bridge. She wouldn't fully relax until her husband was safely back on board.

She hated spacewalks.

Chapter Twenty-one

As his mother floated onto the bridge, Quinn turned up the volume from his father's suit com so everyone could hear his comments. Quinn knew from the drills they had held about using space suits, that reports needed to be as continual as possible. Sure enough, his father was obeying that rule.

"Magnetic boots working optimally. Reaching top of ship and heading starboard. Attaching second tether."

"What happens to the first one?" asked Allison.

"He attaches it to the same ring as the new one so it won't drift away." Lenore peered at Allison. "Don't you remember that from the drills?"

"It's been years, Mom. I can't remember every tiny detail." Allison turned back to her console although Quinn could tell her attention was on her father's voice.

All three looked up as they heard a slight 'thudding' above their heads. *That would be Dad.* He could hear him walking slowly toward the exterior of the environmental controls, the magboots' vibrations reverberating through the hull.

Quinn watched his mother in the command chair, her finger hovering over the communication switch. *She looks nervous. Mom and Dad always said that space was unforgiving and that we should avoid situations like the one we are in.*

Quinn suppressed a snort at his flare of annoyance. Yet another reason to grow up on a planet and not a ship. *Alli and I are lucky to have survived until now.*

"Approaching area," came the report and the footfalls did fade. If they opened the environment hatch, they could probably hear but there was no reason to. Yet.

"I think I see the problem." A sound like a grunt came over the com. "Ran out of line. Attaching third cable, thank you for that." Pause. "Yep, it's a very small leak. Looks like oxygen by the crystallization. Or even the liquid waste system, not exactly sure."

His mother pressed the com button. "Probably oxygen since that is where the extra power is going."

"And it is just a large enough stream to push us off trajectory after a significant time, thus the thruster's extra work."

"Micrometeorite?" asked Lenore.

Quinn noticed that his father's lengthy pause after the question caused his mother's mouth to tighten.

"Wrong angle. And the placement is behind this outcropping, kind of difficult to reach. Let me angle myself closer. Hm... wait. There's something... Oh shit!"

A dull 'whump' sounded through the hull and a sizzle of static showed Diarmin's communications had cut off. Quinn's anxiety soared. He couldn't remember his father ever swearing like that.

"Diarmin, come in. Diarmin, report." Lenore was pressing the communication hard enough to turn the end of her finger white. "Alli, external scan please. Quinn, can we angle the cameras to get a view along the starboard side?"

Quinn struggled with the camera controls, trying not to panic. And it didn't sound like Allison was keeping it together very well either.

"I can't read the suit, Mom. What happened? Why won't Dad answer?"

"Can you read any life signs at all? Even a floating object the size of..." she swallowed. "The size of your father."

"There is a tiny flutter, but I'm not sure..."

"Keep looking, Quinn!"

He jumped. Her voice was not quite a barked order. His answer was not good news.

"This is the best I can do." He put the visual up on the screen. The camera barely registered the side of the nose of the ship and only stars floated in the background.

"Diarmin, report!" Lenore's lips nearly disappeared, so tightly was she pressing them at the lack of answer.

"What's wrong, Mom? What happened?"

"Here is what we are going to do. Allison, you keep working on locating anything that could be your father. Quinn, you are going to help me suit up. I am going out after him."

"But what happened?" Allison's voice was nearly a wail. Quinn put a hand on her arm trying to reassure her, but he wasn't much calmer.

"I think he found an EMP mine and set it off."

"But an electromagnetic pulse will fry his suit's systems," said Quinn but regretted it when Allison's hand flew to her mouth, eyes widening in horror.

Finally, his mother appeared to notice Allison's distress and pushed herself toward Allison. She gripped the chair with her left hand so she could lightly grasp Alli's shoulder with her right. "Look, Alli. Those space suits are designed to hold thirty minutes of air and pressure in case of total failure. If we keep our heads, there shouldn't be any problem getting him back before that time is up. Your father is probably fine but since communications are offline as well, he can't talk to us. Stay calm and continue to do your work as brilliantly as ever and we will be laughing about all of this soon."

"Okay."

Quinn could see his sister visibly calming but long experience told him his mother was not.

"Let's get me into a suit, Quinn."

He nodded as he unbuckled and wondered why she was more worried than she let Allison believe.

As they pulled his mother's suit out of the engine room, she put it on without the inner layer.

"What about this?" he asked, holding up the undergarment.

"No time. I won't be out there long enough to need it."

"Why isn't there time?" Quinn felt his adrenaline go into overdrive. He grabbed his mother's helmet before she could. "What aren't you telling us?"

"Give that here, Quinn."

"Not until you tell me. I get you not telling Alli, but I need to know. In case you don't come back." He was surprised at his own words, but the anxiety was mixing heavily with anger.

His mother's eyes snapped fire, but he stubbornly kept the helmet out of reach.

"You are right. You need to know." Lenore looked down at their floating feet for a breath then looked him straight in the eye. "Those mines sometimes explode with shrapnel designed to cut through not only suits but cables. It is possible he could be floating free, farther away every second, with his suit depressurizing rapidly. There is no way to know until I reach him."

Quinn nodded as he handed the helmet over, fear threatening to overwhelm him. He took a slow breath through his nose and out his mouth like his mother had been teaching him during her fighting training. He felt his mind settle as he turned his adrenaline into a useful tool.

"Then I will prep the shuttle. In case I need to come after you both."

Through the helmet's faceplate, Quinn could see his mother's eyes widen. But they went almost instantly back to normal as she nodded.

"Good idea. I hope it won't be necessary. Those cables are tougher than they look." She briefly gripped his shoulder. "And so is your father."

They both pulled themselves up the ladder and opened the hatch to the airlock.

"Everything all right?"

Quinn turned, startled that he hadn't heard anyone coming, but then again, there were no footfalls in zero g.

"Kurla, everything is fine. Please return to your cabin."

"I'll take care of this, um, Captain." He was proud he stopped himself from saying "Mom". Since the hatch was open, she nodded and entered the airlock. Quinn secured it behind her and turned to Kurla.

"Please, Ms. Plaad. We need to work. Please go back to your cabin."

"But I want to help," she said.

Any other time and Quinn would be happy to have that concerned face stare at his while working alongside him.

"If I... if you are needed, we will let you know. Now I need to know you are safe." He gently grasped her arm and lightly pushed her through the door to the lounge. "Strap in. That's an order."

Kurla gave him a smile that was oddly respectful, then nodded and pushed her way through the other door.

Quinn didn't realize he was watching her until she turned back to grin at him right before heading into her cabin. He cleared his throat and went to tell Allison that he was going to prep the shuttle.

Just in case.

***

Lenore tried to settle her breathing as she stepped into the black nothingness, quickly turning so her eyes were on the ship. She had barely made it through this part of her training with the Xa'ti'al and never truly got over her fear. Without her implant, that fear was twice as hard to control, but the horrifying image of her husband possibly drifting farther and farther away with a depressurizing suit spurred her into action.

The airlock had closed so she reached for the tether that Diarmin had secured. Giving it a tug, she realized it was still attached to the other end. Breathing a sigh of relief, she attached her own line to the cable itself, not the ring. She couldn't take the time to walk there, she had to do her least favorite mode of travel, hand-over-hand.

Grasping the secured line, she kept her face away from the void as she pulled herself along as fast as she dared. At the top of the yacht she paused, trying to see if she could spot Diarmin but with no lights working on the suit, it was next to impossible to see him. Grimly she kept pulling herself along.

When she reached the first ring, she unhooked her line to attach it to the second one, but as she grabbed that cable, she nearly lost her own grip as it pulled toward her. Trying not to panic, she reeled it in. It didn't take very long which wasn't a good sign. She examined the end and it looked like it had been sliced clean through. That meant that it had been a shrapnel mine. Her stomach clenched and she again strained her eyes to find her husband.

"Mom?"

Allison's voice in her helmet startled her, the reaction causing her to start drifting away from the ship. She pulled herself back down and planted her boots on the hull.

"Mom! You haven't checked in. Are you there? You are supposed to give running commentary."

Since Allison's voice sounded like it was filling with anxiety again, Lenore tried to reassure her. Not easy when her own guts wanted to scream.

"Sorry, Alli. I am here. I'm simply concentrating on doing my job. You know I don't usually talk a lot during a mission." She tried to chuckle, but it didn't sound very comforting. *Get Diarmin back, then she will be fine. We all will be.* "Attaching second line now and heading to the third."

Lenore really didn't want to, but she grabbed a protrusion on the ship and pulled her feet off. *I am tethered, I am tethered.* She kept up the chant and pushed herself toward the next handhold. It was the quickest way, but she didn't have to like it.

She reached and grabbed the handle, carefully sighted on the next and within sixty seconds, she was on the other side. Peering down she could vaguely make out a drifting line. Panic swelled in her, her mind imagining the worst despite the fact she kept telling herself it was probably the other half of the broken cable.

"Heading down starboard side." Lenore planted her feet and made her way to the third ring. Keeping her eyes firmly on her goal instead of looking around in a panic, she walked as fast as she dared. When she saw the ring, her breath came out in an explosion. First, for reaching the end of her cable and, second, for seeing that Diarmin's third safety line was still attached to the ring. It was pulled taut which indicated a weight at the other end.

"Alli. Do you have a fix?" Lenore grasped the loose line as she let her eyes slide along the one hopefully still attached to her husband.

"I think so. There is something out there that seems to be maintaining the same distance almost directly to starboard."

"That makes sense. The cable seems to go up for me but since I am standing on the side of the ship, that would be starboard."

But Allison didn't sound reassured. "The problem is that the heat signature is so faint that the computer goes back and forth on whether it is there or not."

"Don't worry, Alli. The suit is probably keeping the computer from registering body heat."

"Come on, Mom. I can scan through walls and ship hulls; a single suit isn't going to stop it."

A wry chuckle escaped Lenore. "You are right, my genius daughter." She sobered. "But the point is that it does read heat so that means the suit hasn't lost all atmosphere. I am going to reel him in now."

"Shuttle prepped and standing by," came Quinn's voice over the com. "And by my count, we are out of safety lines so be careful."

Lenore tucked her foot under a handle so she wouldn't be pulled off the hull as she pulled down on the cable. *If there is still heat, Diarmin must still be alive so why didn't he pull himself in? Is he unconscious?* Lenore tried not to let her thoughts run away with any dire possibilities, which would cause her to yank too hard.

Hand over hand she kept pulling, occasionally glancing up to see if she could spot Diarmin. She felt it was taking far too long but a glance at her suit chronometer showed that she had been outside only fifteen minutes. She looked up again and could see a blot against the starry background. She switched her helmet light to a narrow, bright beam, and it lit up Diarmin's suit.

"I see him!" she said, wincing at the echo of the yell in her helmet. She pulled again but her foot slipped, and she felt her boots lose their magnetic grip. Fortunately, her line was at its limit so she only drifted about a meter. Keeping hold of Diarmin's line, she grabbed her own to reset her boots onto the hull and continue pulling. She concentrated on her breathing, trying to ignore the sweat she could feel starting to drip down her temples.

As the suit got closer, Lenore could see Diarmin's hands. His left hand was holding his right arm and his right hand was pressed to his stomach. The faceplate didn't seem to be damaged even though he was still too far away for her to see his face.

When he was about eight meters away, she could see that his eyes were open, but so was his mouth, either showing the lack of oxygen or heat buildup inside the suit. *That means the emergency supply was running out, or the suit had been compromised. Probably a tear or two which is why he is not moving his hands to help pull.*

Six meters.

She started to breathe easier as a relieved smile crossed his face.

Five meters.

Without warning the line gave a twitch. Diarmin hadn't moved that she noticed, but she could see his eyes widen as he looked at the line she was pulling on. There was an obvious split in the cable fairly close to his body. The twitch must have been it further separating, and now it looked to be only a single slender wire.

Lenore stopped pulling, afraid to break the line. *Besides, he's close enough to drift the rest of the way.*

But as she stood there, quite aware of the seconds ticking away, Diarmin didn't appear to be drifting any closer. She noticed him lightly jerk his head as if trying to point at something to her left. As she looked that way, her light showed a sparkling trail of ice coming from the ship. The leak was still there and pushing the ship away from Diarmin. Not very fast, but enough to keep him from drifting close before his suit gave out.

"Alli. Turn off the environmental systems. Just the oxygen." Maybe that would stop or at least slow the leak. Even so, she knew it wouldn't be enough.

Lenore turned her helmet light back to Diarmin. She had two choices. *Give a hard yank and hope that's enough momentum to bring him in or keep pulling very gently and hope the cable won't snap.* As the light hit Diarmin's face, she could see the same thoughts in his eyes. As he shifted slightly, Lenore could see a small stream of air between the fingers on his stomach. He rearranged his hand and it stopped, but the cable started to slip through Lenore's hand as he drifted away. She grasped it tighter, stopping the momentum but could see his mouth moving and guessed he was cursing himself for letting his hand slip.

That hole must be getting bigger. We are running out of time.

She began her hand-over-hand tug again, trying to be as gentle as possible.

Four meters. It was working.

Three meters.

Lenore's entire focus narrowed to the slow progress of the line growing shorter way too slowly. A glance at Diarmin's face showed his eyes starting to drift close.

Two meters.

Suddenly the cable snapped. Lenore reached her hand up, but he was still too far away. Desperate, she jumped off the hull to grab her husband, hand still extended, but her tether stopped her. She saw him reach for her with his left hand.

"Don't!" she cried, but he couldn't hear her. His suit puncture caused a stream of air to push him away. He put his hand back, but it was too late. He was floating away from the ship again.

Lenore wrapped the end of the newly broken cable around her left hand and wrist twice then gripped it in her fist. She pulled the cable still secured to the ship so her feet were back on the hull and looked up again for Diarmin.

In those few seconds, he had drifted back out to about four meters. She knew she only had one shot. Taking a breath and slowly letting it out, she detached her safety line and pushed off as hard as she could.

The distance between her and her husband closed quickly, and she reached for anything to grab on to. She missed his toolbelt but managed to grip the arm that covered his stomach tear. It leaked very briefly but Diarmin stopped it and Lenore hooked her arm through his, determined not to lose either grip.

Though they were still heading away from the ship, Lenore wrapped the loose cable around Diarmin so she could have a free hand. She reached above her head for the emergency attachment that would hook her suit to his, transferring air and removing carbon dioxide using her own PLSS. Diarmin's eyes flew open and she could see him taking a deep breath. His small smile reassured her, but they were still on the clock.

Making sure they were securely attached to each other, Lenore began to pull both of them toward the ship. It was slow but steady and she didn't take a full breath until her feet were on the hull. Since Diarmin's systems were down, his boots didn't have the magnetic effect so she kept hold of him.

"I've got him," she said. "Quinn, meet us at the airlock."

The trip back was agonizingly slow, and Lenore was reaching exhaustion. Weightlessness while hauling another body was no easy task. As the airlock cycled, she could see both kids looking in, concern clear on their faces. When the hatch opened, both of them reached to help pull them through the hatch and into the lounge where there was more room. Quinn popped off his father's helmet and Alli helped Lenore with hers.

"I can't tell you how good it is to see your faces," Diarmin croaked. He licked his lips and Lenore noticed he still had his hands over the suit punctures. Gently she removed them as she felt the tears in her eyes. *The usual letdown after stress.* "Quinn, he is dehydrated. Help me get him out of this suit and into the medbed. Alli, go warn the passengers and turn the gravity back on."

As Allison floated her way back to the bridge, Quinn helped remove the suit. Diarmin was still conscious but very weak and Lenore was beginning to feel the effects as well. Quinn tugged at the pressure undergarment a little too fiercely.

"Why...is...this...so hard?" he ground out between pulls.

"It's supposed to be skintight," said Lenore. "Careful." She had noticed Diarmin wincing with each tug. "Ease up a bit, Quinn. It's easier to peel it off rather than pull."

"Good thing I had the pressure suit," said Diarmin. "It kept me alive." His voice was merely a whisper now. As the suit peeled down past his stomach, Lenore saw the reason for his pain, a jagged cut where the suit had been torn.

"Attention. Full gravity will resume in ten seconds. Please secure yourselves."

They all made sure to orient themselves with their feet toward the deck, Lenore and Quinn helping Diarmin as they pulled off the last of the inner suit. Suddenly weight returned and they were pulled the last inch down. Lenore managed to stand on her shaky legs but Diarmin kept going until he was in a heap, hand on his stomach again.

"Should have maneuvered him above the bed while still weightless," said Quinn with a grunt as he helped her lift Diarmin.

Supporting Diarmin's weight with his arms around their shoulders, they managed to get him into the bed. Lenore rummaged in the drawers for a couple of specific tools. She found the subdermal scanner first and ran it over Diarmin's wound. When it beeped, she looked at her son.

"Quinn. Go get him some water please," she said.

As soon as he left, Lenore held up the small forceps. Diarmin nodded, knowing the beep indicated shrapnel. Using the scanner, she located the piece and extracted it while Diarmin bit his lip against the pain. Lenore quickly covered the wound with a healing patch that also included painkillers and blood coagulants. She had just begun hooking up IV's when Quinn came back with a cup and straw. Allison showed up as Diarmin sucked down the water.

Lenore activated the various medical devices. "Fortunately, there was no damage to your inner organs, just that nasty cut. Rest now." She could tell he was about to lose consciousness, but he had one more thing to say.

"You know. I never fixed that leak."

Chapter Twenty-two

Allison gazed at her dad's sleeping face. Then she looked at the rest of the family doing the same and noticed that her mother still had her spacesuit on though she had removed the gloves.

"Alli," she said. "Stay here with your father. Quinn, go to the bridge and monitor from there as I go back to fix that leak."

"No. You're exhausted," said Quinn. "I'll go."

"Absolutely not," she said. She pushed past Quinn to retrieve her gloves and helmet from the lounge. Quinn followed her and Allison could see the angry stubbornness starting again in her brother's face. She hovered in the doorway to watch.

"Why not?" he demanded. "I can do it, and, in your condition, you may make a mistake. What if there's another mine?"

"If there happened to be another, it would have been set off by the first. Besides, it has been years since you have worn your suit, and it probably won't even fit you anymore."

"Then I'll wear yours. I'm about the same size as you now," he said, crossing his arms.

Lenore looked at him, blinking rapidly as if she hadn't realized that fact until now.

Honestly, I didn't realize it either, thought Allison

The two stared at each other and Allison thought hard for something she could do or say to keep both of them from another fight. She got an idea and delved into the drawers below the medbed. *Aha, there it is!* She grabbed the bottle and an injector and dashed into the lounge.

"There is no way, Quinn," her mother was saying, but Allison interrupted her.

"Mom, he's right, you're exhausted and Quinn, you are an idiot to even think about going out there. Here." She shoved the injector and bottle at her mother. "This is an energy boost. It will get you through what needs to be done."

At first, her mother looked angry at being interrupted, but Allison could see her weary mind working out what she had said. Soon a small smile was replacing the anger.

"Good idea. I *am* a little tired." She filled the injector with liquid from the bottle, pressed it to her neck, then handed it all back to Allison. "There. It should kick in about the time I get through that hatch. Satisfied, Quinn?" She didn't wait for an answer but put her helmet on and headed for the airlock.

Quinn's face was still angry, but he turned and went up the ladder to the bridge. Allison followed her mother to close the hatch behind her.

"Be careful, Mom," she said. Her mother patted her on the shoulder and stepped through. The hatch closed and Allison went to put away the medicine supplies. She simply couldn't watch her mother go back into danger yet again today.

***

When Lenore returned from patching the leak, Diarmin was already sitting up.

"Hey," she said, holding out a gloved hand. "It hasn't been that long. You need to rest." Lenore looked around. "Where's Allison?"

Diarmin started pulling off all the various devices despite Lenore's protests. "Bondle wanted to check on his cargo so I sent her down to the bay with him. Stop that," he said, batting away Lenore's hands that were trying to push him back down to the bed. "I'm fine."

"No, that's the meds working."

"I need to—"

They were both interrupted by boots on the ladder, Quinn coming down from the bridge. Lenore noticed the angry look was gone but there wasn't any warmth in his face either.

"Quinn, tell your father he needs more rest," she said, trying for a pleasant tone.

"Why should I?" he said, not quite surly but close. "Neither of you listen to my opinions anyway."

Lenore felt her mouth drop open and wanted to reprimand her son, but the words wouldn't come. The look of surprise on Diarmin's face showed he felt the same.

"Did I miss something while I was out?" he said, half-jokingly.

"I came to report that the oxygen controls are back online and power output is nominal. I am now going to check on our other passenger."

Before either parent could respond, he abruptly turned and disappeared through the door to the lounge.

"What was that all about?" asked Diarmin.

"I'll tell you later. I need to get out of this suit." She reached down and picked up the pile of cables, both whole and pieces, that she had dropped when trying to keep Diarmin on the medbed. A wave of weakness washed over her, and she struggled to straighten back up. The energy drug was wearing off.

"Now who's the one needing rest?" asked Diarmin as he helped her up. The wince as he strained his injury showed he wasn't back to normal either.

"We both do," she said. "I will stow my suit and the cables, then get some sleep."

"And I need to get this ship moving again. I don't like being a sitting duck."

Lenore looked at the chronometer on her suit. "It hasn't even been three hours yet."

"That doesn't matter." He looked directly at her. "You saw the leak. You know."

She hesitated. She'd seen it and had been trying not to think about it, but she didn't back down from the intense gaze. "Yes. Where the leak was. And the mine. It was no accident."

Diarmin nodded.

"Sabotage."

***

"Have you recovered from zero gravity, Kurla?" Quinn asked after he politely rapped on the open door.

Kurla jumped to her feet at his entrance. "Of course. I have been in weightless situations before." She moved closer and lowered her voice. "But I did overhear Mr. Bondle saying he needed to take a couple of those anti-nausea pills."

As she leaned in for that whisper, Quinn caught a waft of flowery scent. Perfume? Shampoo? He wasn't sure but the wonderful smell made him quite aware of his own sweaty state after all the activity. He took a step back, not wanting to offend Kurla in any way.

She looked at him but didn't appear insulted. "You, however, look worn out. Is everything okay with the ship?" A small crease appeared between her eyes and the concerned look made him want to undo that step back.

"Everything is fine. Just a maintenance issue." He cleared his throat, trying not to laugh at his own understatement. But he didn't want her to worry about all those things he was stressing about.

"That's good," she said. She put a hand on his arm. "You still look like you need a break. Let's go play a game in the lounge. Or watch a vid."

"Uh, thanks but I am still on duty," he said, regretting the words.

"You have been on duty ever since I got on board. Doesn't your Captain allow for some time off?" Kurla shook her head. "The only downtime I have seen you get is when you are sleeping. And sometimes you don't even get that, doing the night shift." She put her hands on her hips. "Everyone needs some free time to shake off the stress of the day."

"Oh, well, yeah I get free time. Just usually not while we are on... uh... have passengers aboard." Quinn wasn't sure why he was having trouble talking to Kurla. He had played many roles in his various disguises, making up stories on the spur of the moment.

"Come on," she said with a sparkle in her eyes. "I will grab a snack from the galley, and then you and I will sit on the bed and watch a fun vid." She took his arm and propelled him toward the bed. He was flustered enough to let her. As the back of the bunk hit his legs and he sat down heavily, he realized he had to leave before he found himself spending the rest of the day in her cabin.

Kurla turned to presumably get food when an announcement came over the ship speakers.

"Navigator Mikin, please report to the bridge."

Quinn leapt to his feet, guilt sweeping through him at sitting on this girl's bed, even though he knew nobody could see him.

"Excuse me, Kurla," he said as she was still standing in the doorway, blocking his exit. She looked angry.

"Every ship I have been on, the crew gets a few hours a day to themselves. You need to ask for better treatment." Her arms were crossed again, and she looked like she wasn't going to budge.

"As you have said before, you are used to large ships. Things work differently on small yachts such as this one. Please move so I don't have to forcibly move you." He grinned to show he was teasing.

Kurla smiled back and held her hands up. "Yes, sir. I will obey." She moved out of the way, smiling the whole time and he was very glad the tenseness between them was gone.

And relieved that he hadn't needed to actually move her. He wasn't sure he could have done that simple thing.

He strode out the door and stopped right before he entered the lounge to look back. He figured she would be looking but was still pleased that she did.

"If you ever get a break, we will watch that vid," she said. The fingers of her left hand wiggled in a wave, and she disappeared back into her cabin.

Quinn stood there like a fool, staring until he heard a throat clearing. He turned to see Bondle trying to get through and back to his cabin.

"Oh, um, my apologies, Mr. Bondle." He felt his face flame red from embarrassment and braced himself for a comment or at least a knowing look.

The scientist merely nodded and disappeared into his cabin.

"Navigator Mikin, report to the bridge please."

All the good feelings drained away as anger replaced them. He stomped back through the lounge fighting the urge to shout that he was coming. Why was he the one to take care of things when his parents needed a break? When would he get his?

Chapter Twenty-three

The family was back on the bridge, having staggered the sleeping periods so everyone had gotten some rest. Diarmin felt an odd sense of déjà vu with the exception of the pain above his navel that told him things were different than the last time they were all here.

The silence along with awkward shuffling and tapping of keys showed that he wasn't the only one to feel a little strange. His eyes roved over his family in their usual seats.

Lenore had large black circles under her eyes. *Yes, I was wounded but she did all the work, first bringing me in and then repairing the leak.* He tried not to feel guilty about being stupid enough to set off the mine despite the fact that it had been well hidden. Right before the kids had come up to the bridge, he and Lenore had decided that the only place that the sabotage could have taken place was while they were docked at Sultra. *When* it had been done was the mystery. Daviss hadn't found them by the time Kurla was aboard and they had taken off shortly after. The fuel attendants? But why would they? Bondle might have had an opportunity while they were docked but Diarmin was positive he hadn't come out of his cabin during that time. And since they had left, their passengers hadn't any chance to roam outside. So where, when, who and why the sabotage was still unknown.

Quinn was being perfectly pleasant in a stilted way, as if he was constantly striving to keep a temper under control. Lenore had explained their argument to him, but that didn't seem like something that would keep Quinn angry for such a long time.

Allison was the best rested of them all. Not only did she need less sleep, but she had been on the least stressful end of the entire disaster with the leak. She had been worried and scared, but she was still young

K.A. Bledsoe

enough to slough off the past easily. Was that all it was with Quinn? Getting older and dealing with new feelings and emotions?

Diarmin caught Allison glancing at everyone else just like he was. When their eyes met, he grinned. *She is just like me. And Quinn is just like Lenore who has always been emotionally volatile even with that blasted medplant dampening her emotions.* He sighed, almost wishing for another emergency so the family would be working harmoniously together again. He cleared his throat and tried for something to break the silence.

"All systems working efficiently," he said to no one in particular. "Looks like the patch is holding up fine."

"So, Mom," said Allison. "You were going to tell us a story before we were so rudely interrupted."

Lenore gave a half smile. "I don't know if I feel like a story now."

"Aw, please?" said Allison. "I really want to hear it. Maybe Dad can tell it."

Diarmin felt his gut drop and stopped his hand short of holding his wound. He was still having trouble reliving his past and in his weakened state, he knew he wasn't up to actually talking about it now.

"I can tell it," said Lenore. Diarmin shot her a grateful look and she nodded slightly to show she was aware of his issues. "How about you, Quinn? Shall I talk about the third time we met?" Her voice had a slight edge to it. *She also senses his moodiness is not improving.*

Quinn nodded then turned his chair enough to listen. He wasn't quite facing them, but it was better than nothing.

"It might not be with its usual dramatic flair but here goes," said Lenore.

"I was on a mission for the Xa'ti'al, preparing to set out, when I saw your father walking towards me and the vehicle I was packing. I wasn't happy to see him since I had figured out that sometimes the Xa sent outsiders to watch agents for their first few missions."

"You were a Xa, Dad?" asked Allison.

"No, not at all. I was only an observer. The Xa did hire out sometimes for specialized skills and they worked with a few trusted individuals. The observers were usually not Xa because then the rookie agents would get suspicious. I was one of five outsiders they occasionally hired to observe."

112

"But he wasn't there to observe that time," said Lenore. "Instead, he told me the person who had contracted the mission had sent him along as a guide since he had grown up on that planet."

"What planet was that?" asked Quinn.

"Nogus Twain," she answered. "Enough questions or we will never get through this story. Anyway. Kel, as I knew him then, showed me that he did indeed know his way around, so I reluctantly accepted him as a guide. We drove through the swamps to the criminal base I had been instructed to infiltrate and obtain valuable documents from. Working together, we set a decoy and broke in through the front door."

Allison was biting her lip, clearly holding back from asking for details. Lenore didn't seem to notice, focusing instead on telling the story in the shortest way possible.

"I started down the right-hand corridor but Kel indicated I should go left for my objective. Since he had been very well informed up to this point, I listened to him. Well, I shouldn't have." Lenore gave him a comical frown and he stuck his tongue out at her. Allison giggled and there was even a shadow of a smile on Quinn's face.

"I found myself in a bare room instead of the main file storage facility. Cursing to myself, I retraced my steps and went to the room where I was supposed to go in the first place. I walked in on Kel staring down another man who had dark skin and hair very similar to his. Wondering why he was wasting time, I stunned the other man and headed toward the computers. At first Kel was shocked but when I reassured him that I only stunned the other, he recovered quickly. As I prepared to download what I could from the computers, he stopped me, saying that my mission only mentioned printed files and that he would deal with the computers. Though I wondered how he knew what exactly my mission was, I searched through the printed files until I found the name I was hired to find. I pulled that file along with as many others as I could fit in the bag, standard Xa'ti'al procedure, take all you can. When I glanced at Kel, I noticed he wasn't downloading data but destroying it.

"I began to complain but shots came through the doorway. We had to concentrate instead on getting out of there. Taking out three guards, Kel led me to the roof where there were vehicles to escape in. We flew to the nearest city and ditched the vehicle. I went with Kel back to a hotel room where I confronted him about his deception."

"Where you kicked my ass again," he said with a chuckle. Lenore tossed a look at him as if annoyed he interrupted. "Oh, sorry," he said, but he still had a smile.

"I told him I'd had enough. How did he know so much, why did he misdirect me and who was that man that made him freeze? At first, he wouldn't talk but gave in quickly when it became clear I wouldn't take silence for an answer. He said he was the one to contract the mission and had asked for me personally because I was the only Xa he could trust. 'Trust with what?' I asked. He told me to check the file I was supposed to steal. I did and there was his picture with the name Diarmin Kelton. He asked me to destroy it, putting all his faith in me that I would help him. When I hesitated, he showed his trust by explaining that the man had been his old boss and he no longer wished to work for him. It was the only way he could disappear."

Lenore paused for a breath and looked at Diarmin. There was so much more she was leaving out and he knew it would need to be told later, but for now the kids were simply taking in what she said. She skipped over the last details and wrapped up the story.

"I felt for him and was impressed by his willingness to tell me everything. I had never had anyone trust me like that so I followed his request. And since he had wiped the computer records, he was no longer on a printed file and would be very difficult for his former boss to locate."

When Lenore stopped talking, there was silence for at least ten seconds. Diarmin was still trying to shake off the vivid memories the story had brought back.

"That's all? You're stopping there?" asked Allison. "Did you become friends after that? And you said you infiltrated a criminal base. Does that mean you worked for a criminal, Dad? And did you really grow up on that planet or was that part of your cover story? And what about—"

"Is that another person we have been running from all of our lives?"

Everyone froze at Quinn's interruption. It wasn't just the question but how he asked it. Diarmin could see the anger in his eyes and wondered where exactly it was coming from.

"What is that supposed to mean?" asked Lenore. She stood and put her hands on her hips, eyes flashing just like Quinn's.

Uh-oh.

"Exactly what I meant," said Quinn, crossing his arms and standing as well. "You always had us believing it was only the Xa'ti'al or someone like those pirates that Alli hacked. Now we find out that Dad has also made his fair share of enemies."

Diarmin idly checked the scanners and found both of the passengers in their cabins. *Good.* He had a feeling this was going to get loud.

"Quinn, it's always been like this, why are you angry?" asked Allison. Diarmin could tell she was confused and uneasy.

"That's right, Alli. It's always been like this, traveling on a ship, running constantly, unable to stop and live even for a short time on any planet. Mom grew up on a planet and now we know Dad did too. We have never stayed in one place long enough to make any friends, meet nice people, have a normal life."

"Normal," said Lenore, her voice actually getting lower which wasn't a good sign. "We have given you a life far more normal than ours ever was."

"If it is so normal, how many other people do you know who grew up on a small ship like this?"

Lenore couldn't answer and neither could Diarmin though he wished he could. He tried to defuse the tension.

"Quinn, we don't know that many people. I am sure there are plenty of other families like ours."

"Ha, there aren't." Quinn flicked a hand at Lenore. "Didn't you say you were the only Xa who ever left? How can there be someone like us if that's true? We change our identities all the time. You couldn't have found a nice out-of-the-way planet to live on?"

"Then, when we were found, and yes that is *when* not *if*, we would be trapped with no escape. At least in a ship we have mobility."

"You mean you simply wanted your freedom at everyone else's expense."

"Quinn!" Diarmin couldn't believe he had said that. Quinn looked remorseful for a heartbeat but then stubbornly set his chin and stared back.

Lenore opened her mouth to argue further but the pinging from the command console stopped him.

"Transition coming up," said Diarmin. Everyone took their seats, but not without a few upset glances at each other. Not a word was said except those necessary to the procedure. When it was done, Diarmin tried to defuse the tension. "See, nobody following us."

"This time," grumbled Quinn. He locked down his board and headed down the ladder. Lenore started to follow him but Diarmin held her back. Not until she got her own temper under control. The silence as she fumed was unsettling. Allison's soft voice cut through the tension.

"I like living on the ship," she said.

Diarmin smiled at her and Lenore slowly walked to her, gently patted Allison's shoulder, then left down the ladder.

"What was that all about, Dad?" asked Allison.

"I don't know. I was hoping you would."

"Quinn's been moody, halfway between giddy and moping ever since…" she trailed off and bit her lip.

"Ever since what, Alli?"

"Well, ever since Kurla came on board. He likes her, you know."

Diarmin's eyebrows shot up but he brought them back down. He should have been first to notice that and thinking back to Quinn's blushes and attitude, Diarmin knew his daughter was right.

"Thanks for waking me up to that fact, Alli. We will figure out how to handle all this."

"I hope that doesn't mean we are going to live on a planet." She shuddered as she turned back to her console. "All those people, yuck."

Diarmin smiled to himself, thinking she might feel different when she hit puberty like Quinn. Then he felt his forehead wrinkling. Was that all it was with Quinn? Hormones? It seemed to answer the question, but it still didn't feel like the answer. Diarmin remembered the talk he had with Quinn when he was thirteen. It was clear he had been going through puberty then so why, when he was nearly sixteen, was he so angry? This girl? Kurla was really a young woman, though he thought of her as a girl.

"Can you hold down the bridge?"

"Sure, Dad."

Diarmin vacated the command chair and offered it to Allison, but she waved it off and pulled up some work at her own station. So different from Quinn who was so eager to sit in the big seat.

He descended the ladder and walked down the hall, not sure if he should go talk to Lenore or Quinn. Since Quinn's door was closed as he passed it, he figured he would talk to Lenore. Maybe she would have some insight to news of Quinn's new crush.

***

Quinn lay back on the bed. Not his own but the one in the third guest room. When he approached his cabin, he realized he really didn't want to have a big discussion and the first place his parents would look would be his cabin. He shut the door as if he were in there then headed through the lounge to the extra cabin. It was a little crowded with the treadmill and other excess stuff tossed in here to make room elsewhere, but it was also nice and quiet.

He covered his eyes with his arm. He wasn't used to this kind of anger. Why did he seem to have a short fuse lately? Grimly he forced himself to face the fact that maybe it was still a reaction to his recent kidnapping. *No. I was restless before that. It's what led to me trying things on my own. Maybe if I had had more experience on planets, I could have avoided being taken.* Reluctantly he admitted that it wasn't true. It had been lack of experience with criminals, not planets. He took a long, slow breath in then let it out in a huge sigh.

"I'm sorry, I didn't know anyone was in here."

Quinn sat up at the voice and found himself staring at Kurla.

"I…I just came in here to… to get away…"

Kurla nodded knowingly. "I get it. I've been in that mood many times, just needing to be alone. I was going to try the treadmill like you suggested but I will leave you in peace," she said with a smile.

"No, no," Quinn said as he stood. "I can go." He stopped as she put a hand on his arm.

"I can exercise later. In fact," her eyes searched his face as her head tilted. "It looks like you might need a friend more than you need to be alone. What's wrong? Anything I can do?" She sat on the bed, hand still on his arm gently pulling him to sit next to her.

"It's nothing really."

"Now, I can tell you are upset. I have seen that look on my face in the mirror quite often."

Quinn now looked directly at her, realizing that sitting like this they were eye to eye. He couldn't believe that this self-assured woman was ever conflicted like he was, but he was encouraged. He wasn't quite sure what to say. He couldn't tell her the details about his family, but he had to say something.

"I guess I have been thinking about what you said earlier and that maybe I'm feeling like living on a ship is, well, kind of limiting. That I might like to live on a planet for a while."

"So why don't you?" she asked.

He was surprised by the question. Did she really not know how young he was? "I have duties here I can't abandon."

"I see." She looked toward the wall and clasped her hands around one knee, leaning back slightly. "You can't apply for a job on a planet? From what I saw the other night on the bridge, you know your way around computer systems."

"Doesn't everybody?"

Kurla laughed. It was very pleasant, and Quinn felt his lips stretch in a smile in response.

"Oh, no," she said. "I myself don't know one end of a computer from the other. I can use one only if it has voice access and even then, I can't always get it to tell me what I want to know."

"I suppose growing up on a farm with little technology doesn't help you learn about computers."

"Nope." She turned back to him. "Why don't you get off with me? New Drea is fairly large. The Order would be happy to speak for you. You can easily find a job or even go to school for some specialized training."

"School?" His stomach had swooped when she suggested he go with her, but it twisted when she mentioned school. Maybe she did know he was too young.

"Sure. There are lots of advanced schooling choices. For computers, science, technology, business, whatever you want to learn. What would you like to do?"

"I don't know. I have never thought about it." He had of course, but that was working on his disguises and helping the family with missions. Before she had asked, Quinn hadn't thought about any possibilities other than the family business.

"Well, think about it. We have, um, is it two days when we reach New Drea?"

"We reach the Reese system in two days and yours about thirty-six hours after that."

"So over three days to think about it. Maybe I will try to talk to the High Priest and see if he has any more suggestions."

"Thank you, Kurla. That is very thoughtful of you."

She dismissed the compliment. "It's what we do, help others. And you can help me too." She stood and Quinn was on his feet in the next breath.

"I can?" he asked.

"Yes. You can show me how to use this treadmill."

They both laughed and Quinn couldn't believe that only a few minutes ago he had been angry.

Chapter Twenty-four

Lenore was idly flicking through screens on the terminal in their cabin when Diarmin walked in. Her body was tugging at her to start pacing but she was doing her best to resist the urge. She had no idea what she was seeing because her thoughts were on her son. From the look on her husband's face, his were too. She closed the screen and turned her chair to face Diarmin as he sat on their bed.

"Anything interesting?" he asked.

"No, just letting my mind wander."

"I thought you might be looking up helpful hints on dealing with adolescents." His wry smile showed he was being half humorous and half serious.

"I think you and I have read all there is this past year." She shook her head, not wanting to say what she was about to. "I hate to admit it, but Quinn is right. Our situation is unique. We aren't going to find any advice about rearing children while on the run from a variety of criminals."

"Stop that. You know why we did what we did."

"I know, but I can't help thinking maybe we should have tried to put them in a school, give them a permanent home."

"They have a permanent home."

"A ship is not permanent. It can be blown up or captured. But a planet will always be there for a certain nostalgia."

"Really? Are you nostalgic about your home planet? Or, er, well the planet you grew up on?"

She gave Diarmin a sour look. "You know I'm not, same as you." She felt her lips tighten. "But Quinn didn't pick up on that with the story. He focused on his issues."

"Speaking of which, did you know he is attracted to Kurla?"

"Huh. I should have guessed. She is an appealing young woman. How do you know for sure?"

"Alli told me. I don't think I want to know how she found out."

Lenore gave a short laugh. "Probably not." She looked at her husband's worried face. "Don't worry, it's not a big deal."

"Maybe not for you but we don't know about how it will impact Quinn. She might only be here for a few days but even such a short time can have a permanent impact on a young man. It's strange, but I thought you would be more bothered by this news. Don't you remember your first crush?"

"I spent my teens training with the Xa. Doesn't leave much room for a crush." Lenore always hated the references to her past so she tried to change the subject. "My worries now are the present and whether this anger of Quinn's is temporary or quite valid."

The look on Diarmin's face told her he knew what she was avoiding but he didn't pursue it. "Valid?" he asked. "What's that supposed to mean? Emotions are always valid, but do you honestly think he might be right, that we should have raised them on a planet?"

"Maybe then Alli wouldn't be so introverted. And both could have had real friends, maybe two or three crushes by now. Not be running for their lives every time we are in normal space."

"I said it when I came in and I will say it now. Stop it. We can't change the past. We had good reason for doing what we did. And…" Diarmin paused for a slow breath. "You are right in that we need to tell them the entire stories of our past. Then Quinn can at least understand why things are the way they are. And maybe that living on a planet is not necessarily a good thing. Like our childhoods. I think we have been trying a little too hard to protect them from seeing the dark side of people and the universe. It's time they knew it all."

"All? Are you sure?" Lenore asked but she could see his pinched look turn into determination and perhaps resignation.

"Yes, all. Even the fact what I used to be. And the exact reasons why I quit and you left the Order. When they know all of that, then they can decide."

"I suppose that is what scares me," said Lenore. "Eventually, they will move on and create their own lives." She turned back to the terminal. "I just hope we haven't ruined them for normal."

"And what if they want to leave sooner rather than later," Diarmin said under his breath as he left, but Lenore heard him just fine.

***

As soon as her father had left, Allison flicked back to the scan of the ship. She felt a little guilty at the semi-spying, but she didn't like her family to be at odds. Her father went into his cabin where there was another heat signature, most likely her mother. But Quinn's room didn't have anyone in it. Instead there was one in the spare room and another moving down the corridor toward it. Since the last blip showed someone in Bondle's room, her bet was on Kurla.

What a coincidence. Not. Allison admitted to herself that she didn't like Kurla, but she wasn't sure why. Was it because Quinn liked her? Was it because she was too friendly and Allison didn't understand that mind set? Was it simply her usual dislike of strangers? No, Dad doesn't really like her either and that was before he knew about Quinn's feelings.

She found her fingers moving unconsciously on the keyboard and then the conversation in the spare room was coming through the speakers. She felt even more guilty but couldn't stop herself from listening to Kurla and Quinn. She was tempted to turn on the video but kept herself from going that far.

As the conversation progressed, Allison grew more and more uneasy. She couldn't see their faces, but, by the tone of their voices, she could tell Quinn was happier than he had been all day. *Obviously he would like her. She's been the only young woman we have ever really spent any time with.* Allison bit her lip at the thought, not wanting to agree with the idea that being raised on a ship was wrong.

She turned her attention back to the conversation, but it didn't calm her. Quinn was thinking about leaving? Her stomach fell. He wasn't even an adult yet. Could he leave if their parents didn't let him? If they held him here, that might make things worse and he might get angry enough to go anyway. Should she say something to her parents? She didn't want to lose her big brother.

A beep pulled her attention back to her console. Her fingers danced over the keyboard, bringing up the program that had indicated a problem. She had noticed an occasional glitch in the recordings that she shouldn't have been keeping so she had run a diagnostic on the communication systems to find any problems. That beep indicated an anomaly, but the computer wasn't sure what it was.

Pulling up the base codes, she quickly scanned through the data, looking for anything out of place. *Nothing... nothing... there! Wait, there's something else too.*

Hm, one thing out of the ordinary could be a simple error. Two things, however, meant this wasn't simply random interference. She settled down to hunt the source or sources.

Two hours later Allison still hadn't solved the issues but instead noted more problems. The first issue proved to be very cyclical, occurring every thirty minutes. *Doesn't feel like a random malfunction there.*

But the second issue happened once, at a very specific time.

While they had been out of transwarp, dealing with the leak.

It looked like data had been erased for a five-minute block. *I suppose it could have been the result of the EMP mine.*

Yet, that didn't feel quite right. *I'll find it out if I have to search all night,* she thought, glad for something to occupy her.

But though the project was engrossing, she couldn't get the thought of Quinn leaving out of her mind.

Chapter Twenty-five

Dinner was a quiet time. Lenore was on the bridge and Quinn had said he was going to eat in his room. When he had said that, Diarmin noticed the worried look on Allison's face but since Kurla was staying at the table, he put it down to Alli's usual dislike of discord in the family.

The conversation between the two passengers and himself revolved around asking if they were comfortable and needed anything. They assured him they were fine, and silence descended again. Bondle looked deep in thought, most likely pondering some science and unaware of the awkwardness. Kurla was obviously aware and appeared slightly uncomfortable, but she did nothing to try to break the tension.

"I'll go see if the captain wants anything," said Allison and she exited as if escaping. Diarmin did as well by taking his dish to the recycler and cleaning the galley even though it was Lenore's turn. Kurla handed him her plate and utensils and left for her room. Diarmin got so involved with cleaning, he barely noticed Allison come in for dinner for Lenore. He started on an inventory of the foodstuffs they had left and was interrupted by Alli.

"Here." She handed him some more dishes.

"Is she done already?"

"No, these are Bondle's."

Startled, Diarmin looked at where Bondle was seated but it was empty. "I didn't even notice he had gone. Do you know if he went back to his cabin?"

"He was gone when I came in."

"Would you check if he is in the cargo bay? It's a little early but he might be doing his nightly check."

"Sure," Allison hesitated as if she were going to say something. Diarmin thought about prompting her but she abruptly turned and headed out the door, presumably toward the cargo bay.

Shortly after, he had finished cleaning and met Bondle at the top of the ladder to the bay.

"Have a good night, Mr. Bondle."

Bondle mumbled something similar and vanished into the lounge. Diarmin went down, nearly running into his daughter.

"All okay?"

"Yes. He was already down here, examining a sample when I got here."

"Wait. He was actually examining a sample?"

"Yes, why?"

"Well, so far he merely checked the monitors of the crates, never opened one." Diarmin felt a surge of concern.

"It was only a small opening and he didn't open the vial, just ran a scanner over it then put it back." Allison pointed at the lower corner of the crate's monitor. "He entered some code here to close the opening, but I didn't see what it was."

"That's okay, Alli. I am sure he would have told us if there was anything to worry about." But just to be safe, Diarmin was going to run some scans of his own. "Thanks for helping out tonight. One more transition tomorrow afternoon and the day after the cargo will be gone and we'll be paid."

He was happy to see the grin on his daughter's face. "And get some more real food."

"First on the list." He smiled back but the smile faded as he noticed Allison hesitate again.

"What is it, Alli?"

"One of the diagnostic programs showed some anomalies in the communication system. I ran some analyses when I was on the bridge but haven't found anything definitive. I, um, wasn't sure if I should report it until I had something significant, but I figured it couldn't hurt to tell you."

"Put the information on a pad and I will look at it. Thanks for letting me know. Have a good night, Alli." She waved and was gone up the ladder.

Diarmin ran a scan for foreign substances or viruses around the six-alls, careful not to scan the cargo itself as Bondle had warned. Nothing out of the ordinary. He'd ask Bondle tomorrow why he had opened the crate for the first time since he boarded. He put the scanner away, feeling his worries about Quinn return. He paced around the bay for at least another hour, mind wandering and wishing there was an easy answer to their problems with Quinn. Nothing became any clearer, so he decided to try the thing that usually ordered his mind, tinkering. Since it had been quite a while since he had sat at his workbench, he lifted the cloth that covered it and idly stared, wondering which project to work on. Absently he began to gather his implements, mind still on the current difficulties and what to do about it.

When he found himself digging in his toolbox under the bench, he came back to awareness of his surroundings. He had wasted several hours in the bay and done nothing. He also abruptly realized he had been looking for his specialized microtool since he had sat down but there was no sign of it. He rooted around the rest of his work area to no avail. He felt his lips tighten as he considered the possibility of theft. Taking inventory of everything, Diarmin discovered there were several more items missing including the latest microreceiver patch for Quinn. Everything was there the last time he worked at his bench, but he realized that was several days ago. Maybe one of his family had borrowed his things. Perhaps Quinn tried out the microreceiver and used the microtool to examine it.

Diarmin's lips tightened further as he took a deep breath through his nose. Nobody ever disturbed his work, but he had to check even though it was very late. He replaced the cover and went to go wake his children and collect Lenore as well.

When they were all seated in the lounge, children blinking sleep out of their eyes, Diarmin went to the door to the passenger cabin corridor and closed it. He noticed Allison's eyes widen and Lenore's narrow. Quinn just blurted out.

"Why did you do that? We haven't closed it since our first passenger came aboard."

"We have a very serious discussion and I don't want to be overheard."

"Why not on the bridge?" he persisted.

"Quinn, I know you are tired but if you stop asking questions and simply listen, it will become clear." Diarmin was losing patience but he regretted his tone when he saw his son's face show annoyance rather than remorse.

"When I went to do some work a while ago, I noticed that several items were missing. Did any of you borrow them or even move them elsewhere for any reason?" All three shook their heads as he expected. He wasn't looking forward to what came next.

"What's missing, Dad?" asked Allison.

"My microtool, one of the new transmitter patches, a small pack of various electronics and other small items. Nothing very valuable, but that is no excuse for theft. We will have to search Bondle's cabin as he is the only other of us to have been in the cargo bay."

Quinn cleared his throat and all three looked at him. Diarmin was surprised to see Quinn's ears slightly tinged red.

"Um, well. Bondle isn't the only one. The other night when I was on duty, I was wandering the ship and ran into Kurla in the cargo bay. She wasn't carrying anything though."

"And just why didn't you report this, young man?" asked Diarmin, aware his voice was fairly gruff. Probably not the best tone since Quinn seemed to get more defensive than usual.

"She said she was just stretching her legs and forgot that the cargo bay was off limits. I believed her and like I said, she wasn't carrying anything." Quinn crossed his arms.

"And she has no pockets?" asked Lenore. Quinn reddened further but didn't answer as she continued. "A microtool and patch are very small." She glanced at Quinn and finally appeared to notice his red face. "But just because she was there doesn't mean she is guilty."

Diarmin narrowed his eyes at his wife but noticed Quinn's slight relaxation. Was her last sentence intended to placate Quinn or did she truly suspect Bondle? *It doesn't matter.*

"We'll search their cabins simultaneously," he said.

"I'll search Bondle's," said Lenore and she bounced up and toward the door.

"Then I will search Kurla's," he replied.

"I'll go with you, Dad," said Quinn.

Allison made an exasperated sound and Diarmin privately agreed with her. "No, Alli will help me search Kurla's"

"I guess that means I'll go with Mom then," said Quinn with a surly tone.

They stood in front of the doors. Diarmin raised his hand to knock but Lenore hissed at him.

"No, I would prefer to respect their privacy, but we need to just enter so they don't have time to get rid of any evidence."

"At least let's knock first," he said.

Lenore looked like she didn't want to give even that small warning, but she nodded at him.

They both typed in the override opening sequence in case the doors were locked. They simultaneously knocked on the doors and then opened them a breath later. Diarmin took a single step into Kurla's cabin.

Kurla sat up quickly on the bed, causing the light blanket to slither to the floor. She was wearing a very thin, lacy sleep garment and made no effort to cover up. Glancing back at Allison's wide eyes made Diarmin very grateful it hadn't been his son behind him.

"What's going on? Some sort of an emergency?" asked Kurla and her eyes slid from Diarmin's to look at Allison.

"I apologize for the rude entry, Ms. Plaad, but we have a situation." He reached down, grabbed the blanket and held it out to her. She rose to take it and then tossed it loosely around her shoulders, covering up nothing. "Please remain by the door while we search your cabin." Diarmin could hear Lenore's voice and assumed she was saying something similar.

"Search my cabin? Why?" She moved to the door with the blanket still hanging off her shoulders.

Diarmin turned to answer but she was looking out the door, probably trying to see Quinn. He gritted his teeth at the attempted manipulation but kept searching, keeping an ear out for Quinn. He hissed at Allison to catch her attention and jerked his chin at Kurla. Understanding his request, Allison tried to put herself between Kurla and the door while responding to her question.

"Well, um, Kurla. Some valuable items have gone missing so we are searching the cabins, Mr. Bondle's as well as yours to see if, well..." Allison trailed off.

"To see if I stole them?" She put her hands on her hips. "Why would I steal anything?"

"Perhaps you merely borrowed them?" asked Allison, her voice exaggerating a sweet tone just shy of mocking. "Sometimes items can make a person mighty curious."

Kurla's mouth worked as if she wanted to reply to Allison but held herself back. Finally, she looked at Diarmin, her chin raising slightly. "Go ahead, look. You won't find anything." Diarmin didn't comment that he was already looking but simply kept on. She stood right inside the door but kept looking out over Allison's head.

Lenore came in to announce that Bondle's cabin was clear, Quinn following, his face turning the brightest red Diarmin had ever seen. Trying to ignore the fact that Kurla edged closer to his son, Diarmin picked up one of the robes on the floor and felt a suspicious lump. Sure enough, there was an inner pocket that held the microtool, patch, and other missing items. He held them out for all to see.

"Those aren't mine," said Kurla loudly, letting the blanket slip from her shoulders as she gestured wildly. "They were put there by someone else. To make me look guilty."

"Why would someone do that, Ms. Plaad?" asked Lenore. Diarmin moved closer to his wife, recognizing that tension in her shoulders as anger and a readiness to take down an enemy. Guilty as she appeared to be, Kurla was still a very young woman.

"I never lock my cabin so anyone can come in at any time." Apparently, she also sensed Lenore's anger as she retreated to the far wall of her cabin, wringing instead of waving her hands. Allison squirmed out the door, away from any confrontation but Quinn planted himself between his mother and Kurla.

"That is how but not why," said Diarmin.

"I don't know. To throw suspicion off of themselves? Why would I take whatever that is?" She jabbed a finger in the direction of Diarmin's hand then went back to wringing. Now there were tears in her eyes. *She is either very skilled at manipulation or truly innocent.*

"May I speak to the High Priest? Perhaps he can settle this," said Diarmin.

"He might be the one who did this!" she shrieked.

"Or he could prove your innocence," said Quinn.

"But—" Suddenly her body straightened as her hands stopped wringing and dropped to her sides. "I apologize. I was conserving my energy. What has occurred?" Her voice had deepened.

Diarmin explained the situation to the priest. "We were hoping you could shed some light on what may have happened."

Kurla, or the High Priest, slowly shook her/his head. "I am sorry. I fade in and out of consciousness quite often. It is dangerous to take control like this. We run the risk of damaging Kurla's psyche and my spirit. I can neither confirm nor deny the accusation."

Lenore huffed out a breath and Quinn shuffled his feet awkwardly in the silence.

"I may, however, offer a temporary solution," said the priest.

Diarmin and Lenore nodded.

"Confine us, or the girl, to this cabin for the duration of the trip. When we reach our destination, I will again take control and deliver her to the Order. They will know how best to deal with the problem."

"That sounds reasonable. Thank you," said Lenore and Kurla's body went slack for a mere heartbeat.

"No no no! You can't lock me up. I'd go crazy. I need space. I am not used to being on small ships much less in one tiny cabin." In one stride she reached Quinn and gripped his shoulders. "Please don't let them do this."

Diarmin headed to rescue Quinn who was doing nothing to help himself, merely staring wide-eyed at Kurla's hysterics. Lenore got to Quinn first and forcibly separated them.

"Ms. Plaad. Control yourself or I will have to sedate you," she said with a slight push. It didn't appear that hard but Kurla stumbled back and fell onto her bed. She sobbed.

"I thought you were my friend," she spat at Quinn. Quinn said nothing, but pivoted and headed out the door, shoving past Allison in the hall. Allison stared at her parents very briefly then turned to follow her brother. Diarmin and Lenore left, closing and locking the cabin.

"That was…unpleasant," said Lenore. "I will see if she wants breakfast after she calms down."

"Is everything all right?" asked Bondle who was standing in his doorway.

"Yes," said Lenore, but she also disappeared through the lounge door.

I guess it's up to me to explain, thought Diarmin.

When he was finished, Bondle looked very uncomfortable. "I am sorry this happened. And since there is no real proof, I would be happy to remain in my cabin as well except when I need to inspect the vaccines."

"That is very gracious of you and we will send someone to accompany you when you need to inspect them or if you need anything. I do have one question, however." Bondle nodded so he continued. "Our computer officer noticed you removed a specimen from the cargo container. You've never done that before, why now?"

"Oh, I was simply checking to see if the cultures were still active. I can't tell the exact specifications from an external examination. Remember, if the cultures go inert—"

"They will be useless, I know. Well, were they fine?"

Bondle bounced on his toes. It took Diarmin a few seconds to realize that Bondle was happy.

"Very fine. They are reacting exactly as I hoped."

"Reacting?"

The bouncing stopped. "Um, bad choice of words. I mean that they should be chemically active even past our scheduled landing. Which means that they will have the best chance of working at maximum capacity."

"Ah, I see," Diarmin decided to let the matter drop. "Would you like something to eat?"

"Yes, thank you." Bondle retreated to his room as Diarmin went to fix him something from the galley.

Chapter Twenty-six

The entire family was together for the first time since Kurla's house arrest. It had been twenty very uncomfortable hours where nobody wanted to talk to anyone else. Meals were solitary, either in cabins or in shifts. Lenore had never felt so helpless. It didn't help that, with the exception of the theft, this trip had been routine, and she was feeling restless. She knew she should be grateful for the lack of excitement since that excitement usually meant danger for her and the family. Taking action was how she solved problems and she would be happy for something to divert her attention from the family's problems. The simple act of a course change was a welcome distraction.

Normally, only Diarmin and maybe Quinn would take care of the course change, but Lenore wanted everyone together. She had thought for days on how to bridge the awkwardness and finally figured that nothing could be done until the passengers were off the ship.

She glanced around, everyone sitting in their usual seats, staring at their displays and pointedly not at each other. She cleared her throat but the only one to glance at her was Diarmin.

"Is there a way to shorten our course at all? Get to the Reese system a little faster?" she asked.

Diarmin tilted his head at her as if silently asking her what she was thinking, but since both kids had turned at the question, he went on.

"Quinn," he said. "You have been charting courses. Do you have one that will shorten our trip?"

"Of course I do," he said, and his slightly sneering tone hinted at what his next words would be. "But this course was to keep 'out of the way' so it will be harder to be followed. Like usual."

Lenore tried not to bristle at his attitude. Allison had turned back to her board, clearly uncomfortable.

"Why do you want to know?" asked Diarmin, his voice thick with the tone that Lenore thought of as 'exuding calmness' as if he was trying to soothe them all.

"Bondle keeps mentioning his time crunch. I thought we would speed things up to help him." *And get both of them off the ship faster.*

"We haven't had any pursuers in a while. It might be worth a try," said Diarmin.

Quinn grunted which Lenore took as a positive sign, but apparently Diarmin knew better.

"You'd like to add something, Quinn?"

Quinn shook his head and turned back to his board. The relieved look on Allison's face mirrored what Lenore felt in her gut.

It didn't last long.

"Very well, let's calculate a shorter—" Diarmin started but was interrupted when Quinn spun his chair back to face his parents.

"Yes, I'd like to add something." The fire in his eyes made Lenore brace herself.

"Alli and I aren't stupid, you know. You think not telling us everything is protecting us, but we aren't little kids anymore. I know that the guy who confronted you on the planet is probably a Xa. I know that the leak wasn't an accident; the mine proved that. I know you guys talk about it; I see those looks you give each other all the time. I know that your pasts must be horrible, but you haven't said why. I know that we should be even more afraid that nobody is following us because there is something else going on. Nothing is adding up and you both are too obsessed with your secrets to even notice that Alli and I are grown and able to handle it. We have been handling things for quite a while. You deliberately keep us in the dark so we don't know what we might be missing. And maybe we can even help."

"Hey, leave me out of your rant," said Allison, her face showing the first hint of anger, an anomaly to Lenore.

"Fine, then just me. All this hiding and ducking and secrets. You think you are doing what's best for me, but you don't even ask me what I want."

"What do you want?" asked Diarmin.

"I don't know. I don't know enough about the universe beyond this ship to make that choice. Because you never gave me the chance to experience it."

"You've been on plenty of missions," said Lenore, trying to keep her voice down but not succeeding very well. "So don't tell me you don't get any experience."

"The only missions I get to go on are 'safe' ones." Quinn said. "Information gathering. That's it." For emphasis, he made a downward cutting motion with his right hand.

"You're not trained yet."

"And why not?" Quinn didn't wait for an answer. "I know, because you don't want us in danger. But the little training you have given us is defensive. Hell, we don't even know how to use any of those weapons we have. What if someone breaks into the ship? How do we 'run away' from that?"

"So you want training like me?" said Lenore, letting her anger loose like Quinn. "You want to be a Xa'ti'al?"

Quinn paused for a moment, leaned back in his chair and crossed his arms. "Maybe I do. I have no idea what they are really like. All I know is that you say, 'they are bad.' At least when I was little and you said not to touch the hot stove, you explained that I would burn myself if I did. Now you just say 'no' to everything without telling me why not. I'm sick of it."

Silence descended on the bridge which wasn't good. As it lengthened, Lenore searched for something to say but could find no words. She looked at Diarmin for help, but he was only shaking his head. She opened her mouth to break the heavy stillness but was interrupted by a 'ping' from Quinn's console.

Quinn turned to it, still smoldering. "Transition in ten seconds."

"Acknowledged," said Diarmin.

The seconds ticked by very slowly.

"Coming out of transspace in three...two...one..." Diarmin's fingers flew over the control board while Quinn put the course up on his display. The ship shuddered very slightly and the viewscreen showed the normal starry background.

The ship turned and headed in the correct direction to the next jump point. "Fifteen minutes...mark," said Diarmin. He sighed and turned to Quinn. "Look. I understand what you are saying but—"

The rest of his sentence was drowned out by the ship's alarm.

Everyone responded instantly, and Lenore was obscurely proud that the tension on the bridge didn't hamper her family's abilities at all.

"There is a very large ship out there, angling directly into our path," Quinn reported.

"We are receiving a request for communication, more like a demand," said Allison.

"Let's hear it," said Lenore. She knew what everyone was thinking.

The Xa'ti'al.

Diarmin's attention were firmly riveted to the controls. *Most likely planning an escape.*

"This is Central Galactic Patrol Ship *Sentinel Five* calling the *L'Eponge Carre*. Please shut down your engines and prepare to be boarded."

That was the name the ship had been using for their current mission. *This must be something recent*, thought Lenore. She opened a channel.

"This is Captain Fleming. For what reason are you requesting to board?" She glanced at Diarmin, but he shook his head which meant there was very little chance of escaping the huge ship.

"We have been given information that you are carrying dangerous and possibly illegal cargo and have been ordered to investigate. Please cease your evasive maneuvers or we will be forced to consider you hostile and take appropriate action."

With her finger on the mute button, Lenore said to her family, "Well?"

"I might be able to get away if I have a perfect shot and get very lucky," said Diarmin.

"Except I am detecting a scattering field that will prevent the transspace bubble from forming," said Quinn. "And they will be in range in less than a minute so there is no possible way we can continue on our current trajectory."

"Do you think it's a trap?" asked Lenore.

"The ship's ID matches their engine specs," said Allison. "And it is listed as the correct ship assigned to this quadrant."

"It's twice as big as any other ship we have encountered which is typical for the patrol ships in this sector." Diarmin grimaced. "I think we have no choice but to do as they say."

The com beeped again as if impatient. Lenore unmuted it. "Acknowledged, *Sentinel Five*. Our ship will reach zero velocity in five standard minutes. We will await the boarding party at the side airlock."

"Acknowledged, Captain Fleming. *Sentinel Five*, out." The com went silent.

"That gives us no more than ten minutes," said Lenore.

"To do what?" asked Allison.

"The only thing they could possibly be referring to is Bondle's cargo," said Quinn.

"Exactly. Diarmin and I will question him right now. Quinn, you check on the cargo and make sure anything in the cargo bay that may be the least bit suspicious is out of sight." Lenore was feeling her adrenaline rising and ignored the slight rush of enjoyment she was getting out of some action. "Alli, make sure those files we pulled from the slavers are well hidden, even to the point of pulling them from the computer to hide on data sticks if necessary. And kids," she said as they paused in their descent down the ladder to follow her instructions. "I would like you to stay out of sight if possible."

Both nodded, and Lenore ignored Diarmin's eyebrows lifting at that last directive.

To forestall the question she knew was coming, she spoke. "Let's go see if Bondle knows what is going on."

***

"I really don't know what it's all about."

While Bondle's words seemed sincere, Diarmin couldn't help but wonder if someone could be that into their own little world to not even be aware of other possibilities.

"Think, man," said Lenore, and the stiffness in her voice told Diarmin she was only a step away from gritting her teeth. "Why else would they be stopping us? Who knows about the cargo?"

Bondle spread his hands, his nervousness becoming more and more palpable. "Only myself and my assistant. My home planet doesn't even know. I…" He looked down at his feet. "I didn't tell them. Didn't want them to raise their hopes in case…well, you know, in case the medicines don't work."

"Either you are lying, or your assistant turned you in," said Lenore, the acid clear in her voice.

"It's not illegal, I promise. It is as I told you, medicine that I created so it is owned by my government who sponsors me. I don't know why someone would say it is illegal or dangerous and I don't know what else to say to convince you." Bondle looked near tears so Diarmin took control of the conversation. No sense alienating the one man who could convince the patrol that the cargo was safe.

"Mr. Bondle. Is it possible that the planetary government where your lab was located found out about and reported an illegal landing?"

Diarmin ignored Lenore's sour glance. He didn't need the reminder that he had not bothered to hide his takeoff.

"I suppose that is the most likely scenario." Bondle rubbed his chin. "They could have figured where the ship landed and questioned my assistant. Assistant Mill was supposed to keep quiet that we transported something off the surface, but he hates to lie so he may have said something." He looked back up and must have seen the anger still present in Lenore's eyes. "But he would never have said that the cargo was dangerous. It isn't in its current state, I swear." He held his hands out in entreaty. "Let me contact Evan to verify if he said anything. And tell him that our planetary government will pay any necessary fines."

The airlock alarm on the other side of the lounge began hooting.

"Unfortunately, we have no time," said Lenore. "That alarm means the shuttle from the patrol ship with the boarding party is angling to dock." She spun and started for the airlock.

"You'd better come, too, Mr. Bondle," said Diarmin. The man nodded and followed, the worried look still clear on his face.

"I am detecting three life signs on the shuttle," said Allison from her room as the three stood near the airlock. "Standard shuttlepod registered to the *Sentinel Five*."

Lenore nodded and Diarmin could see she had her gloves on and the look on her face told him she was mentally assessing her ability to deal with three should they choose to be hostile.

Or if it was a trap.

K.A. Bledsoe

Quinn also stuck his head out of his room. "What about Kurla? Do we tell her about any of this?"

"No reason to," said Lenore. "She lost any privileges concerning ship business with her poor choices. Now back into your rooms and don't come out unless we say so."

Diarmin wondered if his wife noticed the flash of emotion in their son's eyes.

The light next to the airlock door turned green at the exact moment that the hooting stopped. With the pressure equalized, Lenore opened the lock which showed a uniformed man standing in the connecting tube. He was impeccably dressed in the standard light blue patrol outfit, the bars on his chest showing the rank of lieutenant and several commendations. His cap was tucked under his arm as he walked through the airlock. The two men behind him were similarly dressed but with their caps firmly on their head. The one who came in behind the lieutenant was a corporal and the trailing one a private.

"Thank you for allowing us to come aboard, Captain Fleming." The lead man gave a short nod. "Lieutenant Sherrod Hammins."

Lenore nodded as well and indicated the lounge. "You didn't leave us much choice, Lieutenant. I hope we can clear this up as soon as possible. We are on a deadline."

The three passed Lenore and went directly to the lounge. Hammins turned back to Lenore. "We will be as prompt as we can be while being completely thorough."

Diarmin grimaced inwardly. In other words, not quickly at all.

"If we can inspect the cargo first, ma'am?" said the shorter of the two younger men.

"Certainly. This way gentlemen." She led the way to the cargo bay, the three officers behind single file with Bondle next and himself bringing up the rear. As they all gathered around the six-alls, the corporal pulled out a scanner.

Bondle pushed forward. "Wait!" Diarmin could see the sudden tension in everyone so he stepped in front of Bondle.

"This is the man who owns the cargo, Mr. Ven Bondle."

"Ah, yes, Mr. Bondle," said Lieutenant Hammins. "We have your name as the first to question."

138

"Ask me anything just don't scan the cargo. It could damage the contents which are very fragile."

Diarmin thought guiltily of his own scans and hoped he hadn't damaged any of the medicines. But then he caught himself. He never actually scanned the containers, just the bay. And he also realized he'd been more trusting than usual. What if the reason Bondle didn't want the cargo scanned was not because the contents were fragile, but because they were indeed something different? Something dangerous.

"We need to determine if the cargo is hazardous as reported. If we cannot scan it, we will have to open it."

"No, no. That would be even worse. If you have a micropolaron scanner I will allow it. I have one in my cabin."

"Which could be altered to show any readout," said the private.

"I would never—"

"Excuse me, Lieutenant Hammins," said Lenore. "You said this cargo was reported hazardous. By whom?"

"I am afraid we cannot reveal our sources, Captain." He looked about to add something but the corporal chimed in.

"Lieutenant, I have a micropolaron scanner on the ship. I can get it and return in fifteen minutes."

"Very good, Corporal. Please do that while I remain to question Mr. Bondle and the crew." Hammins pulled out a small pad and tapped on it before looking back at Lenore. "Captain, my report says there are four crew on this ship and I only see two. I will have to question the others as well."

Diarmin could see Lenore struggling to keep her anger from showing so she merely nodded, turned and stomped up the ladder.

Hammins turned to Diarmin. "Is there a place we can sit for the interviews?"

"The lounge will do. I will show you."

The lieutenant nodded. "Mr. Bondle, you shall be first," he said as he gestured the scientist to precede him up the ladder.

"No," he said. Everyone froze at the reaction. The private was the one to speak up.

"Are you refusing to cooperate with an official investigation, Mr. Bondle?" he asked.

Bondle's bravado was brief as all eyes turned to him, the lieutenant's slightly narrowed. "N- not at all. It's just, I mean there can't…" He straightened his shoulders as if gathering his courage. "I simply will not leave the cargo unattended with a stranger in the room who might damage the contents." He held his hands up. "Unintentionally, perhaps, but I can't take the chance."

"Very well, Mr. Bondle. Private Levi, you will accompany us."

Diarmin thought the private looked a little angry, almost to the point of defying the order. But the private noticed Diarmin's eyes on him and the anger was gone. Everyone clambered up the ladder. Diarmin handled the airlock for the corporal's departure while the others went to the lounge.

When Diarmin entered the lounge, the lieutenant was seated at the table with the private standing at attention behind him. Bondle sat across looking very uncomfortable. Lieutenant Hammins paused in taking a breath, probably for another question, and looked pointedly at Diarmin.

"I will check on the rest of the crew," said Diarmin, then left the way he had come. He could hear the questions continue immediately so he figured the family needed a plan. Quinn's door was open so he headed into his cabin.

"Good, you're here," said Lenore. Allison and Quinn were seated on the bed, set looks on their faces. "I have briefed these two on what type of questions they will be asked and how to respond. You know the drill."

"Act innocent of everything, stay in character and give away no information for free," said Diarmin.

"Yes. And I will insist on being present for each being questioned."

"Well, Bondle is coming under fire now."

Lenore cursed as she disappeared out the door and presumably toward the lounge.

Diarmin turned toward his children. "Well. Ready for your first official questioning by the law?" He grinned, hoping to put them at ease. Allison chuckled weakly but her eyes were wide. Diarmin hoped it was only nerves, not fear.

Quinn said nothing, face completely devoid of any emotion.

Diarmin wasn't sure what that indicated. With a pang of regret, he realized he could no longer read his son's emotions. One thing was very certain. When all this was over, they all needed to sit down and have a very serious family discussion, dealing with Quinn's accusations and finding some way to resolve the differences that had sprung up between them. The discussion would be perhaps the most important one of their lives.

Chapter Twenty-seven

As Lenore walked into the lounge, Bondle was just standing up.

"Ah, Captain," said the lieutenant. "I am ready to speak to you and your crew. Are you first then?"

Lenore was trying very hard not to grit her teeth at this self-assured young man's attitude. He was just short of being pompous and arrogant. If it wasn't herself and family coming under fire, she would admire this capable and efficient young man.

"You may start with my crew, but I insist on being present." Before Hammins could answer, she stepped back into the corridor and motioned at Allison who was first out of Quinn's cabin. She reentered the lounge.

"Captain, I usually don't permit—" he began but cut himself off as Allison came into sight. The muscles along his jaw bunched and Lenore suppressed a wry laugh that at least she had got him to grit his teeth. It was obvious that Allison was a minor and there was no legal reason why Lenore couldn't oversee the questioning. It also gave Lenore a chance to hear what everyone said, and she could make up stories to cover any error if she went last as planned.

"Very well," was all he said as he waved Allison toward the opposite chair. Bondle left through the other door toward his cabin, but not before shooting a worried look at Lenore. *I will have to question him myself later. Who knows what things they asked him?*

Allison wasn't even fully seated when the lieutenant began.

"State your name and title please."

"Cathy Mikin, computer tech," she answered, nearly matching his terse delivery. It wasn't quite mocking but close.

"And how long have you been aboard this ship?"

Lenore answered before Allison could. "That question is not relevant for your purpose here."

"I need to know if she was on board when the cargo arrived."

"Then ask that specifically."

Lieutenant Hammins gave a respectful nod to Lenore, obviously aware that she knew questioning tactics and wasn't going to fall for any of them. "Very well. Ms. Mikin, were—"

"Yes, I was here," she said. She looked sorry for her interruption but did not bite her lip, twist her hair or give any other tells that Lenore had warned her about. The officer ignored the interruption and kept going. He asked the usual, did she overhear anybody mention anything about the cargo being dangerous, any suspicious activity, and several other routine questions. Allison answered them perfectly, with an almost bored expression, until a certain question.

"Did you know that the submitted permits were forged?" Hammins's face registered satisfaction at Allison's surprise.

"What?" she said. "That's impossible. I checked it…are you sure?" She shook her head. "Boy, I blew that one." She turned her head toward Lenore. "Apologies, Captain. I should have caught that." She turned back to Hammins. "How did you know? Can you tell me so I don't get duped again?"

Lenore decided to intervene before Allison overdid it. "Leave it for now. We will discuss it later."

Allison's shoulders slumped as she dropped her head and mumbled, "Yes, Captain." Her dejection seemed so real that Hammins looked uncomfortable at getting her in trouble.

"It wasn't easy to catch. Could have fooled anyone," he said. He returned Allison's smile and said she could go. Lenore knew the interrogation had been relatively easy and realized maybe this Hammins wasn't as tough and seasoned as he appeared to be.

Quinn must have been waiting by the door because he came in as soon as Allison stood. He walked to the chair without even glancing at his mother. While she thought it was good that he wasn't showing anything the officer could use against him, she didn't like his completely shuttered face.

The questions began along the exact lines as the ones Allison had been asked. Hammins was careful not to exceed his prerogatives with the questions and Quinn was done very quickly as well. With each interview taking five minutes or less, they might all be finished by the time the corporal returned with the scanner. Quinn stood and left, as emotionless as he had been when he answered all the questions. Lenore thought she saw the lieutenant's eyebrow twitch as if in question to Quinn's attitude, but he didn't stop Quinn from leaving. Diarmin entered, passing Quinn and Lenore noticed her husband glance at Quinn's face but within an eyeblink, he hid the fatherly concern and was all business for the patrolmen.

"Bondle told me that you often oversaw his daily inspection of the cargo. Why? Did you have concerns that there might be a problem?" Hammins leaned forward slightly.

Wow, just jumped right in, didn't he? But if he thinks Diarmin can be intimidated or startled into revealing anything, he is wrong.

"Standard procedure," Diarmin said, a hint of chill in his voice. "If you hadn't noticed, many of the ship's systems are down there. I wouldn't want anyone to accidentally damage or even brush up against sensitive machinery."

"Ah, sensible precaution," Hammins answered, ignoring the jab about not noticing. "Did you ever have any reason to question Mr. Bondle about the cargo?"

"We did before he was brought on. He assured us that it posed no danger. Passive scans of the six-alls revealed no leakage of any toxic substances."

"Did you scan inside the six-alls?"

"Of course not, at Bondle's request. He told me the same thing he told you, that scans may damage the cargo."

"Were you aware that the permits from Bondle were false?"

Diarmin allowed his eyebrows to rise but said he wasn't aware. Lenore began to wonder if the lieutenant was thinking she was in cahoots with Bondle and trying to determine if the rest of the crew were innocent or guilty. The rest of the questions were harmless and Diarmin was dismissed as the hooting of the airlock began.

"Let the corporal in, please," Lenore said to Diarmin. "And bring him here."

"Aye, Captain." He nodded and left. Lenore knew he understood that no stranger was to be unsupervised aboard this ship.

Lenore moved to sit in the chair, but the lieutenant stood.

"If you don't mind, Captain. I would prefer to continue the questions after the cargo has been scanned."

Lenore caught herself about to grind her teeth again but nodded. "I will inform Mr. Bondle."

Hammins looked like he was going to protest but instead headed for the airlock. Lenore went to fetch the scientist, glancing at Kurla's closed door. *Hm, wonder what she would make of all this.* Bondle's door was open and he leapt to his feet as soon as he caught sight of Lenore. He grabbed his scanner and followed Lenore to the cargo bay. Thoughts of the girl were forgotten.

***

Allison had retreated to her cabin, but Quinn was tired of hiding. His parents hadn't told him to keep out of sight after the questioning, so he took advantage of the crowded ship to tuck himself into a corner of the cargo bay before everyone returned to scan the six-alls. He only had a few moments to ponder the situation before the shuttle returned. He was very edgy and didn't know exactly why. The questioning had gone well, almost boring. In fact, he felt like he had been dismissed as irrelevant by the lieutenant. Though he was glad he wasn't under suspicion, it still felt a little insulting. After all, Quinn was capable of doing much more, and, in fact, wasn't as naive as the officer thought.

But Quinn wasn't so caught up in himself not to notice how the rest of his family was feeling. His mother was holding back anger as well, but that was because she didn't like officials aboard her ship. She was barely tolerating the passengers and Quinn got the feeling that after this mission, they wouldn't take on any others in the future. He snorted. That would mean no chance of meeting someone new anytime soon.

His father was tense and worried, but Quinn knew it wasn't all about the patrolmen. *Maybe a little worry about Bondle and Kurla but for the family, too. I don't know.* But that annoyed him further. Maybe Allison was still too young, but he was old enough to strike out on his own. He had skills and could make it probably anywhere if they would just let him go. Maybe they were afraid he would slip and leave clues for the

Xa'ti'al to find his mother. *I am as good at disguise as anyone and they found her anyway with no help from me.*

Allison. He was worried about her, though. She didn't want to meet people, preferred being by herself. These extra three patrolmen were almost more than she could take. That wasn't good. What if she had been the one to be captured by the slavers? She wouldn't have lasted a day, delicate as she is. But maybe that was even more of a reason for Quinn to leave. Show her that there were good things to be had outside of the family. It might even encourage her to go to a school and make some friends. So that settled his mind. He would start looking for a good opportunity to find something else, so he could learn new things and grow without his parents molding him their way.

Through his musings, he'd been aware of the return of the shuttle and now heard footsteps descending the ladder. He pulled back a little further in the niche with his father's workbench and watched the group.

First came his father, followed closely by the corporal who was holding a rather wieldy instrument that Quinn assumed was the micropolaron scanner he had gone to get. The lieutenant was followed closely by the private and they all gathered around the closest six-all. Quinn saw his father open his mouth as the corporal lifted the scanner, probably to tell him to wait, but more footsteps indicated that his mother and Bondle were entering the bay.

"Thank you for waiting for the owner of the cargo to be present, Lieutenant Hammins," said Lenore.

The sour look on the lieutenant's face said he didn't appreciate the sarcasm, but he nodded in an attempt to be gracious. Bondle went straight to the new scanner and acknowledged it was the proper one and wouldn't harm the cargo. Everyone stood silently as the corporal held the bulky scanner under one arm while holding up a wand to the six-all. He waved it from top to bottom, repeated the process for each side of the six-all and again with the other three. He said nothing during the process and his expression did not even flicker. The lieutenant's did, however, when the corporal presented the scanner readout to him.

"Well, I am afraid our information was correct," he said to no one in particular. "The scanner is detecting radioactive particles in each cargo container."

Each person's reaction was different. His father's eyes widened slightly, his mother's narrowed, the private smirked and Bondle protested loudly.

"Impossible! There is absolutely no possibility of radioactivity in those samples." He practically lunged for the corporal's scanner. The lieutenant stepped in between them and held up a hand.

"Mr. Bondle. I cannot deny the readouts." He shoved the pad in front of Bondle's nose. "With this evidence, I must insist that the cargo be opened."

"No no no no!" said Bondle. He waved his own scanner at the cargo and held it out to Hammins. "His scanner is faulty as you can see. Mine shows no radioactivity."

"Another reason to open the cargo."

"This cargo bay is not hermetically sealed. If the cargo is damaged in any way or even one sample container breached, it could cause a chain reaction and destroy the cultures that I have worked so hard to create." His shoulders slumped. "Please, officer. I need these medicines for my planet. My people are dying. Isn't there something you can do?"

Lieutenant Hammins actually appeared to believe the man, hesitating with his response. Quinn thought he was the one being naive. Obviously that's what someone would say if they were shipping dangerous illegal cargo. A glance at his parents showed them watching everything very carefully but not engaging at all. *What are they waiting for?*

The corporal cleared his throat. "Sir, if I may. Back on the local patrol base we have the lab next to the medical facilities which is large enough for one six-all, and the containers can be examined safely in that environment."

"Will that be satisfactory, Mr. Bondle?"

"I suppose I have no choice." His entire body showed defeat.

Good, thought Quinn. *Get this guy off this ship as well as his dangerous cargo.*

"It is not satisfactory to me, Lieutenant Hammins," said Lenore. "I contracted with Mr. Bondle to deliver him and his cargo from Drenon to Reese. The detour will be an unacceptable delay."

"Ah, but you and your crew are not needed anymore," said Hammins, the look on his face one of superiority. "My main ship is equipped with a boarding field that allows me to transfer the six-alls safely. I am confiscating the cargo according to regulation four-six-one of the illegal shipping codes."

"But my cargo needs to be delivered within three days, four at the most," said Bondle. "It will be useless after that."

"Should the cargo prove harmless, I will personally guarantee to deliver it on time, Mr. Bondle."

"Thank you, sir."

"But that is not—" began Lenore.

"Captain Fleming. You have no legal right to protest. Might I suggest in the future to examine permits more carefully so you can avoid a similar situation."

The complete blanking of emotions from his mother's face might seem resignation to most, but Hammins should watch out. He had just made an enemy.

"Mr. Bondle gather your things. We will return to the ship and prepare to receive the cargo."

Bondle nodded and hurried up the ladder. The private leaned over to whisper in the lieutenant's ear. The lieutenant nodded and turned again to Lenore who was standing, arms loose at her side, saying nothing.

"Our scans indicate that there is another person aboard who I haven't questioned."

"Another passenger," said Diarmin quickly.

He's probably afraid Mom will lose it any minute, thought Quinn.

"May I speak with this person?"

"She has nothing to do with this situation," said Lenore through stiff lips. "She boarded separately and is traveling to a different destination."

"Nevertheless, regulations stipulate that all witnesses be questioned."

Lenore didn't even bother to answer, simply turned and left up the ladder. The rest followed, Diarmin last to leave. Quinn followed the group all the way to Kurla's cabin.

Lenore knocked on the door then input the code to unlock it. Kurla stood, looking startled at the lieutenant pushing past Lenore to speak to her. But before he could get a question out, Kurla took the initiative.

"Oh, the Order be Praised, I am rescued," she said, reaching for the lieutenant.

"Rescued?" he said as he took a step back from Kurla, raising his hands in an unconscious attempt to keep her at bay. She saw this and stopped her approach.

"These awful people have locked me in my cabin for no good reason," she said, clasping her hands together and looking down. Quinn heard his father snort before he responded.

"She was caught with items stolen from our ship and restricted to her quarters," he said.

"I didn't take anything. I don't know how those things got in my cabin." She looked at the patrolman and emphasized each argument with a begging flourish of her clasped hands. "They locked me up without proof. A cruel punishment to someone who grew up on a large farm. I have been suffering from horrible claustrophobia for days."

"It's been thirty-six hours and she has been well cared for."

"We shall take her off your hands, Captain," said Hammins. "We have ways to determine guilt or innocence, all harmless and ethical of course."

"Oh, thank you, thank you," said Kurla as she grabbed his hand. "I am grateful...wait...no you can't—" Her face changed as she released Hammins' hand. "That would be acceptable," said the deepened voice.

"What?" Hammins blinked at the sudden alteration.

Lenore quickly explained about the High Priest, although her expression showed she wasn't liking how this was going.

The Priest continued speaking. "Kurla is under my guardianship so you have my permission to proceed with these tests." Kurla's body turned to face Lenore. "Captain Fleming. I apologize for all the inconvenience. Once this is resolved and I am back home, I will make sure you receive adequate compensation from the Order." The body bowed again and when she straightened, all could tell it was Kurla again.

"Very well. Private Levi, please assist the lady with her possessions and escort her aboard the shuttle. Captain." Hammins gestured towards the lounge, leaving the private and Kurla to packing. As the rest of the people went into the lounge, Quinn stayed in the corridor within earshot.

Hammins continued. "I am relieving you of all responsibility for the girl. As for the cargo and Bondle, at this time it appears you have either been duped into carrying illegal cargo or are simply in the wrong place at the wrong time. Unless I find evidence to the contrary, you are free to go after the cargo is aboard my ship. However, if I find any evidence of your collaboration in anything unlawful, I will press charges."

"I assure you, Lieutenant, you will find no such evidence," she replied. Quinn had to admire his mother's restraint. Surely she must be itching to take down the officer. Through the doorway he saw the lieutenant nod, point the corporal toward Bondle's cabin, and then turn toward the shuttle. Bondle exited, nearly running down the corporal. As they all disappeared out of Quinn's sight, he took a few hesitant steps towards Kurla's cabin. She was closing her small bag, the private waiting politely. Quinn cleared his throat, wishing the private wasn't there.

"I, um, wanted to say goodbye, Kurla," he said. She looked at him with anger and hurt in her eyes and he couldn't leave it at that. He felt she had been used by either the Priest or Bondle and didn't deserve to be labeled as a thief. "I am sorry about everything. I don't know what happened. If I could help I would but..." *So lame Quinn.*

But Kurla's face softened. "Thank you. I am hoping these nice men can prove my innocence and then I can go home." She smiled at him. "I meant it when I said you can come with me. I... I'd still like that. But now isn't the time." She gave him a quick kiss on the cheek. "Thank you for believing in me. Goodbye." She left quickly, the private trailing in her wake.

Quinn rubbed his cheek. Maybe he could find evidence to prove she had been framed.

Chapter Twenty-eight

As soon as the questioning was over, Alli headed back to her room. That wasn't to say she didn't know what was going on, however. She pulled up her newest program which allowed her to listen to any or all the rooms of the ship. Guilt suffused her as she knew she was going against her parents' wishes about spying, but for some reason she felt compelled to know what was going on. The program had video capabilities as well, but she didn't usually use those. She hadn't listened in on anyone privately in their cabins, but she heard everything that had occurred on board since the patrolmen arrived.

Well, to be completely honest with herself, she made the program right after the theft so it would record automatically whether she was watching or not. She felt that had such a program been in place, it would have proven beyond a doubt that Kurla did steal Dad's stuff. And then she could show it to Quinn so he would stop mooning over her.

The questioning of Quinn went about the same as with her although the officer didn't ask him about the fake permits. Allison was privately pleased that she managed to turn her surprise at the question into surprise that they were fake. Quinn wasn't the only one who could act.

Ah, now they were questioning Dad. The questions seemed basic and routine and a little boring. When the corporal returned and everyone descended to the cargo bay, she couldn't help herself. She activated the video as well as the audio. She listened to what everyone was saying, but she really was interested in her parents' reactions. As she zoomed in, she caught sight of Quinn lurking in the corner. Typical, although she realized she was doing the same thing. *But I am being more subtle, Quinn.*

As she attempted to focus on her parents, the video fuzzed out and back in several times. *There's that stupid glitch again, but I've never seen that happen before. Maybe when I transferred the controls to my room instead of the bridge it caused a slight distortion in the transmitter. Or maybe looking for the problem made it worse. I never got the chance to give that pad to Dad. Probably ought to now, though there is nothing conclusive yet. Oh, hold on. They're leaving the cargo bay.*

Alli followed all the action in the cargo bay and back to Kurla's cabin. She couldn't believe that the cargo was dangerous, but she was glad that Kurla was leaving. When the groups split, she wasn't sure who to listen to even though both would be recorded. She decided she wanted to hear how the cargo was going to be transferred but instead found her hand turning up the volume in the corridor outside Kurla's cabin. As she listened to her brother and Kurla, she grew angry.

Kurla mentioned again that she wanted Quinn to leave with her. Was he seriously considering it? He didn't say that he couldn't or wouldn't, just stood there dumbly staring with that goofy look on his face. Allison got the sinking feeling that if Kurla hadn't been taken into custody by these officials, she would be trying harder to convince Quinn to leave the family and go with her.

And it looked like Quinn would go.

***

As the hatch slammed shut, Lenore stood with her arms crossed staring at it, trying to keep anger under a tight rein. *There goes all chance of getting paid,* she thought as the patrol shuttle pulled away with both passengers. Lenore realized she couldn't count on the word of the priest. What if Kurla was found guilty and retained so long that the priest's awareness dwindled to nothing? *No, we can't count on that money.*

Lenore felt her lips tighten and was aware of Diarmin coming to stand next to her. She didn't look at him and was obscurely pleased that he didn't try to make her feel better in any way. He knew her well enough to know an arm or word of comfort would have the opposite effect. Now she was annoyed that he could read her so well. So much for the vaunted Xa'ti'al abilities to suppress emotion. Then she remembered her bioimplant that helped suppress emotions was gone and training couldn't quite keep up anymore.

"Bridge or cargo bay?" he asked.

"What?" Annoyed again, Lenore grimly admitted to herself that she was letting the strong emotions distract her.

"Well, someone needs to be on the bridge for the field docking maneuver and someone in the bay to make sure the transfer of cargo goes smoothly. Which do you want?"

It took several moments before she responded, and it wasn't to answer the question. "That cargo would have earned us enough money to get the defensive systems for the ship. And have plenty left over."

Diarmin nodded, crossing his arms as well. "Yes. I don't mind losing the money for Kurla's trip; that was just extra. But the cargo..."

"I didn't trust Bondle, but I figured I could handle him."

"The patrol changes things. Couldn't have predicted that."

"I should have," she said in a mumble. Not quietly enough since, out of the corner of her eye, she noticed her husband turn his head toward her. She still didn't look at him, not wanting to see his expression. "Maybe we should have run," she mumbled again.

Diarmin turned his head back to stare at the hatch. "We could still run now. Deliver the cargo to Reese and take whatever they give us."

That shocked her out of her self-absorption enough to look at him. He looked at her and she couldn't read his expression.

"Are you serious?"

Diarmin shrugged, arms still crossed. "Why not? At least we'd get some money out of all the time we've already put into this."

"You know why not. We would become what we have been trying so hard to get away from. That criminal world."

"I said 'We could.' Doesn't mean we should." He gave her a half smile, but Lenore wasn't sure if he was joking.

"I'll take the bridge," she said. "You make sure the cargo bay is secure."

Diarmin gave a quick salute and left for the bay. Lenore stared after him before she left in the opposite direction. As she reached the bridge, she was slightly startled that Quinn was already there in the navigator's seat. She hadn't seen him go to the bridge. She berated herself for letting her awareness slip. She had seen him in the cargo bay and lounge, but she let him be since she didn't exactly order him back to his room after he was questioned. She shook her head as she took the command chair. Sometimes she longed for how everyone followed orders to the letter in the Xa'ti'al.

That thought nearly caused her to spring upright. Why would she think that? Blind obedience was one of the things she had hated. And Diarmin suggesting they steal the cargo and run from the law? Was telling the stories of their past somehow making them revert to who they used to be?

No! She wouldn't let that happen. She shook her head again, quite violently this time, and must have made some sound because Quinn turned his head to look at her oddly. Trying to avoid any questions, Lenore cleared her throat and opened the intercom to Allison's cabin.

"Alli, can we have you on the bridge, please?"

"On my way."

As if in answer, the com board pinged and Lenore answered the hail.

"*Sentinel Five* ready for docking sequence." The voice belonged to the lieutenant. "Please transmit the specifications of the cargo bay opening so we can adjust the field."

"Acknowledged," she responded then opened the cargo bay com. "They are on their way."

"All prepped here," was Diarmin's response. Allison clambered up the ladder and took her station.

Within five minutes, the large ship had expertly maneuvered into place and extended the field that would become a barrier to space, a force-field airlock that allowed both cargo bays to be opened in space. Lenore alerted Diarmin and told Allison to put the cargo bay on the monitor. She complied just in time to hear the echo of the airlock at the top of the cargo bay ladder slam shut. Diarmin would wait until the all clear was sounded that the field was stable so the atmosphere wouldn't be sucked out when the bay opened.

Another five minutes and the private and corporal were in the bay, activating the anti-grav platforms. The camera showed Diarmin with his arms crossed, offering no assistance and with a look on his face that probably mirrored hers earlier. The cargo disappeared from view and

Lenore could feel the vibrations through the deck of the cargo bay doors closing.

"Thank you for your cooperation, Captain Fleming. I hope it won't be necessary to be in touch soon."

"Agreed. Fleming out." Lenore chose to ignore Hammins's awkwardly phrased comment which could be taken either as a polite farewell or subtle threat.

Diarmin appeared at the ladder and continued to the science seat. "Well," he said as he sat down heavily. "That's that."

Quinn nodded, his face grim. Allison stared with wide eyes and Lenore said nothing. The silence on the bridge stretched on as she sunk deeper into introspection.

"What course should I set?" Quinn finally asked.

Lenore looked at Diarmin. Should they get supplies, look for another job, head for the nearest planet? She and her husband stared at each other as if they could communicate telepathically. Why wasn't he saying anything? Why wasn't she?

"Something feels off," were the words that came out of her mouth. Instead of questions from the others, all Lenore saw was nods and relief.

"I've been feeling that since they first hailed us, but events moved too quickly to think about what was happening," said Diarmin.

"Do I set a course?" asked Quinn.

"No," said Lenore. "Let's do some investigating of our own. I want some answers."

Chapter Twenty-nine

An hour later, the family gathered in the lounge with their findings. Each had their own assignments, but Diarmin felt that his discovery might be the most important. As soon as Quinn took his seat at the couch, Diarmin tossed three devices on the low table between everyone.

"What are those?" asked Lenore as she picked one up. Each of the kids also grabbed one to look at closer.

"I'm not sure. As you can see, they have been damaged beyond recognition, but I can surmise what they used to be by where they were found."

"Where?" asked Allison and Quinn at the same time.

"One was in the cargo bay, just across from where the six-alls were, one in our cabin and one on the bridge. I didn't check in your kids' cabins."

"Some kind of surveillance devices," said Lenore, her face grim.

"Probably," said Diarmin. "I will have to take them apart to see if they were video or audio or both." He knew his lips showed a grim line. "They were hidden very well, in plain sight yet camouflaged to match their surroundings exactly."

"Who do you think put them there?" asked Quinn.

"I don't know. I ran a scan for fingerprints and DNA but found nothing."

"I didn't find anything like this in Bondle's cabin," said Lenore and Quinn shook his head indicating he had found nothing in Kurla's. "Or anything else odd. Only what you would expect to see. And they left nothing behind. Did you have any luck, Alli?"

Allison was peering intently at the device, muttering to herself.

"Alli, what did you find?" Lenore asked.

"That's it!" Allison cried, causing Diarmin to startle slightly even though they were waiting for her to speak.

"What's 'it'?" asked Quinn.

"These devices must have been interfering with our communication systems within the ship, though I'm not sure how far back the glitches go." Her voice devolved back into a self-absorbed mutter. "Maybe if I look at the time indexes and cross-check when they first appear—"

"Alli!" said all three other family members simultaneously.

"Huh? What?" Allison looked up, blinking as if she had forgotten everyone was there.

Diarmin sighed, knowing she did that when she was thinking hard about a tech or computer problem. "Explain, please."

"Oh, sorry." She grinned, slightly embarrassed. "I had seen some anomalies in our communication systems, mostly inter-ship, but often enough that I kept looking for what might have caused them. Diagnostics showed nothing but if these are surveillance devices, they probably interfered with our systems when they would send out a signal." She turned the device over to examine closely. "If it weren't slagged I could try it out, see if it creates the glitch, in fact, maybe I could..."

As she trailed off, Lenore rolled her eyes and Diarmin could see she was trying to be patient. But it wasn't her best quality.

"Why didn't you tell us about these anomalies?" she asked.

"I told Dad, but we haven't had time to talk about it. I thought they were only a problem I needed to correct in the systems. I never would have guessed it was this. These devices explain everything. Well, almost."

"Almost?" asked Quinn.

"Well, there was one instance where the anomaly wasn't an interference but instead a... I don't know how to explain it in layman's terms... maybe like a camouflaged pulse laid over a random static burst that was then deleted—"

"Never mind explaining the anomaly," said Diarmin. "What do you think caused it?"

"More importantly, when did it occur," said Lenore.

Diarmin looked at Lenore and saw the beginnings of anger. Not at Allison but at the discovery. *She suspects something.*

157

"As to the cause, I am not sure, but I can tell you exactly when." Allison looked at her mother as if she didn't want to tell her. "It happened while we were dealing with the leak and the, well, you know."

Diarmin felt his gut tighten though he had half-guessed that answer because of Lenore's reaction. The look on his wife's face now could only be described as thunderous.

Several moments passed without anyone speaking. Lenore was the first to speak, her expression now one of determination.

"Okay. We will consider what exactly that means, but for now, Alli, please report on what you found while we were searching the cabins."

"Well, depends on what you mean by 'found.'" Allison tucked her feet under her on the couch and fiddled with the ruined device. "I tried to contact the lab using the code that Bondle had initially called us on but received no answer. I also hacked the city's database and could find nothing, no news reports or even private government documents that had any mentions of illegal cargo. The only mention of the lab is when it was built, corresponding to what Bondle told us."

"Did you hack into the laboratory computers?" asked Diarmin.

Allison shook her head and tossed the device back to the table. "I tried but couldn't find them."

"What do you mean?" asked Quinn.

"I mean I couldn't find them. Which indicates either that they don't have any computers connected to the IGNet or they are simply turned off. Can't read something that has no signal. If I was there I might, but from here…" she shrugged.

"And the patrol?" asked Lenore.

"All legit," said Allison. "Lieutenant Sherrod Hammins has been the commanding officer of *Sentinel Five* for two years and five months, based in the asteroid belt between the fifth and sixth planets of the Welanon system. Their base is small, usually staffed by only three or four, more like an outpost than a large base. The corporal and private were recently transferred there, but such transfers occur every six months to a year, and theirs had been scheduled for sixty-five days."

"So all we know is that someone placed spy devices on the ship," said Quinn.

"It couldn't have been the patrol, they didn't have the time or opportunity," said Diarmin.

"Not to mention no reason to do so," said Lenore.

"So that means that one of the passengers did it," said Allison. "But who and why?"

"I think Bondle was transporting something other than vaccines," said Lenore. "Maybe bioweapons or even explosives since radiation was detected. The device was to keep watch in case anyone got too curious."

"I'm tempted to say Kurla since she was caught with stolen items," said Diarmin. "Why would Bondle bother with planting stolen goods in her cabin?"

"To distract us from his possibly dangerous cargo, by focusing on the immediate threat rather than a possible one."

Diarmin shook his head. "If he used the devices, he would have known in plenty of time to redirect our attention another way. No, it had to be Kurla who planted them, possibly looking for ways to make money other than stealing the small, very valuable items that could be easily hidden in her bag."

"But she has very little knowledge of computers or technology," said Quinn.

"And what makes you say that?" said Lenore. Her tone was sharp and Diarmin suspected she was losing patience with the lack of definitive answers. And she didn't like being caught on the receiving end of deception.

"She said so," Quinn said, his tone defensive. When nobody commented, he went on, carefully avoiding his mother's glare. "She seems too young for that kind of espionage anyway."

Allison sputtered and Quinn looked away, obviously realizing too late what he had said. His own sister could do all that easily. Not to mention his mother had done a lot more when she was a lot younger than Kurla. He mumbled an apology and Diarmin thought he would have to intercede in another argument but apparently Lenore and Allison decided to let it go.

For now.

"There's no proof of who put them there or why. I think the best we can say is that one of our passengers is guilty and the other innocent," said Lenore.

"*Former* passengers," said Diarmin but regretted the words as soon as they were out. Lenore's head whipped around, eyes narrowing at him.

"Former?"

"They are not our problem anymore. Let the patrol sort the whole mess out."

Lenore gripped the arms of her chair and stared. Diarmin stared back to show he could be as stubborn as she could. The silence stretched on, Allison and Quinn taking turns glancing at both parents.

Finally, Lenore sighed and spoke in that dangerously quiet voice. "For all we know, the patrol may be behind all this. As far as I am concerned, it is my fault if I let harm come to a passenger aboard my ship, blameless or not. If everything turns out to be in order, I will take the heat and listen to your 'I told you so' for as long as you want to say it. But I feel in my gut something is wrong and I need to put it right."

She looked at each of her family's faces in turn as if daring them to argue further. Diarmin was tempted, but he had only brought up the possibility of leaving so all possible choices were discussed. Privately, he thought she was right in that they couldn't leave either Kurla or Bondle to be a pawn in whatever was going on.

"Okay." Lenore nodded decisively. "Allison, contact the planetary authorities on Drenon and see if they can't get in touch with the lab, more importantly with the assistant. Then help your father with finding out anything you can about those devices. Quinn, search your and Allison's cabin for any similar devices. I will locate the base so we can be on our way within the hour."

***

At exactly one hour after she issued her directives, everyone was in their seats on the bridge with the exception of Allison. After sending the coordinates to Diarmin so he could set course for the base, she paged her daughter.

"Alli, we're heading out. We need you up here."

"Give me a minute. Wrapping something up."

She closed communications without waiting for Lenore to answer. Lenore looked at her husband, but he answered before she could ask.

"She never came to help me with the devices which is unfortunate because I found something that I need help deciphering."

Five minutes later the ship was ready to leave, and Lenore was itching to go. She reached out to call Allison again but the sound of footsteps on the ladder stopped her.

"Sorry it took so long but I found some things you need to see," she said.

"Good, because I found nothing," said Quinn.

"I might have found something, but you go ahead, Alli," said Diarmin.

"You can tell us on the way to the base. Diarmin, let's—"

"Wait, Mom," said Allison. "You need to hear this first. Won't take long."

Lenore gestured for her to continue, trying not to be annoyed at being interrupted or for the delay.

"First, I contacted Drenon to see if they could check out the lab. I posed as an investigator and they were only too happy to help, once they verified my ID of course."

"ID?" asked Quinn.

"Sure, I always keep a few in my database ready to go in case of situations like this," she explained. "Some can be adapted to whatever occupation I need but there are a few standard ones like an investigator, physician, and even a researcher. You'd be surprised how many people will just give information away if they think they will be in a book about—"

"Back to your report, Alli," said Lenore, well aware of her daughter's tendency for tangents.

"Oh, yes. Well, they sent someone to the lab and found that it had been broken into. They discovered, um…" As she trailed off, her face took on a pinched look that was relatively new. Lenore thought she knew what was coming.

"They found Assistant Mills. He was dead. Extensive blood loss from possible torture." She swallowed, her short phrases indicating her distress. Lenore's heart went out to her, but Allison gamely went on. "Unfortunately, the security tapes were wiped, and they could find no other immediate evidence. I convinced them to turn on the computers so I could see what I could find. They were damaged, but I did find some evidence that the system had been hacked shortly after we picked up Bondle. Later that day, in fact."

"By who?"

"That I don't know. Yet. If it is possible, I will find it." Her fierce tone proved her determination. Quinn reached out and put a hand on Allison's shoulder very briefly. He understood his sister's feelings about death more than anyone, and Lenore briefly wished again that she had her son's empathy.

"Mill's death is unfortunate. But we need to get going."

"Wait, there's more," said Allison. She sat at her station and punched at the keyboard. "I got curious about who might be hacking in so I backtracked the records of the patrol. This is what I found." One last harder-than-any-other punch of a key and the main screen showed two pictures of patrolmen, a corporal and private.

"Who are they?" asked Diarmin.

"They are Private Levi and Corporal Zachariah."

"But those aren't the men who came aboard," said Quinn.

"Exactly." Allison's mouth was set in a grim line.

"The ones who came on board must have taken their identities." Lenore's teeth gritted, her lips probably in a grim line identical to Allison's. "It may be neither of our passengers are to blame for any of the problems, especially the confiscation of the cargo."

"Unless they are working with Bondle?" asked Quinn.

Diarmin shook his head. "Why would they need to hack into the computer system if they were working with him?"

"At least now we know who to watch out for. Anything else, Alli?"

She looked down, shuffling her feet. "Well, I did find another data blank. It happened after I began investigating so I missed it because I was only checking out previous occurrences."

"When did this other one happen?" asked Diarmin.

Allison shot a quick glance at her brother before she turned over a pad to her parents. Lenore looked over Diarmin's shoulder at the readout, although with that glance at Quinn, she had a good idea when the data blank had occurred.

"When?" asked Quinn, obviously irritated at being left out.

Diarmin hesitated in answering but Lenore would not hide things from her son anymore, especially after his outburst earlier.

"Right after Kurla was restricted to her cabin," she said, watching Quinn for his reaction.

His face flushed slightly. "That doesn't mean anything."

"This blank is most likely someone sending a signal, hidden within our own systems, then erased to cover their tracks," said Diarmin. "I have, um, seen something similar."

Lenore nodded. She had, too. She turned back to Allison. "Can you find out where the signal came from?"

Allison shook her head. "All I know is that it was from somewhere on the ship that was not our own systems."

"See?" said Quinn, angrily. "It could have been from either of our passengers. Or from someone outside the ship trying to access those security devices." He crossed his arms, determined to be stubborn.

"Your father and I will see if we have any better luck, having experienced this before," said Lenore. "We need to get going. Anything else, Allison? About this, the patrol or the lab?"

"No, but I will keep digging." She turned to go but Diarmin called her name. She turned back and caught the pad he tossed to her.

"First, check out what I found on the devices. There are fragments of a program and an indicator of a master device that may have controlled all three. See what you can decipher. We may need that information before we reach the base."

Allison nodded and headed back down the ladder.

"Take the ship to the patrol base," said Lenore. "I'm going to prep."

Chapter Thirty

Diarmin maneuvered the yacht into orbit around the asteroid that housed the base. As Quinn put the tiny asteroid on the screen, Diarmin realized that Allison was correct in her assessment that it was really more of an outpost than a base.

"We're in range, Alli," said Diarmin. "Open a channel please."

Allison hit a couple keys and nodded to her mother.

"Base five-seven. This is Captain Fleming calling for Lieutenant Sherrod Hammins. Please respond."

The family waited, tense, for an answer. Nothing. Diarmin felt alarms going off in the back of his mind. His wife seemed calm as she hailed again.

"Repeat, base five-seven. This is Captain Fleming calling for Lieutenant Sherrod Hammins. Please respond." As the silence stretched, Lenore repeated the message once more, this time asking for anyone to respond.

All eyes on the bridge glanced back and forth at each other. Without a word, Lenore shot out of her chair and down the ladder. Diarmin knew she was going to don all her gear, not just the basic prep she had done earlier.

"Alli, can you get a read on the base?"

"No clear readings of any kind, but I don't know if it is because of a scattering field or the artificial atmosphere surrounding the base. All I can read is that there is one large building, but no life signs or other ships are detected."

"Keep checking." Diarmin stood. "Quinn, keep repeating the hail and let me know the instant either of you find anything."

Quinn nodded and Diarmin headed for their cabin. Sure enough, Lenore was securing the last of her personal devices as he entered. She looked at him expectantly.

"Still nothing. Alli can read an atmosphere so we won't need suits but that's all we know."

Lenore nodded. "Standard for a small patrol base like this one. We go in prepared for anything. Level Five alert."

"We? Who's we?"

Lenore looked at him, eyes slightly narrowed. "You and I of course. The kids are safer on the ship."

"Maybe Quinn should go with you and I can be the back-up."

"Absolutely not." She shoved past him and pulled the weapons bag out of their closet.

"Quinn has been training for missions. We need to start including him more." Despite his arguments, he began to arm himself as well. *Old habits,* he thought.

"Not this time."

"You heard him as well as I did. When will be the right time?" He lowered his voice. "If it's not soon, it may be never."

She snapped the last blaster in place and looked directly at Diarmin. "When we have at least a vague idea of what we are going into. When we have a clear plan. Quinn hasn't enough experience to know what to do on the spur of the moment. Another time." She left the cabin. Diarmin knew better than to argue with her when she was focused on upcoming action. He finished his preparations and followed his wife.

***

Diarmin circled the base once with the shuttle before they landed. Lenore spoke aloud, knowing Quinn was listening back on their yacht.

"No sign of the patrol ship. No evidence of damage to the base. The doors seem to be secure. Diarmin is going to land."

"Acknowledged."

"Be advised that though my implant is designed to pierce scattering fields, we may lose contact once we are inside the atmosphere."

"Understood."

Lenore grimaced at Quinn's terse responses. He didn't sound happy. He had argued like his father that he should go to the base, leaving Diarmin and Allison as back up. Lenore stood firm and tried to make it seem like Quinn was vital on the ship. She had told him he needed to monitor closely in case action was needed. Allison was working on the devices to see if she could glean anything from the program Diarmin had detected. But Lenore knew keeping them both busy wouldn't stop them from doing something stupid if she and Diarmin were to get into trouble.

Well, she simply had to make sure they didn't.

The shuttle was on the ground and she was out the door as soon as it opened wide enough. Her blaster led the way, and she trusted Diarmin with her back. Nothing appeared amiss, but she didn't let down her guard.

They made their way to the door of the base with no problems. Diarmin pulled out his unlocking mechanism, but it wasn't necessary as the door opened at Lenore's touch.

"Not locked," he whispered. "And we were unchallenged."

"Not a good sign," she answered just as quietly. "Ready?"

He nodded and she dashed through the door, eyes darting all around. The entry room was normal with no guard stationed at the window. Since that position should have been covered by the private, she wasn't surprised to find it empty. The door to the inner section of the base was also unlocked, and this time it was Diarmin's turn to leap through while she kept an eye out for an ambush. Nobody was in the room but for the first time, there were signs of a fight. Not a huge one, a couple of chairs tipped over, papers scattered on the floor. The most telling sign was the blaster mark on the wall just over the desk. She indicated the mark with a gesture of her weapon and Diarmin nodded. The blast mark was located slightly above where a head would be seated at the desk. It had been to intimidate the person sitting there, probably Lieutenant Hammins.

They slowly approached the open door on the other side of the room. If it was a standard base, it would lead to the galley and cabins of those stationed there. The two paced the corridor, past the first cabin, obviously for the highest ranked officer. The open door showed a mess as if it had been looted. The door on the left held a room with two beds and foot lockers. Nothing was out of place except unmade beds, so the evidence seemed to support a coup by the two false patrolmen. The galley was empty, not even looted though Lenore wouldn't blame them since patrol rations were only eaten when there was nothing else to be had.

Past the galley was one more door. This one was locked, confirming Lenore's suspicions that not all of the patrolmen and passengers had been involved in the theft of the cargo. The door most likely led to the brig, and the fact that it was locked meant whoever took the ship wanted to make sure the others stayed put. Diarmin attached his device and had the door open in ten seconds. Not letting down her guard, Lenore peered around the corner and saw two cells. The one on the left was empty, force field down, but the other contained at least two people talking quietly that she couldn't see from her present position. The rest of the room was vacant, so she eased in as quietly as possible and beckoned Diarmin to follow.

As she came into full view of the cell, she noticed Bondle and Lieutenant Hammins sitting on the bed. The scientist seemed to be unharmed, but the lieutenant had a blood-soaked cloth awkwardly tied to the left side of his head down over his eye. Bondle looked up immediately.

"Captain!"

Despite his injuries, Hammins stood and tried to shield Bondle with his body.

"Sherrod, this is ridiculous. They're friends." Bondle gently pressed the lieutenant back to the bed. Hammins sat down hard, just short of collapsing, nearly displacing the cloth. Bondle sat next to him to adjust the makeshift bandage before he looked back at Lenore. "You are friends, aren't you?" His eyes looked worried.

"Since we are here to get you out, it should be obvious we aren't working for whomever did this to you," said Lenore.

"What's the code to open the cell?" asked Diarmin.

Hammins mumbled the proper sequence and the force field vanished as Diarmin typed it in. Lenore indicated the door they had come through to Diarmin. He nodded and placed himself at the door, blaster ready. Lenore helped the lieutenant to his feet, noting he had a slight limp.

"Do you have a medical bay?" she asked.

"At the other end of this corridor," he said.

She and Bondle arranged themselves on either side of him, his arms around their shoulders, and slowly helped him to the bay.

"What happened?"

"Mutiny," spat Hammins. Lenore could see the fire in his uninjured eye and was glad to see his spirit wasn't at all diminished.

"A little more detail would be helpful, Lieutenant," she said. When he opened his mouth to answer she stopped him. "Let's let Bondle answer first then you can add your account."

He looked about to protest when he nearly tripped and grunted with pain. He nodded so Bondle spoke.

"We had just landed and were sitting at Sherrod's desk. I was giving my account of everything and he was writing up an official report. Suddenly, the corporal simply came over, pulled his weapon and shot at the wall behind Sherrod, um Lieutenant Hammins."

The first name meant that the two had been in the cell for some time and Bondle was just realizing that their newfound familiarity may not be appropriate. Lenore ignored the correction.

"Go on."

"Hammins reacted as any officer would and jumped up, reaching for his own weapon but the corporal was now pointing his gun right at his face. We were helpless then and obeyed the demand to head for the cells. Right after I went in, Sherrod attacked the corporal and they fought. He would have succeeded, even broke the man's wrist I think, if the private hadn't come in and shot at Sherrod. The blast caught him in the side of the head, and I am afraid he may lose his left eye."

They had reached the medical bay and eased the lieutenant onto the bed. Lenore gently placed the IV cuff around his arm and activated the medbed. It would diagnose and dispense the proper medications and even fix whatever damage it could. It wasn't very sophisticated, however, and she privately agreed that Hammins would probably lose his eye as she unwrapped the cloth from his head.

"What did they want?" she asked Bondle.

"They didn't ask for anything, just locked us in here. Oh, the private asked why they didn't just kill us and the other said...let me see if I can remember exactly. He said, 'Boss said we may need the scientist,' and then something about how the goody-good lieutenant would die soon of his wound anyway."

"What happened to Kurla?"

"They took her," Hammins said, his voice hoarse but reviving somewhat now that painkillers had entered his system. "They needed a hostage, they said." He tried to sit up, but Lenore pushed him back down. He protested. "I need to file a report. Need to go after her. And the ship. Can't believe a patrolman would betray..." His words started to slur. In his weakened state, Lenore held him down easily.

"Lieutenant Hammins, those men were imposters. Probably killed the real Levi and Zachariah and assumed their identities," she said.

"All the more reason to contact headquarters. They need to know." He tried to disengage the IV cuff. Lenore held firm.

"Of course, Lieutenant, but let the medbed stabilize your wounds first or you will pass out in the middle of your report." She pushed some additional buttons.

"Thank you, Captain Fleming. I owe you one." He relaxed back and his eyes began to flutter close. His last words came out as a mumble but were understood. "Call me Sherrod..."

"Is he okay?" asked Bondle.

"He will be. I sedated him for now," said Lenore. "He doesn't need to be filing reports with those wounds."

"But my cargo, and Miss Plaad—"

"We will take care of that, Bondle. Now it's time for us to talk." Lenore took Bondle's arm and steered him out of the room and back to the front office, beckoning to Diarmin to follow as they passed him. All three sat and Lenore didn't hesitate.

"Tell us, Mr. Bondle. Why would they steal a cargo of plague medicines? Unless you have been lying to us from the start."

He raised his hands at her imperative tone. "No, no, I didn't lie! They are vaccines, it's just that...well... I didn't tell you everything about them." His shoulders slumped and he looked down. Lenore said nothing, just kept glaring, knowing he was going to tell everything.

"Remember I had said that the cultures weren't dangerous to you because they haven't been purposed yet? Well, this vaccine is designed to adapt to the particular strain introduced into it. You inject a few diseased cells and it adapts to destroy that particular disease. This is how I am hoping to eradicate the rapidly mutating plague on my planet."

"If it works like you say," said Diarmin, "it can be adapted for almost any cure in the galaxy. That would be very valuable to anyone bringing it to market."

Bondle nodded but the look on his face turned even more anguished. "Yes, I was hoping that would be the case and my planet could begin to recoup its horrible losses. But there's more." He stopped and ran his right hand through his hair in a nervous gesture. After several false starts, Lenore spoke for him.

"The cultures can be purposed for negative effects as well, can't they?"

Bondle swallowed and nodded, eyes still on the floor.

"So, we are talking about potential bioweapons as well," said Diarmin, voice grim. "Now we know why they had to keep you alive, to create more if they can't figure out how to themselves."

"Who knows about the other possible applications of these vaccines?" asked Lenore.

"Only myself and my assistant, Evan Mill. Everyone else only worked on sections, never the entire strain." He shook his head. "I am sorry. I probably should have said something, but I didn't want my creation to be used as a weapon. It is supposed to heal."

Lenore's heart went out to the man. She knew how he felt. Obligated to keep secrets, but secrecy could damage in the long run. She put a hand on his shoulder.

"I should tell you that your assistant is dead." There was no easy way to say that.

Bondle's head came up and the shock was too real. "No! How? Why?"

"We think someone wanted information, but Mill wouldn't give it," said Diarmin. "He gave his life protecting your creation."

Lenore peered sideways at Diarmin. They had never really discussed or concluded that, but he was probably right. And trying to comfort Bondle whose gaze had returned to the floor. Bondle was fighting tears, but now was not the time for grief. She stood and that got his attention.

"Where are you going?"

"I am going to find that patrol ship and those men."

Bondle looked up at her from his chair. "And my cargo?" The hesitant look in his eyes told Lenore that he wasn't sure what she intended. Fighting down anger at the implication that she would run off with his cargo, she replied, trying not to grit her teeth. He had been through a lot and these new experiences told him he couldn't trust anyone.

"Mr. Bondle. You signed on as a passenger. I am bound by my honor as a captain to see that you and your cargo reach your destination intact."

His reaction was not what she expected. He leapt up and threw his arms around her. "Oh, thank you, thank you, thank you, Captain. You have no idea what that means to me."

Stiff and fighting the urge to shove him away, Lenore looked at Diarmin and saw him trying not to smile. That drained the tension from her, and she relaxed her posture and gently disengaged Bondle. "You are welcome. By my calculations, we have two days to deliver your cargo, Mr. Bondle. We need to get started."

Chapter Thirty-one

Allison was going to wait on the bridge until her parents returned, but when Quinn vacated his post as soon as they signaled the shuttle's return to the ship, she changed her mind. She downloaded everything onto pads as quickly as she could, wanting to catch up with her brother. Her mother's vocal implant was still transmitting, and she caught a few words that she didn't quite understand.

"...makes no sense. Why would they take the girl? Bondle would be the more likely hostage. Something is not right here, Diarmin."

But she had no time to listen further as she saw the shuttle was nearly to the ship.

As she descended the ladder, Quinn exited his cabin with his pack on his back. She followed him to the shuttle's docking port but was surprised when he opened the weapons locker and grabbed a blaster to hide in his pack.

"Do you even know how to use that?" she asked him, wondering at his odd behavior.

"Stay out of it, Allison," he said, voice gruff.

Allison was startled at his tone. He had never spoken rough to her, even when he was angry with his parents. He had always been the gentle big brother. This new side of him scared her. It didn't seem like Quinn at all.

A few minutes later, their parents irised open the shuttle bay door and stepped through. Her mother stopped just inside, brought up short by an obviously angry Quinn standing with both hands tightly clenching his backpack straps. Diarmin barely had room to enter and seemed about to comment until he caught sight of the tense scene. Allison simply stared, not sure what to do.

Lenore's lips thinned as they usually did when she was fighting emotions. Her voice was calm as she gestured at Quinn. "And what exactly is this?"

"I heard everything," said Quinn.

"And?" said Lenore.

The muscles along Quinn's jaw bunched, but Allison knew he wasn't going to back down from whatever this was. She had heard everything too and still didn't know what was in his mind.

"Everyone seems to be worried about getting the cargo back. I noticed nobody even mentioned getting their hostage back." He squared his shoulders and stood as tall as he could. It would have been comical if the situation wasn't so fraught with tension. "I am going to help rescue Kurla."

Their mother simply stared unblinking at Quinn. He stared back, not losing his bravado one bit despite that glare. Allison had been on the receiving end of their mother's gaze more than once and was obscurely impressed with Quinn's resolve. Her eyes flicked to her father, but he was apparently not going to interfere.

"Just because we didn't mention Kurla doesn't mean we aren't going to help her," said Lenore. "It's insulting for you to imply that."

Quinn's jaw bunched again but he didn't waver. "I am going."

"You are not."

They stood there staring, each not willing to back down.

"Enough!"

Allison literally jumped back a foot at her father's near shout. He stepped between the two antagonists and gave each a stern look.

"We don't have time for this now," he said, looking at Lenore. He turned to Quinn. "Quinn, I appreciate you wanting to help and in nearly any other circumstance, I would welcome you along. Your mother and I have already discussed this and in the future, you can be a great help." Allison noticed her mother's expression did not change but her feet shifted as if she didn't agree with that statement. Her father continued. "However," he said to forestall the triumph starting on Quinn's face. "This time we will be facing two men who have already killed experienced patrol officers and an innocent scientist. They are very dangerous and ruthless. It's not the mission for you to test out your *new* fighting skills."

Allison didn't miss that emphasized word and neither did Quinn. He glared for another moment then pivoted and stalked off to his cabin. Diarmin turned to Lenore and the look that passed between them was indecipherable to Allison. Her father turned back to her.

"What have you got for us, Alli?"

Glad for the change of topic, she held out the pads one by one. "This one is what I got from the device program. It shows an external source of activation and control. It took some doing, but I determined that the control device is still activated." She handed over the other pad. "By using one of my tracking programs, I have found that device at these coordinates and moving outward from the base. This last pad shows the signature and engine specs of the patrol ship. Tracking the patrol ship, its course matches that of the control device so I assume it is onboard that ship."

"Excellent job, Alli." He juggled the pads into a stack and looked at Lenore. "Shall we set a course?"

Lenore nodded and they all turned to continue down the corridor. As they passed Quinn's cabin with the closed door, Allison made a snap decision that she hoped she wouldn't regret. She stopped and turned to face her parents who almost ran into her.

"Mom, Dad. There is something you need to see, well, listen to anyway," she said in a soft voice so Quinn couldn't overhear. Her mother simply raised an eyebrow and Allison knew she was pushing her luck, but she simply had to. "In your cabin?" The few steps back would give Allison time to think of the best way to explain why she had what she had.

As they all entered the cabin, Allison closed their door and made her way to the desk with the computer. A few taps and she had the recording she wanted them to hear.

"I know you didn't want me to spy, but I happened to hear a conversation because I wanted to see if I could help talk to Quinn about whatever was bugging him." This wasn't quite the case, but the little deception would at least give her a good reason for disobeying her parents about spying. "This was right after the argument on the bridge about being raised on the ship." She hit a key and Quinn's voice piped out followed by Kurla's. They listened without comment to the conversation where Kurla suggested Quinn leave with her. Even though she knew what was coming, Allison's stomach still dropped as she heard the eagerness in Quinn's voice. She closely watched her parents, but they were too canny to reveal their feelings.

When it was over, her mother spoke. "Thank you for this, Alli. I don't think you need to worry. It's just a conversation." She smiled. "I think teenage hormones are causing these reactions. We just hadn't realized how much Quinn, and you," she ruffled Allison's curls, "have grown. Head to the bridge and pull up the tracking program so we can plot an intercept course. We will be up in a minute."

"Okay," she said and left the cabin. After a few steps however, she stopped and quietly tiptoed back to their cabin. If that conversation was nothing, why did they need to discuss it privately?

"...if you are sure," Diarmin was saying.

"Don't you trust Quinn?" Lenore asked.

"Yes, I do, but this is about something other than trust. I have to admit that lately I have no idea what is going through his head. I can't read him anymore."

Her mother made a sound that Allison couldn't quite fathom. Agreement? A groan? Then she spoke. "Either way, we need to sort it out with him."

"If we still can."

Allison turned and fled to the bridge before her parents caught her eavesdropping yet again.

***

Quinn couldn't sit still. He grabbed his pack that he had tossed on the bed. He unpacked it, neatly laying out the items on the bed, until he realized this was exactly what his mother did before and after missions. Then he nearly shoved everything off the bed until his hand touched the blaster he had stowed there. He picked it up and held it. Allison was right. He didn't know how to fire it, but wasn't the threat enough? If he could bluff convincingly, he wouldn't have to fire it.

Could he, though? What if they called his bluff and he was forced to shoot someone? He'd watched someone he knew be shot. On video and not in person, but it had still been horrible. Visions swam through his mind of bodies in the corridors outside of the slave cells. He'd put that out of his mind, but deep down he knew his mother had probably killed them while rescuing him.

Could I pull that trigger?

That's what stun is for, said the little voice in his head.

That's true. Quinn searched for a switch for a stun setting but couldn't find it. Did this blaster even have a stun setting? He also knew there was a safety but didn't know how to disengage it.

Suddenly he felt his anger rush back. His mother had been giving him and Allison self-defense training and had just started teaching him other fighting techniques. But she hadn't even told them the basics of weapons. What if they couldn't get away but got hold of a gun? They could use that information that she refused to share.

Well, there was more than one way to find out about weapons. He sat at his terminal and started typing in search parameters. If they didn't need him to help rescue Kurla, fine. He would help himself and be ready for anything.

Chapter Thirty-two

As the ship sped to intercept the thieves, Quinn still hadn't made an appearance on the bridge. Diarmin kept glancing at Lenore but she was hiding her emotions well. No punching at the keyboards, no thin lips or bunched jaw muscles.

Strange that she isn't angrier about Quinn. Then Diarmin realized it had nothing to do with Quinn. It had to do with retrieving the stolen cargo. She was in battle mode and mentally preparing herself by emptying her emotions and formulating plans. She hadn't been in that state for a while and, to be honest, since she lost the Xa'ti'al implant, he hadn't thought she would. The implant helped with medical functions, but he had also determined that it suppressed emotion and heightened awareness which helped make the "perfect" soldier. Now Diarmin realized it wasn't only the implant. Training also played a part in the emotion suppression. He just hoped it wouldn't backfire without that implant to get her through it.

And wouldn't backfire on him and the kids.

"I'm reading the ship now," said Allison from her seat. "They are still in transwarp." She typed a little more. "If my calculations are correct, they will need to make a course change within three hours."

"How do you know that?" asked Lenore.

"Because if they don't, they will fly right into a red dwarf star, or close enough to make no difference anyway," Allison said with a shrug.

"Keep a close eye on that, Alli." Diarmin reached for the inter-ship communicator but his wife beat him to it.

"Quinn, we need you on the bridge, now." She closed the circuit without waiting for an answer. Her clipped tones and monotone voice told Diarmin she was all business. He only hoped it wouldn't alienate

Quinn any further. But if the last few days were any indication, it probably would. And Lenore, in this mood, wouldn't even notice, making it worse.

The footfalls on the ladder weren't stomping, a good sign, and Quinn took his seat without comment, his face as emotionless as his mother's. Diarmin felt a wave of relief. Maybe the impending action made them put all the resentments on hold.

"Quinn," said Lenore. "We are currently tracking the patrol ship, keeping pace. It is due to drop out of transwarp at any time in the next three hours and we need to be ready when they do. Since Alli is closely monitoring when they will shift, you will analyze the best way to disable that ship."

"You *need* me to do that, do you?" Quinn mumbled under his breath. But since Diarmin heard it, he knew Lenore did as well. She turned her chair to face Quinn.

Uh-oh.

"Yes, Quinn, we need you. Or maybe not. We could probably manage without you." She ignored his hunching shoulders and reddening ears that told them he was getting angry again. "But the bare fact is that we are about to face a top-of-the-line patrol ship manned by people who we know will not hesitate to destroy this ship. Our shields certainly won't withstand their weapons for long and we need exact timing with an exact shot in order to disable them in the few seconds before they can fire back. So, we might do this without you, but it would certainly help for you to shelve that attitude and assist us so that we have the best chance of surviving long enough to discuss it later."

Lenore swiveled her chair back to her station without giving Quinn a chance to respond. While Diarmin hadn't wanted that kind of confrontation, it seemed to work for now as Quinn said nothing and began to prepare his station for his job.

The next forty minutes were excruciatingly silent. The only sounds were the occasional beep of the computers and rustling of clothing when someone shifted uncomfortably in their seat. When Allison finally announced that the patrol ship's transwarp field was destabilizing in preparation for a course change, the relief at something to do was palpable.

"Based on the specs that Alli provided," said Quinn, "the best way to take out the weapons or engine is to come at the ship from the port side, not behind or underneath."

"Excellent, Quinn," said Diarmin as he adjusted course to do so. "Can you give your mother a specific target?"

"Here." He punched some keys that sent a picture to Lenore's console. "That is where the weapon's control blister is, near the front, and the engine's is at the rear."

"All I see are two dots on the hull," said Lenore.

"Yes, they are beneath the hull for protection. I estimate at least two direct hits, probably three, for them to fail. With only six concussion missiles, you will have to be very accurate and probably only pick one target to eliminate the shields in that area."

"Shields won't be a problem," said Allison.

"Why not?" said everyone else at the same time.

"These specs were the classified specs, not the public ones. They include the shield codes so, ffffft." She flicked her fingers into the air. "Gone shortly after they drop out of transwarp."

"That would have been nice to know, Alli," grumbled Quinn.

"It should have been obvious," she said haughtily. "They don't put weapons placements on public specs."

"Still—"

"Transition in ten seconds," Diarmin interjected. "And...five, four, three, two...there's the ship."

Despite the tensions, the family went into action immediately. Allison punched in codes.

"Shields down."

"Firing," said Lenore.

"Hull breached," said Quinn. "One more ought to do it."

Lenore complied and the resulting explosion didn't need Quinn's yell of triumph.

The ship responded by turning on its axis and the glow from the engines showed it was preparing to run.

"Diarmin!"

"On it!" He maneuvered their ship for the best possible angle for the engines and two shots later, the engine glow faded, and the patrol ship was dead in space.

A male voice came through the speakers.

"How dare you fire on a patrol ship. You have violated the law and will be—"

"Don't bother," interrupted Lenore. "We know this ship was hijacked and is carrying illegal cargo. Prepare for boarding."

"Well, well, well. Little Captain Fleming is back. Are you pouting that we took your high-paying commission?" From the sound of the voice, it was the fake corporal talking and Diarmin knew the man had made a mistake in talking to Lenore like that.

"Prepare to be boarded," she repeated.

"Feel free to try. We won't surrender."

"I would suggest you comply. You've seen our accuracy. I have no compunction with holing your ship and letting you be sucked into space so I can retrieve the cargo at my leisure."

"I wouldn't hole the ship, we have a hostage in our brig," said the thief.

"We are aware of that, and, while we would rather return her in one piece, I am sure the patrol would understand an accidental casualty," answered Lenore.

Quinn made an odd gurgle, but Lenore ignored it.

Surely he doesn't think she is serious, thought Diarmin.

The following silence indicated he was pondering whether to believe her. Muted mutterings were heard before he responded.

"How about we simply destroy the cargo? Then you would have nothing." The man's voice was close to a sneer, but Diarmin could hear a slight waver. *He knows he has little chance of getting out of this.*

"Look, we can argue all day, but I don't have time," said Lenore. "I don't want a fight so here's my final offer. I am not the patrol or any sort of hero so you let us have the cargo and the girl, and I will look the other way as you escape with a very expensive patrol ship. You won't get a better offer than that."

Mumbled words again as if the speaker was covered, then the answer.

"Very well. You may board through airlock two. Not sure if the cargo-exchange systems work, being shot up and all."

"We will take care of it. Captain out."

"That was easy," said Quinn.

"Yes." Lenore unstrapped and beckoned to Diarmin. "Too easy. We'll be ready for a firefight. I am sure they suspect that we have no intention of letting them get away, much less with a patrol ship." She started for the ladder but turned to the children. Diarmin also paused.

"Both of you need to be prepared. For any situation. Monitor as usual. We know how to take care of ourselves in hand to hand weapons fire. If," she held up a finger, "it all goes wrong, you both return to the base."

"But—" started Quinn.

"No exceptions. The best chance we all would have is for you to contact Lieutenant Hammins. He can call in backup to help."

"I want to go with you," said Quinn. His face showed a stubbornness that Diarmin was beginning to think was becoming permanent. "Three against two is better odds."

"Alli can't pilot this ship if the worst should happen. Do as I say, no exceptions. However," she said before Quinn could argue further. "If we are captured, you may join a rescue party with Hammins."

Diarmin's right eyebrow rose slightly. That may appear to be a consent, but he knew that Lenore had said that because the patrol would never let a citizen go on a rescue mission, much less a teen.

"We are wasting time. Gotta go," said Lenore and she was down the ladder before they could respond. Her voice yelled back up. "Love you kids. Let's go Diarmin!"

Diarmin gave each of them a quick hug.

"See you two soon," he said and then descended to ready himself for what was sure to be a vicious fight.

***

As the shuttle headed for the patrol ship, Quinn figured the fastest course back to the asteroid base while muttering angrily under his breath.

I could have gone with them. I could have helped. I know enough to not be in the way.

But even as he thought that, he knew he couldn't be a good backup. He didn't know weapons and would be a liability. He set his jaw. Maybe it would be better for him to find another place. His mother wouldn't teach him weaponry. She was too worried about keeping him safe to let him do anything interesting. Maybe it was time for him to start learning from someone else.

"Quinn?"

He started at Allison's soft voice. He had forgotten she was there and the look she gave him made him feel a little guilty at his selfishness.

"What is it, Alli?"

"Well, I don't know. I got some funny readings and I'm not sure what they mean. Should we ask Mom and Dad?"

"You know the rules. Level Five Alert means listening only, no communication. And they are docking with the ship now so we don't want to distract them. Show me the readings."

As she swiveled the screen to show Quinn and pointed out her analyses, he got a sinking feeling in his gut.

"Are you sure that's accurate, Alli?"

"Yes. Verified three times."

"Then if that means what I think it means, they are in very serious trouble."

Chapter Thirty-three

After the boom of the syncing docking ports and during the hiss of pressurization, Diarmin turned to his wife, both of them drawing their weapons.

"How do you want to do this?" he asked.

"Let them decide on how we retaliate."

Diarmin nodded, knowing that it all depended on the thieves' first shot. The light turned green so Diarmin hit the panel to open the hatch and ducked back into the shuttle so only his blaster faced the opening.

Immediately after the doors split open, blue fire came cracking through. Stun beams instead of kill shots which meant they would stun the men if possible. Lenore's face took on a grim determination as she pulled a stun grenade from her ammo belt. She nodded to Diarmin and he lay down covering fire as she bent low to get a quick look. It only took a second then she armed the device and lobbed it through the hatch. They both covered their ears and squeezed their eyes shut against the detonation of the grenade. The rain of fire ceased and then both were through the hatches.

Both fake patrolmen were on the ground, one unconscious and the other moaning weakly. Diarmin disarmed the unconscious one while Lenore quickly handcuffed the other and hauled him to his feet. Diarmin picked up the other and tossed him over his shoulder and nodded to Lenore to lead the way toward the cells.

Two corridors later, Diarmin regretted his burden as he was sure the man was drooling down his back, but the brig was straight ahead. There were two standard cells, side by side, a clear wall between them and force fields in the front. One was occupied by Kurla and the other stood open.

"Put him in there," Lenore told Diarmin with a jerk of her head. "I'll switch this one out with the hostage."

Diarmin slowly eased his burden to the bed as Lenore paused in front of the cell.

"Code please," she said, poking her prisoner behind the ear with her blaster. He mumbled some numbers, and Lenore punched them in, deactivating the force field.

"Oh, thank the Gods of Clarity. I am rescued." She rushed over to Lenore to embrace her enthusiastically. "I thought these horrible men were going to kill me. Thank you so much, Captain."

Lenore had to release the cuffed man in order to push Kurla away.

She still wasn't quick enough.

Diarmin pulled his own blaster as he realized that Kurla had Lenore's own weapon aimed at the spot between her eyes.

"I really didn't think I would be seeing you two again," said Kurla. "You both struck me as mercenaries willing to cut and run as soon as the cargo was taken. Ah ah ah," she said, apparently noting Lenore tensing for a reaction. "No trying to resist, I won't hesitate for a point-blank shot. And you over there. Put your own gun down before I mess up your wife's face."

Diarmin knew he had no choice, especially when his "unconscious" prisoner sat up with a smirk and pulled ear plugs out of his ears. The man grabbed Diarmin's blaster and held it on him, not as close as Kurla was to Lenore. He taunted Diarmin by waving a personal shield device in front of him.

Diarmin could see the icy calm in Lenore's eyes despite having her own blaster muzzle held inches in front of her face.

"Binder key, please. No no," said Kurla as Lenore started to reach. "Just tell me."

"Left jacket pocket."

Kurla's eyes never left Lenore's as she dug around in said pocket. Diarmin simply stood, wanting a chance at retaliation but his captor was not taking his eyes off him at all.

"Here we go, Renny," said Kurla. He backed up to her and, still without taking her eyes from Lenore's, Kurla unlocked his binders.

Kurla was well trained.

"Search them," said Kurla after that man pulled out his earplugs as well. He didn't bother with any taunts but Diarmin knew he had had a shield as well.

The blaster point didn't waver as the man she called Renny found and divested Lenore of her other weapons, the needle gun, holdout blaster and two tiny knives. Strangely, he left her gloves on and Diarmin knew of other devices he hadn't removed. But now was not the time to think about it as Renny left Lenore's cell to come search him. There was only one hidden blaster and a knife in his boot, but those were found easily enough. Kurla slowly backed away, blaster still aimed at Lenore's head, until she was out of the cell. Diarmin tensed in case Lenore had an opportunity while Kurla was still in her reach, but since there were two guys on him, he wasn't sure what he could do.

This wasn't good.

Renny had finished searching Diarmin so Kurla activated the force field on Lenore's cell and then Diarmin's as the men exited.

"Hob. Go." Kurla pointed down the hall and the other man nodded and left for some obvious previous plan. Diarmin's stomach sank as it was most likely to take the shuttle and retrieve the children. He fought down panic and saw Lenore's throat moving ever so slightly. She was using her subvocals. *Maybe she has a plan, some message to the kids.* But the panic still kept coming.

Kurla turned to Renny and gave him Lenore's blaster.

"Watch them."

Suddenly a loud boom of decompressing atmosphere reverberated through the ship followed by an alarm. Lenore and Diarmin were protected from vacuum behind the force field, but Kurla and Renny had to grab onto something before they were sucked out of what was evidently an opening or hole in the hull. After only a few seconds, however, a clang was heard, and the negative pressure let up. *Hob must have closed the breach.* Kurla, breathing heavily and looking quite angry, yelled into her wrist unit.

"Report!"

"The shuttle disengaged from the ship, apparently remotely, leaving the hatch open to space. I managed to close it before I was pulled out."

Kurla turned back to Lenore.

"Somehow they knew. Ah, of course." She took the weapon back from Renny. "Search the man for a patch behind his ear." Her smug smile was almost more than Diarmin could take. Renny entered the cell and pulled off the receiver patch as well as the transmitter patch on Diarmin's throat, then headed for Lenore's cell. As Renny searched her again, Diarmin noticed the anger on her face. He knew she was showing that anger on purpose so as not to tip them off that she had any sort of transmitters.

"She's clean, no patches."

The cells were reactivated and Kurla returned the weapon to Renny.

"No worries. We have an alternate plan." She grinned at Lenore. "And you two fetch the most money anyway. The children are merely a bonus. I'm going to see if the computer has fixed those engines yet."

Her wrist bleeped and a voice came out.

"The shuttle has returned to their ship and it looks like they are preparing to transwarp."

Kurla looked annoyed, but Diarmin couldn't tell if it was because the kids were leaving or because Hob had reported where anyone could hear.

"Acknowledged. Get on those repairs."

"So. Running away, are they?" Kurla's head swiveled between her two prisoners. "Typical kids."

She turned and left.

Well, now what? Standing wasn't doing him any good, so he walked to the bed and sat, not at all amused when the man's blaster followed his every move. What could they do behind a force field? Well, a lot, but he and Lenore would have to plan. The clear wall between the cells allowed them to see each other, but they couldn't speak as long as they were being watched. As Lenore also headed for her bed, she looked at him directly for the first time since they had been captured. He couldn't help but feel a rush of guilt. They'd been played. By a girl barely older than Quinn. Anger and guilt now played equally in both their expressions.

Lenore finally broke the silence. The thick wall made her voice seem like a whisper, but he could easily read her lips. Especially because she echoed his current thoughts.

"At least the kids are safe."

***

Lenore couldn't relax. She wanted to pace but wouldn't give their watcher the satisfaction of knowing how upset she was. It had been nearly two hours since the shuttle had left and the only capitulation Renny had made was to get a chair. He still twitched every time they moved or spoke so they had no chance of divining an answer to get out of this mess. Since their guard's attention was still sharp, she had to take a chance on a different form of communication. She didn't know how much Diarmin remembered about the Xa'ti'al hand signals but figured that would be the least chance of the guard figuring out what they were saying.

"Well," she said aloud. "We have earned the stupidity of the year award." With her hands she mimed another sentence entirely: *Children to base yet?*

Diarmin's eyes widened only slightly and he answered aloud. "Yes, we have. Add gullible to that award and we well deserve it." His gesture was crude, but she knew what he said. *Two hours to base. There soon. Plan?*

They continued the idle chatter, to Renny's obvious annoyance, angling their bodies so he couldn't see the silent communications.

Lenore: *You have any equipment?*

None. You?

Gloves, belt, bra.

Diarmin's eyes lit briefly before he schooled his expression. He knew that "bra" meant her EMP device was still there. It was indeed their best shot, but he asked the one thing she wasn't sure about.

Force field?

She shrugged. It would render the blaster useless, but she wasn't sure if it would take out the fields to the cells. The electronics of cells were often shielded against just such an effect or else prisoners would get free when ships were attacked by an electromagnetic pulse, a common weapon of pirates.

Another plan?

She shrugged again. They needed that watcher out of the way. If only they had a distraction.

Kurla entered the brig, that superior smile still on her face. Lenore vowed to herself that she would punch it off later.

"Well, engines are nearly back online." She turned to Renny. "Help Hob prepare the ship for flight." He left, taking the blaster with him. Kurla turned back to her prisoners. "Weapons will take slightly longer but will be fixed by the time we reach your ship."

"Reach our ship?" asked Diarmin. "How will you find it?"

"The same way you found me, I assume. The tracking system should be up and running within minutes. Those devices are very handy."

"So it was you who planted them," said Diarmin. Lenore always hated these kinds of conversations, but she knew it was the best way for them to get information.

"Of course. It's how I got the codes to open the six-alls."

"Why go after our ship now?" asked Lenore. "You already have the cargo."

Kurla threw her head back and laughed. Lenore had a feeling she wasn't going to like the answer at all.

"That cargo was just a lucky score. My real mission was to capture you, *Lenore*." Her smile turned malicious and the way she drawled the name told Lenore exactly who had hired this woman. Kurla continued with her gloating. "Thank you for delivering yourselves to me so easily," said Kurla. "I didn't think the plan would work but apparently, the chief knows his stuff."

"You have me. Why go after my ship?"

"For the bonus, of course. The whole family brings quite a hefty sum. Besides, with a few modifications, your ship will suit me just fine. A patrol ship is too easily tracked."

Footsteps approaching made her turn.

"Renny. I told you—"

"Communications are out," he said. "Inside the ship as well as external. Hob sent me here to inform you."

"Damn that Hob. He probably short circuited something when he rebooted the system." She grimaced, her gloating vanished. "Let's go help that oaf fix his screw-up." They both turned to leave but was stopped by someone in the doorway holding a blaster.

"Not so fast, Kurla."

It was Quinn.

Chapter Thirty-four

Lenore's heart squeezed which nearly robbed her of breath. Quinn was supposed to be safe at the patrol base. Now he was here and most likely to be captured as well. And where was Allison?

Kurla recovered from her surprise quite quickly. "Hello there. Renny, this is that talented young man I was telling you about."

The man nodded and Lenore could see Quinn's eyes narrow.

"I am sorry, what was your name again?" she asked Quinn.

"Why does that matter?"

"We have to know what to call you if you are going to be on my crew," she said, voice now taking on a tone that Lenore could only describe as silky.

Quinn surprise was evident. "What?"

Kurla shrugged. "I was serious when I suggested you get off the ship with me. We have been looking for a fourth for a while but haven't found anyone suitable." She grinned at him. "Until now."

"You're crazy," said Quinn. "I heard what you said about your mission. To capture us."

"That's true, but from what I have seen, you are worth more than that part of the bonus. Your talents are wasted with them." Her hand swept back to indicate Lenore and Diarmin and she unobtrusively took a step forward. "And we can teach you so much more, especially how to handle weapons." She took another step.

Quinn wasn't fooled.

"You mean handle like this?" He thumbed off the safety and switched from stun to blast. Lenore knew she hadn't taught him how to handle a weapon and for the first time, began to worry, not about Quinn's safety, but about what he was thinking. Quinn took two steps into the room which stopped Kurla's approach and made her and Renny back up a few steps. "Release them now or I will simply kill you and do it myself."

"Wow. I believe you. Don't shoot." Kurla raised her voice slightly, "I said, 'don't shoot.' That means you too, Hob."

In the doorway was the third man. Holding a blaster on Quinn.

"Good idea. He might take me out but not before I shoot you," said Quinn, voice rough.

"I told you he was good," said Kurla, glancing at Renny. "He even managed to slip on the ship unnoticed. I assume you are also responsible for our communication failure?"

Quinn nodded. "And overrode the docking alarm and hatches to get on."

Kurla applauded. "So clever. Better than what they did." Again, she waved her hand and Lenore fought to keep silent. Clearly they couldn't have gotten on the way Quinn had since they'd tipped their hand when they fired on the ship. She knew Quinn was smart enough to see this.

"Now, let's all think this through. Even if you take me out, you will be dropped a second later by Hob and you will fail. But," she held up a finger. "If you join our crew voluntarily, I will promise you they will not be harmed."

The tip of Quinn's blaster wavered slightly, and Lenore's gut tightened. She could see on his face that he was actually considering it.

"Why would you offer that? Won't you lose your bonus?"

"The reward was for a live delivery of the woman and the bonus for delivery of the others, dead or alive."

Lenore actually heard Diarmin's intake of breath, but it was nothing compared to her own shock and renewed hatred for the Xa'ti'al. That comment showed her that, because of her encounter with Daviss, the Xa no longer wanted her back to rejoin them. Only for revenge.

"So, how would that work then?" asked Quinn. Lenore hoped he had contacted the patrol and now was stalling to give them time to get here.

"We would deliver a body similar to yours with the face destroyed and say that you were killed while attempting a rescue. Come now. We can either fake that, or it will be the truth. Which will it be?" Kurla cocked her head. "We can give you a brand-new identity and you won't ever have to worry about any further pursuit."

Lenore hated to see how that comment appealed to her son.

"Wouldn't those who are offering the reward know the difference? DNA and all that?"

Kurla shook her head. "They know very little about you and the girl. A few blurry photos and general description, that's all. A side effect of being off the grid your entire life."

Quinn appeared to consider this information for a few moments. "What about the priest?" he asked. "What does he think about all this?"

Kurla laughed so hard she nearly doubled over. Quinn's eyes narrowed again as she tried to catch her breath.

"Oh, I have so much to teach you," she said, wiping her eyes. "There's no priest. It's a ruse that I have used several times to good effect. As you can see, there is so much more to a disguise than wigs and makeup."

Quinn nodded. "You fooled me."

"So, you will join us?"

Quinn's mouth thinned as he glanced briefly at his mother and father. Lenore held her breath as he looked away, guilt on his face.

"Only if you swear to not harm them," he said. Diarmin gave a small gurgle that Lenore felt in her heart.

"I already promised that," said Kurla, annoyance in her voice.

"One more thing." Quinn brandished the blaster again and Hob's finger tightened on the trigger. "You let my sister go. For good. She is with the patrol by now and I doubt you would want to tangle with them."

"You are right." Kurla lifted her chin. "You have my word. We will not pursue her, now or ever."

Renny started to protest but Kurla cut him off. "That's my order. This young man will repay tenfold our loss of that part of the bonus. The kids aren't worth that much anyway." She held her hand out.

Quinn's hand wavered slightly but he didn't lower the weapon. "How can I trust you? Be sure you won't go after my sister? Or hurt them?"

Kurla lowered her hand and looked annoyed again but answered. "Trust goes both ways. I think I have something that will establish our trust, but I need something from you as well. How can you prove your trustworthiness to me?"

"There is an item in my jacket pocket that should be a start."

A smile spread across Kurla's face. "I was going to say the exact same thing. We are very similar creatures, you and I." She held her left hand away from her body and slowly reached her right hand into her pocket. Quinn tensed but there were no tricks. Kurla pulled out a small device that easily fit into the palm of her hand and held it up.

"Renny. Do you know what this is?"

"Yes, it is the control for the snoop cams."

"And what happens when I destroy it?"

"You would lose the ability to track the cams."

"You see? I would have no way to find your ship and sister. I will destroy it if you can earn my trust as well. And if you stay, you can be assured of your parents' wellbeing. Come now, your turn."

Without lowering the gun, Quinn reached his left hand into his own pocket and pulled out a small cube that was obviously some kind of electronic device. He took a deep breath and let it out slowly.

"This... this device is unique. It masks any transmissions within a certain area. Even," he hesitated and wouldn't look toward his parents. "Even very strong implanted tech."

The surprise on Kurla's face was only there for a second until the smile returned. "Ah, so that's why she didn't have the patches."

"Yes. My father and I have been working on this for quite some time."

Lenore whipped her head toward Diarmin who looked away from her glare. Could it be true? Why would they both betray her like that?

Kurla echoed her thoughts. "Why would you do that?"

"It was designed to hide her bio signs from detection. The side effect we couldn't counter was complete cutoff from any transmissions. If you use this, you won't be able to detect any biosignatures."

"Since they are in the cell, I won't worry about that," she said. "Toss that to Renny here to verify it isn't dangerous."

Quinn complied and Renny mumbled that it seemed to be a suppressor of a sort, nothing like an explosive.

Lenore kept saying to herself. *He's faking. He has to be. He wouldn't do this to us.*

"Very well." With a flourish, Kurla tossed the control to the floor and ground it under her heel. "There. I think we have a good start. The rest of trust needs to be earned." She held out her hand again.

Quinn engaged the safety and handed her the blaster. Hob slowly lowered his though he kept alert.

"Welcome to the crew," said Kurla. "Your first order is to set up that device so she can't send any messages."

Quinn nodded and took the device to hook on to the cell door just above the control pad. Lenore couldn't stop her feet and she took three long strides until she was in front of her son on the other side of the force field.

"Why?" She stopped herself short from saying his name, but she wanted to.

He wouldn't look at her and she thought he wouldn't reply but as he pushed the button to activate the small device, he finally talked.

"This way, I know you will be healthy and able when you get to where you are being taken. And my sister and I have a chance for new lives." He didn't give her a chance to answer, simply turned and walked away. Despite telling herself he was acting, doubt crept into her heart.

"Can I ask you a question, Kurla?" asked Quinn.

"Of course," she said.

"Why did you steal those items?"

"Aha, want to learn something already?" As Quinn nodded, Kurla glanced at Lenore with a grin then linked her arm through Quinn's and started out the door. "If you want to appear helpless, act like a victim. Also, the stolen tools gave me a reason why I was in the cargo bay, distracting from my true purpose for being there. Nobody thought to look for hidden devices, did they? So, what you need..."

Her voice faded away as she moved out of earshot. Renny shot them a malicious smile before he also disappeared down the corridor after them.

The strength left Lenore's body and she sank to the floor. The horrible scene that had just played out had distracted her from the fact that she and Diarmin were to be handed over to the very people she wanted to see the least.

But the hurt of losing their son was a hundred times worse than knowing they were going to be delivered to the Xa'ti'al.

Chapter Thirty-five

Allison shifted, trying to relieve the cramp in her left leg. Of all the things she had ever done, sitting squeezed into a tiny storage space for hours was her least favorite. She found a more comfortable position and eyed her pad yet again. Aha! Two heat signatures were in cabins, most likely getting ready for bed. She waited for another fifteen minutes or so but two were still on the bridge. She wished she had a better scanner so she could know who was where.

After hacking into the patrol ship's computer, Allison had programmed its computer to ignore her bio signs and anything related to the shuttle. After Quinn left, she eased out of the locker where she had stowed away and sneaked on board the ship when all the other bio signs were in the brig. Despite her efforts to sabotage the repairs to the ship, the computer had told her when they had finished. The ship had jumped to transwarp about an hour ago.

Now, since it looked like at least two were going to sleep, Allison went to work. Using her hook into the ship's computer, she overrode the locks on the cabin doors, locking the two in the cabin. She watched the sensors carefully but the two in the cabins did not move at all. She didn't dare use the same stratagem on those on the bridge because there they could override her commands. But she was running out of time. She had to start the next phase of the plan or they would all pay the price.

***

"Mom. Dad. Anybody awake?"

Lenore almost didn't catch the whisper. It wasn't coming from her audio implant and turning her head slightly, she saw nobody else in the brig. She quickly stuffed the EM device back into her bra and pulled on her gloves. She'd been trying to rig up something to short out the force field of the cell but hadn't quite succeeded despite Diarmin whispering advice when he could. She noticed Diarmin in a listening pose as well. He looked at her and tapped behind his ear, but Lenore was already raising her hand to her ear. She activated her enhanced hearing implant and listened again.

"Come on, someone be there. I can't go any louder."

The voice sounded like it was coming out of the box that Quinn had attached to the outside of the cell. Lenore stood, eyeing the security cameras as she strode to the box. Diarmin followed on his side of the wall, getting as close as he could to her.

"Alli, is that you?" Lenore whispered, feeling a little silly at talking to a box.

"Yes, it's me. Your implant isn't receiving so I tapped into this little device. It isn't hooked up to the ship so I figured it wouldn't be traced. I still need to whisper though because I couldn't hack into any systems in the brig, so the security video and audio are still working."

"I have my hearing maxed so talk as softly as you need. Where are you?" She assumed on a patrol ship shadowing the stolen vessel.

"In a storage closet two corridors away from the cargo bay."

"What?!" Lenore's heart sank as she realized her daughter was exactly where she didn't want her to be. Diarmin hissed at her and she lowered her voice again.

"How?" she asked, wanting to say so much more but needing to be wary of any watching eyes.

"I stowed away on the shuttle and after Quinn got off, I found a good hiding place in this closet. Except it's quite cramped and I can't do all I wanted."

"Look, Allison. You need to get back on that shuttle and get out of here."

"They've locked it down and I haven't hacked those codes yet. Concentrating on getting you and Dad out."

"We'll be fine. You leave!" Lenore couldn't help her voice raising again.

"Ow, Mom. Not so loud. Anyway, I can't access the systems of the brig to let you out. They are on a separate grid than the rest of the ship. I can't even cut power to that section. Probably a failsafe built into patrol ships to prevent exactly what I am doing. I need to come to you to let you out. Just wanted to give you a heads up so you will be ready."

"Don't you dare, Alli," Lenore said in a rough whisper. "You stay put." A quick glance at Diarmin showed that his anxiety levels were perilously close to the maximum like her own.

"It's okay. I have got two of the others locked in their cabins. The other two, I don't know which, are on the bridge...oh, oops. Crap!"

"Allison," said Lenore.

No answer. Lenore looked at Diarmin and the fear in his eyes echoed that in her heart.

"Allison!"

The box was silent but suddenly that was her secondary worry as Kurla and Quinn came into the room. Quinn was walking in front of her and Lenore noticed that Kurla was wearing a blaster. So, she still didn't quite trust her newest crewman. Lenore's relief that they hadn't discovered her daughter must have showed as Kurla's eyes narrowed.

"Why would you be happy to see me?" asked Kurla. "I am here to get some answers as to why you two are talking in whispers." Her head swiveled between her prisoners. "You could have talked from your beds. Why are you standing here? Attempting to get out?"

Lenore took a step back. "Just restless and bored. Got anything to read on this ship?"

Kurla laughed sourly. "Reading? That should be the least of your worries. Now, what exactly are you up to?"

A face popped around the door frame and it took all of Lenore's will not to react. She thought Diarmin was completely stone faced as well but Kurla either noticed or heard something. She spun around to face Allison, hand going for her blaster.

"Don't," said Allison. "I really don't want to shoot you." She was in the doorway, at least ten feet from Kurla, but with both hands she held a blaster rifle.

Kurla's hand hovered over her blaster. "Well, well, well. The whole family back together again. You know, little girl, I can see that you are not used to that weapon and I am guessing that I could probably get a shot off with no difficulty. Unlike you, I am very experienced and would not miss. So why don't you be a sport and simply hand over that gun so nobody gets hurt. You can join your parents."

Lenore had come to the same unfortunate conclusion since she could see the barrel wavering and Allison trembling.

"You said you would let her go," said Quinn.

"I said I wouldn't pursue her." Kurla shot a quick glance and grin at Quinn. "But what am I supposed to do when she appears on my doorstep?" She turned back to Allison. "Now be good. I doubt your aim would do more than singe my hair."

"I don't have to aim. This weapon is set on wide beam," said Allison as she gripped the barrel more firmly.

The grin vanished off Kurla's face and her hand stopped its slow approach toward her own weapon. "I see. But if you fire, you will take out your brother as well and you don't want that, do you?"

Allison's eyes flicked toward Quinn and Lenore could see her son give a minute nod. Was he confirming what Kurla said? Encouraging her to give over the blaster? Lenore felt her heart couldn't take any more. She decided to create a distraction, but the decision was moot as everything happened all at once.

Kurla went for her blaster.

Allison said, "Sorry, Quinn."

She squeezed her eyes shut and pulled the trigger.

Chapter Thirty-six

Diarmin blinked the tears away. The blue light had filled the room and he was temporarily blinded. The force field had kept any of the weapon's discharge from reaching inside the cell, but he heard groans and thuds. He fiercely rubbed at his eyes, desperate to see what had occurred. The only comfort he could give himself was that the light had been blue. That indicated a stun shot but he couldn't be sure. He didn't think that rifle had a stun setting.

Through watery vision, he could see someone outside their cells, fiddling with the controls. He thought he could see dark hair.

"Alli?"

"Just a minute, Dad. These controls are tough."

"What...what did you do?" That was Lenore's voice.

"It's okay, Mom. The gun was set to stun. Ah, there!"

The force field fizzled out and Diarmin rushed to envelop his daughter in a hug. His wife was half a second behind.

"Ooof. Okay, okay. I'm fine. Let's get this ship turned around, shall we?" she said.

Diarmin could feel the tears in his eyes and this time they weren't from the stun beam light. "Good work, Pirate Peri."

Allison smiled at his use of her hacker ID.

Lenore went to Quinn, checking his pulse.

"It's okay, Mom. I told you I used the stun setting."

"Not everyone handles stunning well. Also, that stun setting is for large crowds. Point blank and in close quarters like this, it's lucky you weren't stunned as well, Alli." Lenore straightened, apparently satisfied with Quinn's condition.

"Huh. I think I have learned a few things from you guys," replied Allison as she pulled the tiny personal shield emitter out of her left jumpsuit pocket.

"Good girl," said Lenore though her smile was only there for a moment. "Can you reactivate the cells?"

Allison shrugged. "Sure."

"Good. Diarmin, put Kurla in that one." She pointed at the cell that he had just vacated.

"What about Quinn?" he asked as he picked up the unconscious girl.

Lenore looked at her son a long time before answering. Diarmin wondered if she was considering putting him in the other cell. Allison must have thought the same thing because she went to her mother.

"Mom, Quinn didn't really abandon us, you know." She put a hand on her mother's arm.

Now Lenore smiled but Diarmin wondered if Allison saw the sadness in it. "I know. Let's take him to sick bay. Activate the cell, Alli and your father will carry Quinn." She turned to Diarmin. "Meet us on the bridge when Quinn is secure." She turned back to Allison after the force field crackled back to life. "Lead the way to the bridge."

Diarmin gently gathered his son up in his arms and exited the brig as well.

"Okay, Mom. I wish I could have locked the two on the bridge like I did the other two in their cabins but that would have been a waste. After all, the bridge is where everything is controlled so they could have easily opened the door and also discovered my hack so I had to wait until they were in another room. But I was stupid and got distracted talking to you..."

Her voice faded out as they went the opposite way down the corridor and turned a corner. Diarmin knew Allison's constant chatter was simply her working off her nerves. Especially because Lenore was not being maternal but militant, like she always did when on a mission. The family knew she did that, but it didn't make it any easier to deal with.

Diarmin looked down at Quinn's face. Had it all been an act? He had always believed in his son, but he had seemed so sincere.

Either he's a better actor than Lenore or I gave him credit for, or he did indeed...no...I won't believe that he would leave us. He was pretending.

But the doubt in his heart wouldn't be silent.

***

Fortunately, the patrol ship hadn't gone far, and it was only a little over an hour back to their ship which Quinn and Allison had hidden behind a moon. After they reversed course, Diarmin joined them on the bridge and told them Quinn should recover fairly quickly. Lenore kept herself busy while Allison chattered constantly, obviously trying to convince her mother that she and Quinn had planned everything together.

"Although he didn't tell me what he was going to do, just distract Kurla and her cohorts so that when they were no longer suspicious, I would lock them down, then unlock the brig." Allison was sitting at the science terminal, still fiddling with the computer. "But I couldn't unlock the brig and I got confused as to why there were only two signatures in there and four outside. I figured Quinn would be in the cells with you guys but—" Allison abruptly cut herself off with a bite of her lip. She obviously realized she might be getting Quinn in worse trouble. Diarmin was seated at the navigator console apparently ignoring everything but by the hunch of his shoulders, Lenore knew he was uncertain about Quinn as well.

It was a relief to all as the patrol ship shuddered out of transwarp.

"Well, this ship is obviously not completely repaired so, Diarmin, you take it back to the base. I will take our ship along with the kids."

Lenore saw her husband hesitate before answering, but she was too tired to try to figure which of the dozen reasons why.

"I, um. I could use the kids to help me," he said as he stood to take the pilot's chair that Lenore had vacated.

"Fine." She supposed he didn't want her to be alone with them, especially Quinn, afraid of a confrontation where he wouldn't be able to moderate. "Alli, do you have the shuttle unlocked yet?"

"Yes."

"Good. You stay here with your father. I will take Quinn back to our ship."

Diarmin looked like he wanted to protest but knew better. She took pity on her family and softened a little. She put a hand on her husband's arm as he sat in the pilot's chair.

"Look, I don't want Quinn on this ship at all when we return. He needs to be distanced from the situation with no possibility of being considered an accomplice. Alli, you can erase the recordings with your usual skill." As Diarmin nodded she leaned down, lowering her voice so Allison wouldn't hear. "I promise I won't get into anything with him until we are away from the patrol base."

A small smile appeared on his face but didn't reach his eyes. He nodded again.

"Well, see you two at the base," she said and tossed Allison a wave. She waved back solemnly. *She is worried too. We all are.*

Lenore retrieved Quinn from sick bay, still groggy despite the reviving medications that his father had administered. Proof that the stun beam was a little more intense than usual. Lenore thought that maybe he would learn a lesson from this experience, but she wasn't sure exactly which lesson she wanted it to be. She had to help him all the way to the shuttle and he slid from her support into the copilot chair with a thud.

"Mom, I'm—"

"Not now, Quinn. We still have a lot to do and you are in no shape for a discussion."

He fell silent as she undocked and headed for their yacht, drifting in space off the port side of the patrol ship. Not a word was exchanged as they docked and disembarked. The relief Lenore felt upon coming home was overshadowed by the odd grimace on her son's face as they entered through the airlock. She helped him to his cabin and he finally broke the silence.

"I'm better. I can help on the bridge."

"No." Her abrupt denial brought his head up in surprise. Lenore regretted her short temper and tried to smile. "You still need rest. It's a short flight back and I can handle it. Don't make me lock you in." That last was supposed to be a joke but her tone was just a little too sharp. He straightened up, looked her directly in the eyes, pivoted abruptly, and disappeared into his room. For a moment, tears pricked at her eyes. She hadn't meant to hurt him. Or had she? To get even for the hurt he had caused her? His door slid closed on her hesitation.

Fiercely she fought down all the emotions. They would have to deal with this when things were back to normal.

She turned to head for the bridge, trying to ignore her feelings that they may never get back to normal.

Chapter Thirty-seven

Since it was several hours back to the patrol base, everyone got at least two hours of sleep, although Lenore had only dozed in the pilot's seat. They had been on the go for over a day and Lenore knew it wasn't nearly over yet despite the fact that they had caught the thieves. The patrol ship touched down only minutes before she landed the yacht. Quinn hadn't come out of his room or tried to contact her in any way. Several times she had been tempted to go in there but didn't know what to say. She decided to give him time to completely recover from the strong stun shock before starting any conversations anyway.

As she exited the craft through the open cargo bay, she saw Diarmin and Allison approaching. They met up equidistant between the two ships.

"Sherrod gave permission to land and had dozens of questions that I told him needed to be answered in person," said Diarmin.

"Good," said Lenore. "Are the prisoners still secure?"

"I left them where we had trapped them, in the cell and rooms."

"What if they break out of their rooms?"

"I sealed the bulkhead in the area as well," Allison chimed in. "I figure with my scrambled codes it would take an hour to get out of their rooms and two more to get through the bulkheads. I don't think they will try anything, especially since we told them if they did, their rooms would be flooded with a nerve toxin with a paralytic agent absorbed through the skin."

"A nerve toxin?" Lenore didn't think that was standard issue on any patrol vessel that she knew of.

Allison shrugged. "It's really only a sedative but Dad said a nerve toxin would make them think twice."

A smile tugged at the corners of Lenore's mouth. It should probably worry her that Allison didn't blink at a bald-faced lie, but she felt oddly proud. "Good job you two. Alli, you head back to our ship while your father and I take care of the rest of this."

"Sure."

Allison skipped back to the lowered cargo ramp as they headed for the base entrance.

"Do you think the cargo is still intact?" she asked Diarmin.

"I don't know. I examined the six-alls and they don't appear to be damaged, but we are right up against Bondle's deadline of when they will go inert."

"He will have to determine that."

The conversation took only a dozen steps but the door to the station opened and Lieutenant Hammins came out, limping heavily with Bondle hovering as if he wanted to help but the lieutenant had refused. A large bandage covered his left eye and his right arm was immobilized against his body.

"Thank you, Captain Fleming, for the return of the patrol vessel, although I should arrest you for sedating me and leaving without my authorization." His smile made the threat hollow and Lenore could tell that the humor helped to hide his pain.

"You are welcome, Lieutenant." Lenore bowed her head slightly along with Diarmin.

"My vaccines. What about my vaccines?" asked Bondle while shifting from foot to foot so rapidly it looked like an awkward dance.

"The cargo seems intact," said Diarmin. "But I don't know if they are still active. You should determine that." He indicated the way and Bondle proceeded at nearly a jog, pulling his scanner out of his coat pocket as he hurried along.

"While they check on that, let's return to the base, Lieutenant, and I will fill you in on what happened."

"Please, call me Sherrod."

Lenore nodded and began to report as they headed for the entrance. By the time they reached his office, she'd finished her abridged version which left out the capture and subsequent rescue by their children. Sherrod was as surprised as they all were that Kurla was behind the entire scheme.

He shook his head sadly. "She had me fooled."

"She had us all fooled," said Lenore, noting an edge to her voice that showed she was still angry about being duped.

Sherrod began to ask his own questions that, despite his obvious pain and fatigue, were quite insightful. Lenore's respect for the man was raised a notch and she had to think of a distraction before he pulled the entire story out of her. She did not want this man to know that she had been the intended target, not the cargo. Fortunately, Bondle and Diarmin returned before Sherrod could get too far.

"The cultures are still active!" Bondle's excitement was contagious. Lenore was a little surprised at the relief she felt at the good news. She tried to tell herself it was relief that they would be paid, but she knew she felt for the scientist.

"How long do we have?" she asked as she stood.

"I estimate twenty-four hours, no more," he replied.

"Then there's no time to waste," said Lenore.

"Wait," said the lieutenant, holding out his good hand to halt them. He awkwardly got to his feet. "I am the one who pulled you off your course and I gave my word that I would get you to your planet on time."

Diarmin gently gripped Sherrod on the left shoulder and eased him back into the chair. "It wasn't your fault and you are in no shape to pilot a ship. You have enough to do right here."

The frustration on the man's face was evident. "You're right. I already called for reinforcements, but it will be at least a day before they get here."

"And you need to guard the prisoners until they arrive."

"Again, you are correct." He sighed and gave Lenore a rueful smile. "Looks like I owe you even more."

Lenore felt uncomfortable with the praise. "Just doing what I was hired to do. Diarmin, you bring the prisoners to the base's brig while I get the cargo transferred."

"But I need everyone to give their reports," said Sherrod, rising again to his feet.

Lenore pulled a flimsy out of a pocket. "Here is everyone's account of the events. We really shouldn't delay."

Diarmin had already disappeared out the door, Bondle following closely. Lenore stood ready to help the lieutenant, but he was steady in his limping stride as they left the base.

"I would ask you to return to give a fuller accounting, but I am not going to see you again, am I?" asked Sherrod at the door to the outside.

Lenore stopped and faced the officer "You are a very shrewd man, Sherrod. It is a good thing you are also honest. Therefore, I will be honest with you as well. No. We will not be returning."

Sherrod tilted his head, somehow maintaining his dignity even with a bandaged eye. "I meant it when I said that I owe you. If you ever need anything, just ask."

"You can return the favor by not reporting our names."

He grinned. "I get the feeling your name isn't really Fleming anyway."

Lenore smiled back. "Like I said, a shrewd man." She held her hand out. "It was an honor to meet you, Lieutenant Sherrod Hammins."

He took it in his good left hand. "The honor is mine, person who shall remain anonymous."

Sherrod remained in the doorway as she headed toward the ships, feeling a little lighter for the first time in days.

***

As soon as she was back on the ship, Allison headed to Quinn's cabin. The door was closed so she knocked.

"Quinn, it's me," she said. He might not want to open the door for Mom or Dad.

The door slid open and Quinn turned back to his bed without saying a word. Allison took that as oblique permission to enter so she did, a bit hesitantly. She sat on his desk chair, balancing her personal pad on her lap.

"Um. How are you feeling?"

"Okay. Still a little woozy." He was lying on his back staring up at the ceiling.

"I'm sorry I stunned you," she said.

He shrugged. "We knew it was a possibility."

"Yeah, but we didn't know it would be so powerful. Mom said that setting is made for crowds so it was dangerous in a small room."

Quinn merely shrugged again. Allison didn't know what else to say. Since she didn't want to leave either, they sat in silence. After a few moments where they avoided looking at each other, her fingers itched for something to do so she activated her pad. A few taps had her hacked into both the patrol ship and base. A few more taps and she verified that Kurla and her crewmates were still locked up tight, Dad and Bondle were in the cargo bay checking out the samples, and Mom was in the office with the lieutenant. Of the group, Allison figured the one to listen to would be her mother, so she activated the monitor's audio settings. As her mother's voice piped through her pad, Quinn turned his head and appeared to be listening as well.

She turned up the volume and neither made a sound until Bondle and her father had entered the patrol office.

Allison chuckled. "It's funny how Mom worded that whole story. She didn't tell everything, but she also never lied. I need to learn how to do that."

She looked at Quinn and he looked back at her with a smile. She wasn't sure what the smile was for but was glad to see it.

"Alli, please help with the cargo transfer," came her mother's voice through her wristcomp.

"Okay, Mom," she answered. As she stood, she glanced back at Quinn, but his smile was gone, his gaze returned to the ceiling. Allison hesitated, biting her lip. She didn't want to say the next thing but felt she had to.

"Quinn, I…" she swallowed. "I think it's sort of my fault why Mom and Dad are so mad. Well, not mad maybe just upset. Sad? I don't know—" She cut herself off as Quinn sat up to stare at her.

The look in his eyes was not friendly. But she had to get this out.

"I know I shouldn't have done it, but I kind of eavesdropped on you and Kurla in the spare bedroom. I did it because I didn't trust her and wanted to prove to Mom that she was up to something. But instead I heard you talking about leaving and I…well…I got scared. I didn't want to lose you. I played the recording for Mom and Dad because I thought they would, I don't know. Maybe stop you or maybe do some of those things you want to do or, I don't know." Allison's rambling apology stuck in her throat as Quinn sat there saying nothing. She shuffled her feet as Quinn looked toward the floor. "I guess I want to say I'm sorry. It made them think you joining Kurla was real. Except." She stopped but realized she needed to say this. "We never planned that. And I heard everything. And it felt...real. Quinn." Her hand came up but dropped back at her side. "I have to ask. Did you mean it? Did you really want to join Kurla's crew?"

Quinn's head shot up and Allison eagerly awaited his denial. She would even accept anger that she dared suggest such a thing. Instead he stared at her.

"Allison. Where are you?"

The message at her wrist made them both jump and broke their locked gazes. Quinn still said nothing but lay back down on his bed and rolled to face the wall, away from his sister.

Allison felt a weight on her chest as she left toward the cargo bay.

***

The cargo was stored within twenty minutes, about the same time as it took for Diarmin to transfer the prisoners. Two trips each. For Lenore and Allison, one trip per six-all with Bondle nervously dancing around the antigrav floats and muttering to himself. Diarmin, the first trip with the two men, both in binders with Diarmin's blaster trained on them if they so much as twitched. The second was with Kurla whose face Lenore saw as she maneuvered the last six-all out of the patrol ship.

She did not look pleased. Lenore had the feeling that this was the first time the girl had been detained. Perhaps even the first time she had failed in a scheme.

Good. She needs to be taken down a peg.

As Lenore considered that thought, she wondered if the girl knew just how serious her situation was.

She had just finished securing the cargo in their bay when Diarmin entered.

"What took you so long? Kurla make a break for it?" She was joking but her attention was caught with Diarmin's answer.

"Not exactly. She wants to talk to you. Alone."

Lenore looked questioningly at her husband, but he shook his head. "I don't know why, but Sherrod gave his approval if you want to."

Lenore didn't really want to see the girl who had imprisoned her, threatened her family and tried to corrupt her son. But something in her said she should, and there were still some questions unanswered.

Diarmin seemed to agree. "I will prep the ship," he said as he lightly touched her arm. "Go."

Without a word, Lenore left the cargo bay and headed back into the base. As she passed by the office, a glance showed Sherrod at his desk. He looked up briefly but went back to his terminal. The message was clear. He wouldn't interfere.

As she approached the brig, Lenore's hands twitched to pull out a weapon, but she knew that would be asking for trouble. Especially because, depending on what Kurla said, she might do something she would regret.

Standing at the front of the cell, eyes on the doorway, Kurla's chin raised slightly at Lenore's entrance. Lenore had to admire the girl's bravado.

"Thank you for coming," she said.

"Make it quick. I'm on a schedule." Lenore thought she was unemotional but the suppressed anger in her voice was evident. It didn't deter Kurla in the slightest.

"Very well. I want to make a deal with you."

Lenore was too surprised to laugh. "You have nothing I want."

"I notice your son isn't in a cell. Quinn, I believe is his name."

"What's your point?" Lenore crossed her arms.

"It just seems if you are going to arrest the crew and he was a member of that crew, he should be here. If you urge leniency for me, I will keep quiet about his joining the crew." Kurla's voice dropped to just above a whisper and the look of a conspiratorial confidante was almost comical.

"Talk away," said Lenore, purposely not whispering. "First of all, he was acting the entire time. Second, even if he wasn't, there were no illegal acts committed while he was a part of your crew so no reason to arrest him."

Kurla's face turned from pleasant to fierce during Lenore's explanation. Lenore was finding it very hard to maintain her own temper at Kurla's attempt at manipulation. *I need to get out of here.*

"I will not plead for leniency for you," Lenore said. "You have acted with malice, deliberate deception, intent to harm and possibly even murder." She headed for the door, tossing one last comment over her shoulder. "Enjoy your trial."

"I wasn't alone in this. I can tell you who I am working for. Who planned the operation." She tossed her hair out of her eyes. "My snooping devices also told me your daughter's name, Alli. I'll tell them everything I know."

That stopped Lenore cold. Slowly, she pivoted to face Kurla. The triumphant grin of satisfaction on Kurla's face quickly vanished as she caught sight of Lenore's expression. Lenore took the three steps back to the field until the only thing separating the two women was an inch of energy.

"I *know* who you are working for. But apparently you don't know them as well as I do."

Kurla's jaw muscles bunched, but she didn't back down. Lenore wasn't finished.

"I know that those who hired you will not be pleased at your failure. In fact," Lenore allowed herself a half smile. "I will be very surprised if you survive long enough to make it to the trial." Lenore started to turn again but spun back around at laughter. She stared, incredulous, at a laughing Kurla.

"Oh, bravo. That was nearly word for word what I was told you would say."

"What are you talking about?" *This woman has lost her mind.*

"You are wrong. I know exactly who I am working for. You see, Lenore. You were my first solo mission."

Lenore's heart went cold, and she felt her own jaw clenching as she ground out a single word.

"What?"

"I just finished my training as a Xa'ti'al and you were my target."

"You failed."

"On the contrary. I succeeded far better than I ever thought I would. My mission was never to bring you in, but to test you. And gather detailed information about your family."

Without realizing what she was doing, Lenore whipped out her blaster and pointed it at Kurla. The woman merely laughed again.

"Perfect! He said you would do that at the mention of your family and you did, angry eyes and all." She grinned as she pointed at Lenore's eyes, then suddenly sobered. "Killing me won't do any good. I have already sent my data in."

Lenore fought to control her fury at being manipulated. Only one man could have played her so well. Daviss. Now she needed to forget those emotions if she was going to get anything more useful from Kurla.

"You said you were testing me. For what?" She kept the blaster pointed at Kurla though she was sure it wouldn't penetrate the brig's field.

Fairly sure.

"I see no harm in telling you now," said Kurla, lifting her chin slightly. "The Xa'ti'al wanted to see the result of an ex-Xa raising a family. Would she lose her training? Become soft? Or train her children as well as she had been?" Kurla smirked. "It could be an entirely new program for future Xa."

"Why me? Why not breed their own?"

Now Kurla's eyes narrowed, the smirk dropping from her face. "Because, when you left, the order came down to sterilize all future agents. Men and women. Thereby eliminating another incentive to desert."

Lenore shouldn't have been surprised at this revelation, but she was shocked nonetheless. "And I suppose Daviss explained to you the best ways to manipulate me?"

"Of course. I didn't think he could be that accurate, but you did nearly everything exactly as he said you would."

"Nearly?"

"Well, you were supposed to break out of your cell quicker than you did with all the devices we let you keep."

"So those men were Xa as well?"

"Of course. How else do you think they knew how to deal with a stun grenade and fake unconsciousness? And Daviss knew you were on that station. He led you on so there would be time to sabotage your environmental systems."

"So we would have to drop out of transwarp so you could send a message I suppose," said Lenore.

"Obviously."

"Why not take us on our ship when the patrol stopped us? Three Xa should have been able to do that."

"I had my strict instructions and there were two obvious reasons." Kurla appeared to be enjoying telling the tale. "First, because I know better than to confront you in the place where you are most comfortable. Neutral ground is always preferable. And the second I have already mentioned. We were testing you, Lenore. You and your family. How you would react, what your kids would do, everything. Frankly, I was disappointed. I had heard about how good an agent you were, but now I know that you are a fossil, Lenore."

"Oh?" She felt her teeth grinding again.

"Yes. You've grown soft. I guess being a mother will do that." Kurla's voice dripped with condescension. "Removing your medplant just aided in losing your edge." She stared at Lenore. "There is nothing more for the Xa to learn from letting you stay free, so take my advice and run. Run far. But I don't think that will be enough."

A deep breath allowed Lenore enough control to speak.

"You are right. I have let myself become too trusting. But now, thanks to your warning, that ends today. The Xa will never catch me off guard again."

Kurla merely laughed again until Lenore fired her blaster. She had the satisfaction of seeing Kurla leap out of the way despite the force field stopping the shot.

"If I ever see you again, that is what will happen to you," said Lenore. "No hesitations." She holstered her blaster and exited, nearly running into Sherrod. The worry in his good eye calmed Lenore somewhat.

"She is fine." She lowered her voice as Sherrod peered around the corner to verify her claim. "Listen to the brig's recordings and you will know why I did what I did. And Sherrod." Lenore looked directly at him, voice at a whisper. "You can repay me that favor by erasing those records."

He nodded and she headed back to the ship, not even trying to figure out if she was angrier at the Xa'ti'al or herself.

Chapter Thirty-eight

Diarmin had just finished securing Bondle's cargo when he caught sight of Lenore heading for the cargo ramp that was still down. Her face and trudging gait showed that the discussion with Kurla did not go well.

Lenore strode up the ramp, but before Diarmin could ask a question, she spoke.

"Where is my medplant? Have you fixed it?"

Her demanding tone left no doubt she was fuming inside. Diarmin strode to his workbench and reached under it to a well-hidden spot underneath. He pulled out the device and held it out to her.

"I have fixed the basic circuits but, as I told you before, the programs are still unclear, and I don't know if would work the same as before. Besides, our medbed isn't capable of reimplanting and we would have to..." He trailed off as Lenore ignored him to return down the ramp. He followed but she didn't go far, stopping right off the ramp.

She gently placed the device on the ground, then took out her blaster and fired point blank at the medplant.

After all that work to get it functional again.

Lenore bent down to examine the little debris that was left. She scooped it up and handed it to Diarmin. "Destroy the remains, I want nothing left." She started to head back into the ship, but Diarmin grabbed her arm.

"What's going on? What did Kurla say?"

"Let's get off this planet," she said, trying to pull her arm away but he held fast.

"A few minutes won't make a difference. Tell me why you destroyed the one thing you have been trying to get me to fix. And we are talking here, not in the ship where we can be overheard so I want to know everything."

He could tell by her expression that she was preparing to be stubborn again, but then she must have changed her mind. He released her arm as she related the entire story, speaking very fast as if it were an unpleasant task to be done with as soon as possible.

When she finished, he agreed with his assessment. *Very unpleasant.*

"That doesn't explain why you destroyed the medplant," he said.

"Don't you see?" Lenore began pacing, only three steps at a time so she could still talk quietly to Diarmin. "The only person who knew about me removing that medplant was the slaver in Quinn's rescue."

"But you killed him. Right after you pulled it out."

"Yes, and you erased the tapes." She paced a few more times, eyes now turned toward the ground. Diarmin waited patiently, knowing his wife was trying to find the words for a difficult subject.

"I've been wondering how Daviss keeps finding me so quickly. If someone reported us the moment we land or dock at a station, it still takes time to get to a ship and travel. But he's been there within an hour or two." She crossed her arms but didn't stop walking. "He has been a step ahead of me this whole time. I thought I was being sloppy even though I couldn't figure out where I kept messing up."

She stopped and looked at Diarmin.

"I think they have been tracking me through that medplant. It somehow has been sending them signals. It's the only way they could have known it was removed and the only way he could know my whereabouts so accurately."

Diarmin felt his stomach clench at that realization. "And like Kurla said, they have been testing you so that's why they never closed in, always pushing you just a little further."

"Yes, and like a complete idiot, I have been letting them." She put her fists to her temples and bit her lip. "They played me. Daviss has been manipulating me from the start."

Diarmin grabbed Lenore's fists and pulled them away from her head, temples already red from the pressure of her anguish.

"Stop that," he said. "He has not been manipulating you from the start. For one thing, they implemented sterilization after you left so that means they reacted to your desertion, not planned for it. Now, having been unable to bring you back, they are reacting in another way. They probably realized that your emotions would be easier to manipulate now that the medplant is gone."

"You are right. But no more." The determination was back in her eyes, sending a wash of relief through Diarmin. Determination was better than despair.

"No more," he agreed. "Now let's get this mission finished so we can decide how best to handle the Xa'ti'al."

Lenore grinned, but it wasn't a pleasant one. "Absolutely. They have messed with the wrong family."

Chapter Thirty-nine

Quinn felt the ship enter transwarp. By his calculations, he had been in his room, staring at the ceiling for about nine hours. The first few hours he had dozed, still sleeping off the effects of the stun blast. He felt a wry grin. It had been stronger than he thought it would be. The IGNet never mentioned that.

His grin faded as he realized that, despite having lain here for hours thinking on the past days, he had no answers. For his family or himself. He had some vague ideas and feelings but didn't know if he could form them into coherent sentences. Maybe if he identified his feelings, he might have better luck.

First, there was still anger. It felt like he had been angry since Kurla came on board. But he reluctantly admitted his temper had been short for weeks. Since the end of the mission with the princess, maybe even a little during. He thought it was fading with time but instead the situations just switched. Every day had brought something new to be angry about. Even now, he was angry that neither of his parents had come to thank him for his part in their rescue.

Now, Quinn felt embarrassment. He hadn't really helped. He simply focused everyone's attention on him instead of Allison. She had even gotten him onto the ship without detection. His skills hadn't been up to the task and he'd been playing everything over and over in his mind but coming up with no better solutions. And he put Allison in danger.

One huge emotion that took him awhile to identify was doubt. Right now, he doubted himself, his family and even his own intentions. Had he really wanted to join her crew? Did he have criminal tendencies? A stray thought of something Allison had said niggled at his brain but a knock on the door made the thought vanish.

"Quinn?" It was his father. "Are you hungry? Would you like some dinner?"

Quinn rolled off the bed with a groan. He opened the door to see his father with a concerned look on his face. "I'm not hungry," he said.

"Well, the whole family is in there, Bondle is down in the cargo bay keeping a close eye on his cargo, so now would be a good time for us to have a meal."

Quinn was about to refuse again, but the tone of his father's voice indicated that he was expected to be there.

"Okay."

He followed Diarmin into the lounge. Everyone was seated at the table with plates full of food in front of them. Diarmin took a seat and Quinn slowly sat in a chair with a plate. He ate a few bites but the weight of the stares of his family made the food stick in his throat. His mother placed a glass of liquid in front of him.

"This is a strong electrolyte drink. It will help with the aftereffects of a stun blast."

Quinn obediently drank some. It tasted wonderful so he drained the glass. Wordlessly his mother refilled it and Quinn knew they couldn't put off the discussion anymore. He suspected the drink had something else because suddenly his head cleared, and he felt almost normal.

"Are we on our way to Bondle's homeworld?" he asked.

"Yes. It should be another five hours," said Diarmin.

"Two hours to the course change and then three more to finally deliver the cargo," said Lenore. "Bondle should have twelve hours to test the effectiveness of his vaccine."

"Good. I am glad all the...delays weren't...didn't...I mean..." He trailed off.

"We were fortunate," said Lenore. She took a deep breath and pushed her plate away. "Let's talk about that, shall we?"

Everyone else put down silverware and pushed plates to the side.

"Start from the moment we left the ship to board the patrol ship," said Diarmin. "We have already heard Alli's version, give us yours."

"Okay. First, Alli and I knew something was up because Alli had read three biosignatures on the bridge. None in the brig as the man had said. We weren't sure why Kurla was on the bridge with the men, but it seemed wrong. We listened the entire time to your transmissions as you ordered, and when we heard it start to go wrong, Alli accessed her tap into the systems but all she could get at first were the biosignatures. When they put you in the cells, we remotely undocked the shuttle and programmed it to return as you instructed with your subvocals. We hoped at least one would be pulled out the airlock, but he closed it in time." Quinn suppressed a small shudder. Saying that out loud made him realize for the first time that they had tried to kill a man. He pushed the thought away and kept on. "As soon as the shuttle was aboard, we took off to hide. We argued about going to the patrol base, but I didn't want to waste time. I had Alli hack into the entire system again while I came up with a plan and readied weapons."

"Which reminds me," said Lenore. "Where did you learn how to use those?"

"The IGNet. It has everything a person would want to know." He grimaced. "Good and bad."

"I see." She leaned back in the chair, lacing her fingers together over her stomach. The lack of emotion on her face did not reassure Quinn. "Continue."

"The plan was that I would go aboard, distract everyone while Alli slipped on, and then she would go to work." He swallowed. He had to get the next words right. "I knew I couldn't take all of them so I thought I would simply surrender and be in the brig with you. She'd then deactivate the cell fields, and, with the element of surprise, you could easily handle all three. I...I honestly had no idea she would ask me to join her crew. But it was distracting them all and giving Allison a lot more time to find a secure place so I went with it. I also thought that if I could even be trusted a little as a member of the crew, maybe I could do more."

"But why did you have the device that would suppress my implant if you weren't planning on needing something to inspire trust?"

Quinn felt a rueful grin. "I was just using that device to suppress my biosigns." He shrugged. "I didn't know if it would do anything about your implants, but it's all I could think of."

Now Lenore looked accusingly at Diarmin. "So why didn't you tell me the truth?"

"I couldn't blow Quinn's story, could I? And I never really had the chance to later."

Lenore put her elbows on the table, hands on her temples as she closed her eyes.

"Okay," she said, finally. "So far everything you've told me matches with what Allison said." Here Allison nodded vigorously as if by strength of agreement she could avoid her mother's next words. "But, Quinn. I…we…need to know. Was there a part of you that wanted to leave?"

All heads swiveled to look at him. He still didn't know if he could explain, but he had to try.

"I will be completely honest. I have thought about leaving and even said so when I was angrily yelling on the bridge. So, honestly, yes, there was a small part of me that was tempted by Kurla's offer. I was attracted by the thought that maybe I could have some different experiences and learn exciting new things." Quinn tried to ignore the hurt on his family's faces. "But only for a brief moment and do you know why? I suddenly realized that Kurla was the completely wrong person to do that with." He was silent for a moment as he organized his thoughts. "Mom. Dad. Despite the fact that I know you have deliberately kept information from me and Alli, the fact of the matter is…" he shifted his gaze between his parents, trying to show his sincerity. "You have never lied to us. I have had plenty of time these past few hours to think. Now I know that all those things you haven't told us or taught us are for our protection. Kurla was only ever for herself and she lied about everything. When she laughed about faking the priest and said, 'there is much more to a disguise than wigs and makeup,' I knew she had been in my room and gone through my belongings. As far as I know, none of you have ever invaded my privacy in such a way. Well, with the exception of eavesdropping and I understand why that was done." He grinned at Allison's red face. "From that point on, there was zero chance that I would help Kurla in any way." He stopped, even though he felt he hadn't quite explained himself well enough.

"I see," was all his mother said but the tension drained out of the room. "I appreciate the honesty. That couldn't have been easy." She smiled and the relief Quinn felt made him light-headed.

"I must say, Quinn," said his father. "You are an even better actor than I ever thought you could be. But then again, I haven't really seen you working since I am usually on the ship." Now he gave Lenore an almost accusatory look, as if she should have known he was acting.

"Yes, well, you were very convincing, Quinn. And I really didn't think you were able to think and adapt that quickly in a dangerous situation so credit goes to you for that. But there's one more thing I need to say." His mother gave him a stern look. "You disobeyed my orders, put yourself and your sister in extreme danger, and..." she paused. Quinn lifted his chin, determined to take his deserved punishment.

"And we owe you our freedom. Both of you. Thank you, my clever children."

She stood and held her arms out. Chairs slid back or fell over as the other three rushed into a family embrace.

***

A heavy tread in the corridor outside the lounge made them all break apart. Quinn went to right his chair while Allison grabbed a couple of plates. Bondle came huffing around the corner, his face bright pink.

"If I keep climbing these ladders every hour, I will either be in shape or passed out by the time we get to Reese." He looked up, appearing surprised that anyone was in the lounge. Diarmin hid a chuckle. Bondle had been muttering to himself since they came back aboard, concentrating on his vaccines and in a constant state of worry.

"I am so glad you are here, Captain," he said as he shuffled to the table. "I would like to contact Reese right away, or rather the prime planet Reesling."

"I'm sorry," said Lenore. "But we can't transmit while in transspace. Why the urgency?"

"Well as you know these samples are very close to their limit so I want everyone to be prepared. They must be purposed as soon as possible, or I will have to start the process all over again. It's not like Mill can start another—" An anguished look drew his eyebrows together, but he shook it off. "If I can get even a few of these to work, the government will extend the facilities for mass production. That's why I need medical staff standing by so we can have the best chance."

"As it happens, we were just discussing the course change coming up in two hours," she said.

Diarmin kept his eyebrows from raising. They hadn't talked about it at all, but he stood beside her, ready to support any story she concocted. The kids were doing the dishes, but he could tell they were listening intently.

"Ah, so I can talk to someone when we transition, yes?" asked Bondle.

"Actually, that's what we were planning to inform you," said Lenore. She gestured to the table and all three sat. Allison brought over a plate of snacks for Bondle and Quinn a drink so they just sat in the other chairs. Bondle didn't look at anyone else but absently started eating while waiting for Lenore to continue.

"We are concerned about someone who may still be after the cargo," she said. "So that means that we are going to change course in record time. Transitions usually take anywhere from fifteen minutes to a few hours. But I don't want to be in real space for more than sixty seconds, preferably less."

"Then I won't be able to talk to anyone."

"No, but there will be time to send off a message. You have a little more than an hour to compose exactly what you want to tell them. I would also like to send a brief message warning about possible ships following us in, so be sure to send a copy to a government official, as high up as you can, preferably military. We need them to be ready in case any ships are waiting to waylay this one."

Bondle's eyes widened at this comment as well as both kids'. Diarmin had been considering the problem but hadn't had time to talk about it with Lenore. He knew he should be concerned at her telling Bondle without a family discussion beforehand, but it was too late to argue now.

"I understand, Captain. I will go write as succinct a message as I can." He stood and both kids urged him to take the food with him. He absently grabbed the dishes and disappeared into his cabin.

"Good, that's taken care of," Lenore looked at everyone. "Now, let's head to the bridge and figure out how we are going to handle that transition as well as our arrival at the planet." She smiled at Quinn. "*All* of us."

He grinned back and Diarmin felt his spirits lift, even though danger still awaited them all.

Chapter Forty

Despite the tensions on the bridge, Allison couldn't stop smiling. The entire family was working harmoniously again, the troubles, if not completely gone, at least mostly solved. Allison felt they would be fine as long as they were together.

"Time to transition?" asked her mother.

"Five minutes," she replied at the same time her brother did. They grinned at each other then put their attention back at their usual stations.

"Okay let's go over this one more time, just to be sure," said Lenore. "Diarmin, you bring us out of transwarp and Alli will send the messages. I will scan for ships while Quinn will make sure his navigational setting will work."

"I have two alternatives if something comes up," said Quinn.

"Double checking that everyone is strapped in tight," said Diarmin. "I plan on a hard bank the second we come out."

"The message is ready to go. Both sections," Allison added.

"Acknowledged." Lenore pressed a key. "Strap down, Mr. Bondle. This may get rough."

"I am, Captain," came a voice through the speaker.

"Estimation of time it will take to change course?" she asked even though they'd discussed this twice already.

"A few seconds to verify our position, another few to figure new course and the time to get us there," said Diarmin. "Forty-five seconds to a minute."

"Good."

"Sixty seconds to transition," said Quinn.

Everyone sat tense, as the countdown got closer to zero. Allison verified the message was ready and also prepared herself to perform whatever scans she could in the few seconds they had before slipping back into transwarp.

"Five...four...three...two...shift," said Quinn.

Immediately the yacht banked hard to port as well as down. An energy beam lance narrowly missed the ship, proving Diarmin's guess correct.

Allison ignored the viewscreen to do her job. "Shields up. Message away!" She started to collect whatever data she could.

"First and third courses blocked," said Quinn. "Course two is clear."

"Acknowledged," said Diarmin. "You might get one shot off, Lenore. Time to transition...fifteen seconds."

"Forget the shot, just go."

The ship shook as it took weapons fire on the shields.

"Shields stable," said Lenore.

"Hold on," said Diarmin. He took the ship into a steep ascent, curved to port again and then accelerated, pressing the family deep into the seats. Allison couldn't help looking at the viewscreen as a missile headed straight for them. "Here we go!"

The starfield disappeared, taking the threatening missile with it as the yacht slipped into transspace. The family all sighed in relief simultaneously.

"Fifty seconds. Not bad, Dad, considering there were at least two ships, ready and waiting for us," said Quinn.

Allison checked the data she had gotten from her scans and turned to look at her mother. By the look on her mother's face, she had similar information as Allison. Her mother's head came up and eyes locked with Allison's. Her tiny nod told Allison that she could tell the others her findings.

"Actually," she said to Quinn. "There were six ships."

"Six?" Quinn said, eyebrows rising like the squeak in his voice.

"So that means..." Diarmin trailed off as if he didn't want to finish that sentence.

Lenore finished it for him.

"It means that they are stepping up their game."

"They?" asked Quinn.

"You've probably guessed, but I am sure that Alli's data will confirm what I suspect. Those were the Xa'ti'al."

***

Silence reigned on the bridge for several moments. Lenore's breathing was loud in her own ears as she was trying to settle her churning stomach. Her fears weren't for herself but for her family. She'd felt that way since the moment Kurla had mentioned that the Xa wanted her alive but family dead. She'd come to some difficult decisions in the past few hours, one that only solidified with how many ships were actually lying in wait.

"Kids. I need to tell you something."

Quinn and Allison turned in their seats, looking expectant. She was very glad that the anger was gone out of Quinn's eyes, but she was sure it would be back at some point. She took another settling breath then realized she was stalling so she simply started speaking.

"Your father and I have discussed this before and though we haven't talked about it in these last hectic hours, I am sure we are still on the same page." She glanced at Diarmin who had the same expectant look. "Quinn. You were correct in that we have never told you everything and also correct that it was to protect you both. But now, not only do we feel that you are ready to hear the story, with all that's happened, it is a must. So."

She stopped and took another breath but couldn't bring herself to look at her kids. "When all this is over and we are again safe, your father and I will tell our stories." She looked at Diarmin again. His lips had tightened but he nodded at her. "Everything. The good, the bad, and even things you might be too young to understand. You need to know why we made the choices we did and how it shaped our lives. And then yours." She cut herself off, rambling because she didn't want to say the next line. She hadn't discussed this with her husband because her decision had been made moments ago. "After you hear everything, if you think it would be best, I will return to the Xa'ti'al in return for your lives and safety."

Both children burst out with denials and comments. Lenore held up her hand and they fell silent again.

"Don't argue now. Wait until you have heard the entire story. You may change your minds." She tried to grin and lighten the mood. "That is unless it is all made moot in the next few hours." She turned her grin to Diarmin but the blank look on his face made it disappear from her lips.

"I'm going to check if our passenger and cargo survived all the hubbub," he said, unbuckling himself from the chair.

Lenore almost held out her hand to stop him but, as she had told the kids, now was not the time. As Diarmin headed down the ladder, she removed her restraints as well, trying not to regret her words. She felt like she had to say what she said now, in case the worst happened when they got to Reese.

At least now, even if I don't get the chance to tell them everything, they know that my intentions were good.

"Quinn. Time to the planet?"

Quinn turned back to his board but not before Lenore saw a hint of some emotion return to those eyes. She didn't think it was anger but couldn't tell what else it might be.

"Four hours."

"Good. Let's discuss what exactly we will do when we get there."

Chapter Forty-one

Diarmin trudged back to the bridge. He had been trying not to think about the last thing Lenore had said to Quinn and Allison. How could she even consider going back to the Xa'ti'al? Did she forget all the reasons she left? Maybe telling the story to the children will remind her. He was also trying to not regret agreeing to it. What would the kids think when they learned who he used to be? Firmly he shoved the doubts back. They all needed to be at their best for the next hour.

As his head popped through the opening, all heads turned to him. Lenore opened her mouth but Diarmin beat her to it.

"I figured Mr. Bondle should be on the bridge when we arrive. That way he can talk to whomever is in charge." A tip of his head indicated that Bondle was right behind him on the ladder.

"Good idea," said Lenore. She stood as Diarmin took the command chair. "Mr. Bondle, how did the cargo do during the transition?"

"The cargo is fine, but I got rather shook up." He glanced at all of them with a sheepish look. "I am afraid I had to take the rest of the nausea medication to calm my stomach."

"Well, we are hoping the end of our trip will be less challenging." She indicated her chair for him to sit.

"Ah, no. Don't give up your seat for me."

"Mr. Bondle. Regulations are that all passengers must be strapped in for transition," she replied. "Don't worry. I've done this many times." She arranged herself next to him and, using a switch under the science console, raised it so she could access the board while standing.

"Time to transition?" asked Diarmin, trying not to be concerned at his wife not being strapped down. But if it got rough, he needed to be firmly in his chair to pilot and neither of them wanted the kids unrestrained.

"Ten minutes."

"Exact coordinates?"

Quinn punched a few buttons and the information scrolled across the screen.

"That's awfully close to the planet," said Diarmin.

"We thought that it would be best to get the cargo delivered as soon as possible," said Allison.

"I understand," he answered, knowing the truth was that the less time being open to attack.

"My message requested that the ship be allowed to land at the primary medical facility instead of the space station," said Bondle as he fastened buckles and straps. "They have a landing pad on the roof that is not large, but if all other vehicles are moved, you should have no trouble landing with antigrav. It would take too long to transfer the cargo from the station."

"Very well," said Lenore as Diarmin nodded. "You should know, with the message I sent attached to your own, I requested an escort, military-grade if possible."

"We have a small standing security force, but they should be enough to deter pirates," he replied. Apparently, he didn't see everyone's exchanging glances. "Did you give them a description of your vessel?"

"Yes, as well as our identification specs so they won't fire on us as we enter their space."

"Good."

The group fell silent again, working diligently at their posts. As the minutes wore on, the tension rose significantly.

"Thirty seconds," said Quinn. Instead of counting aloud, he put the timer in the corner of the viewscreen. Eyes shifted between consoles and clock.

Diarmin's hands hovered above the pilot controls as the countdown approached zero.

"Transition," said Quinn. The screen resolved to show a planet exactly in front, close enough to see blue and white swirls, yet far enough away to not cause problems with gravity. But their attention was not on the lovely planet but the two ships directly in front.

"Ah, good. Those are our sentry ships. I will make contact for landing—"

He never got to finish that sentence as an orange light surrounded their ship. The wrenching lurch told Diarmin that they were now held in a tractor beam.

"Reese sentry ship," said Lenore. "This is Captain Nora Fleming. We are on an emergency medical mission that you should have been made aware of. What is the meaning of the beam holding my ship?" She covered the microphone and gave a loud whisper to Allison. "Find a way out of that."

Allison nodded as a return message came through.

"Captain Fleming. My orders are to take you to the correct coordinates."

"My pilot is more than capable of landing. Release my ship."

"It's true," Bondle chimed in. "The pilot is an excellent one."

"I have my orders." The line cut out.

"Is this standard?" Diarmin asked Bondle.

"Not at all. I have never heard of sentry ships using their tractor beams for anything other than towing disabled ships to the space station."

"If our shields were up, I could change the resonance pattern to disrupt the beam, but they latched on too quickly," said Allison. Her fingers were flying over her keyboard as well as two pads propped up on either side. "I am attempting to hack in for the command codes."

"Do it fast," said Quinn. "The course they are taking us on leads away from the planet."

"I can't contact the planet. They're disrupting communications," said Quinn. "And our weapons won't activate within the tractor beam's field."

"Let's try this then," said Diarmin. "Hang on tight!"

He put the yacht on maximum reverse and the orange light flickered but held fast. As a slight pulse indicated a switch in the beam, he slammed the yacht hard to starboard.

"That's weakened the hold," said Lenore. "A couple more punches and we won't need weapons."

Tugging the ship in every direction threw everyone around, but Lenore held fast to the console and kept standing. The last pull was straight up, then the orange light was gone.

Diarmin said, "Raise shields" only half a second before Allison yelled, "Shields up."

As the yacht pulled away, a blast rocked the ship.

"Concussion missile," said Quinn. "Energy weapons firing as well."

"How dare they!" said Bondle who was gripping the arms of the chair. "Let me speak with them, Captain."

"I don't think they are listening," said Lenore. "And I don't think these are your people." To her family she added, "The second ship is closing and firing their weapons."

The ship shook again.

"Those are energy weapons," said Quinn. "Three hits, the starboard shields are down to half strength."

"Well, they can't hit us if they can't catch us." Diarmin took the ship into a dive then looped around.

"Firing," said Lenore.

"Minimal damage," said Quinn. "Their shields are just too strong."

"Working on it!" said Allison, fingers still flying.

"We only have two missiles left. We will have to make them count when Alli gets the shields down."

"Almost there. I'm through two of the four firewalls."

Energy blasts continued to rain on the ship. Despite evasive maneuvers, the toll was adding up. *Where are the real security forces?* thought Diarmin.

"They are definitely going for the engines," said Quinn. "Stern shields won't take much more, especially on the starboard side."

"Third wall down," said Allison.

As if that was a sign, a missile tore into the ship, sending Lenore flying. A high-pitched whistle and air being sucked down the stairwell indicated a breach somewhere in the ship.

"Mom!" yelled Allison. She and Quinn went for their buckles to help their mother lying still on the deck.

"Don't leave your posts!" yelled Diarmin. "We can't help her if we are all dead. Quinn, I transferred the science controls to your board. Locate that breach and seal it. Allison, get that hack!"

Both kids looked stricken but Diarmin knew it was the right thing, especially when the ship rocked from another blast. Had they been unbuckled they would be in the same predicament as their mother.

The whistle stopped. "Starboard shields on the stern are completely gone," said Quinn. His voice was rough but steady. "Breach was in one of the guest cabins, so I sealed the lounge door."

"Good job. I will attempt to keep the ships to the port side."

"I'm through!" Allison yelled. "Looking for the shield codes...got 'em!"

Diarmin glanced at the science console where the weapon controls were. They couldn't be transferred. Bondle wouldn't know what to do and he looked like he was trying hard not to pass out. Lenore was still unconscious, and he needed to fly the ship. His heart clenched at what needed to be done, but they had no choice.

"Quinn. You are going to have to fire the missiles."

Quinn nodded and unbuckled.

"Their shields are down," said Allison. "On both ships."

Quinn stood and headed for the science console, steps unsteady in the violently swaying ship.

Suddenly, the screen lit up with an explosion that wasn't on their ship.

"Alli, what happened?"

"It looks like one ship was seriously damaged. And there's a missile heading toward the other."

Quinn made it to the board and his fingers flew. "Four ships are converging on the attackers. From the scans it looks like the same class of ship."

"Hold your fire, Quinn," said Diarmin. "It's about time they showed up."

"*After* I got the shields down for them," muttered Allison.

"Both of the ships that attacked us are heading for space and engaging their drives," said Quinn. "They're gone."

Diarmin brought the yacht to a standstill and all three headed for Lenore. There was a growing pool of blood by her head and she wasn't showing signs of reviving.

"That's a lot of blood," said Allison in a small voice.

"Head wounds bleed a lot and she definitely has a head trauma," said Diarmin, pointing to the cut above her left temple. "It also looks like she fell on her left arm. It's broken and maybe the wrist as well. Someone get me the medical kit." He started cleaning the blood from her face with a cloth from one of his jumpsuit pockets.

As Allison headed down the ladder, a bleep at the console indicated someone wishing to communicate.

"I'll stay with her," said Quinn softly.

Diarmin handed him the cloth. "Keep that away from the open wound."

"I know, Dad."

Diarmin returned to the beeping command console to open a channel. *L'Eponge de Carre.* First officer, here."

"This is Admiral Frisson, commander of the Reese security fleet. Apologies for our delayed arrival. Do you have any casualties?"

"The Captain is hurt, but we are treating her."

"Our medical experts will be at your disposal. Is your ship capable of flight?"

"Yes."

"Then proceed immediately to these landing coordinates at our main medical facility. I'll have people standing by."

The transmission cut off after the coordinates were sent. Allison pounded back up the ladder, medical kit clutched under her arm. Diarmin took it from her and pulled out a scanner.

"Is she all right?" asked Bondle.

Diarmin had nearly forgotten he was there. He ran the scanner along the length of his wife's body.

"She's got a concussion and a couple of broken bones but no internal injuries." He carefully picked her up. "I'll take her to the medbed." He looked at his worried daughter. "Do you know how to hook her up?"

Allison nodded, her left fingers wildly twisting a curly lock of hair.

"Then you follow me and don't worry. She's been through a lot worse than this." He turned to his son.

"Please take Mr. Bondle to the cargo bay to inspect the cargo. As soon as I get her into the bed, I'll land the ship. We will need to be ready to unload."

Quinn helped Bondle to his feet. Diarmin could hear their conversation as he carefully descended the ladder with Lenore.

"It's all my fault. I should have stayed in my cabin and she would have had her chair."

"If you had stayed in your cabin, you'd likely be dead now," said Quinn.

"What?"

"That part of the ship was holed. There is no air in there now." Quinn cleared his throat. "In fact, you might have even been sucked out to space. Like your belongings probably were. Sorry."

"That's okay. It's a good exchange for my life. What's important is in the cargo bay."

The group paused in the corridor, unable to squeeze by while Diarmin settled Lenore on the medbed. "There. I'm for the bridge. To the bay, gentlemen. And soon we will be finished with this mission."

Allison muttered one word as she began hooking the IVs to her mother and activating the bed.

"Finally."

Chapter Forty-two

Lenore came awake suddenly. She tried to sit up but found she couldn't due to the strap on her chest. Her head throbbed horribly and there was a dull ache in her left arm.

"Easy, Mom," came Allison's voice as her face came into view. "You've had a rough day."

"I suppose this strap was your father's idea," said Lenore, trying to think through the pounding in her ears.

"No, it was mine. We all know how you are when you wake up from injuries. Now you just sit there while I fill you in."

"Yes, ma'am," said Lenore with a small smile. She willed the meds to work quickly.

"First of all, the rest of us are fine. You are the only one who got hurt. You have a concussion but no fractures in your skull, what a wonder. But your left forearm is broken with one large break and several smaller ones in your upper arm, wrist and two fingers although how anyone can break only their pinkie finger and middle finger is beyond me."

"The ship?" She remembered the loud explosion before seeing the bulkhead rushing toward her.

"The hull was breached somewhere by the guest cabins. The area is now sealed. Right after you were, uh, injured, I got the shields down. The sentry ships then swooped in and, thanks to me, were able to deliver a couple of damaging missiles. The ships bugged out after that." Allison looked up as the ship vibrated slightly and engines cut out. "Ah, that would be Dad, engaging the antigrav. We must be close to landing at the medical facility."

"Good timing," said Lenore as the last of the medications were pumped into her body. A stimulant by the feel. "Take the straps off, please and hand me that immobilization device for my arm."

"Mom, you are in no shape...okay." Allison did as asked, shaking her head the entire time. Lenore wondered if it was a good thing that her daughter knew her well enough not to argue.

By the time she felt the slight jolt of the landing, Lenore was on her feet with the immobilizing gel pack forming a hard sheath around her entire arm. She tucked it into a sling, patted the bandage on her head to make sure it was secure, and took two steps toward the cargo bay ladder. As she swayed with light-headedness, she looked at Allison still shaking her head.

"Well, Alli. Evidently you're right that I am not particularly well, but I need to see this through. Give me a hand?" She tried for a smile but was sure it wasn't a cheerful one.

Allison grumbled but she answered. "How about a shoulder?" Despite her grumpy mutterings, Allison had a slight smile as if she was pleased her mother needed her. Lenore knew she had to keep reminding herself that she could depend on her entire family if she had to.

The climb down the ladder was awkward with one arm and Allison doing her best to help, but once in the cargo bay, Lenore put her good arm on Allison's shoulder. That steadied her enough to let her reach her son who was standing ready to open the bay doors which also served as the cargo ramp.

"Mom! Should you be up?" He glanced at Allison who rolled her eyes. But he said nothing as Bondle came to him, scanner in hand.

"Captain. I am glad you are okay. I feel horrible that I couldn't—"

Lenore held up a hand to stop him. "What's done is done and I will recover."

"Yes, she will, she's tough. The ship will need a large head-sized dent fixed though." said Diarmin who Lenore hadn't heard approach. "Here, you need this."

Diarmin handed her a personal force field generator, giving one to Allison as well.

"What's this for?" she asked.

"Before we landed, we were notified of the best ways to avoid contamination." He returned to the ladder and closed the hatch to the rest of the ship.

Lenore was startled. *I forgot about the fact that we may catch this plague.* These drugs definitely dulled the brain, or was it the concussion?

Diarmin offered a field generator to Bondle, but he shook his head.

"Thank you, but I cannot work with the samples while wearing one of those. I will have to take my chances."

"What else do we need to do?" Lenore asked, feeling disconcerted at being out of the loop.

"The people meeting us will let us know." Diarmin grinned. "We have been busy while you were sleeping."

The joke eased the tension and the cargo ramp was lowered after everyone's fields were powered up.

"How did the cargo do?" Lenore asked Bondle.

"Unlike you they are carefully wrapped against impacts. But we won't know if the cultures will work after so long until we insert the plague virus in them."

As soon as the ramp was down, Lenore could see several people in white lab coats waiting outside along with a man in an admiral's uniform. He was tall with steely gray hair and mustache, hat tucked under his arm. He strode up the ramp and stopped just before the bay.

"Admiral Frisson, at your service," he said with a slight dip of his head. "You must be Captain Fleming. I'd heard you were injured." He lifted his chin. "Permission to come aboard and receive your passenger and cargo?"

"Granted," said Lenore, and she was amazed at how good that felt.

Admiral Frisson gave one wave of his hand and the group of white-coated people swarmed aboard. Bondle stepped in front of the cargo. His coat was no longer the same pristine white, but his demeanor left no doubt who was in charge of the cargo.

"I am Senior Researcher Ven Bondle. These samples are to be delivered immediately to the lab nearest the worst plague victims. Nobody is to handle the individual vials until I have explained the proper procedures." His instructions continued as they wheeled the six-alls down the ramp and into the building. Lenore was amused to see the shy scientist gone now that he had purpose. Diarmin also had a smile on his face as he watched Bondle give orders.

"Welcome to Reesling," said the admiral. "We rarely let outside ships land on our planet, but we have taken steps to ensure a very small chance to be infected."

Diarmin was the one to speak her thoughts aloud. "Perhaps we should leave."

"You can rest easy. Ven wouldn't have known, but it's only been in the past year that we have determined that the plague is carried within the soil and plants on the planet. As long as you don't eat or drink anything and remain in the sterile medical facility, you shall be fine. We have made sure that nobody who is infected will come near you or the ship, and there are other methods in place. Those personal shields are the extra security." Now he grinned. "And if this vaccine works as Ven says, you won't need to worry at all." His arm swept back toward the building. "Please, let me offer you our medical services. It's the least I can do."

"I am fine. It's only a broken arm." She hadn't been in a hospital since she left the Xa. The need to hide her implants and other secrets had been her priority.

"Nonsense. The bone-knitter will have that fixed up for you in less than an hour."

"Bone-knitter?"

"Yes," the admiral grinned. "I'm sure Ven told you that we have the best medical researchers in the galaxy. We have a device that regrows bones. Developed almost a decade ago. It's just now hitting the market outside of Reese."

"Go ahead, Captain. We'll get started on the repairs," said Diarmin

"Ah yes. About that. Again, I apologize for our late arrival. We were on the periphery of the system and didn't expect you to arrive so close to the planet. Ven said nothing about that. And then the ships that intercepted you were ours, so I assumed they were there to help until the tractor beam. The subsequent weapons fire confirmed that."

"We thought closer to the planet would avoid a confrontation." Diarmin tilted his head and twisted his lips in a rueful look. "We guessed wrong but, fortunately, you arrived in time." Diarmin held out his hand. "It was a pleasure meeting you."

Instead of shaking Diarmin's hand, Admiral Frisson made a circular gesture with his hands that was part welcome and part refusal. She wondered if that was the standard greeting amongst a plague-ridden people or simply because of Diarmin's personal field.

"You may see me again," said the admiral, "but now I will escort the Captain to the proper doctors." He indicated the way to Lenore and smiled at Allison still next to her. "I see you are well supported. This way."

He descended the ramp, only staying a step or two ahead of Lenore, occasionally glancing back to see if he was walking too fast for her. Lenore took a couple of quick steps to catch up, leaning on Allison, the clashing fields only sparking slightly.

"Admiral, pardon me for asking. But you referred to Mr. Bondle as Ven. Do you know him personally?"

"*Ahem*, well, yes. He's my nephew. He sent the message with his requests to me. He is very young despite his intelligence and he was worried that nobody would take him seriously." He glanced at her as they continued walking. "Our planet has had their hopes of new cures crushed many times. As my sister would tell you, Ven would never say he has a possible cure unless he was nearly a hundred percent sure of it. We always thought that if anyone could find a cure, it would be Ven. He was so…determined and let nothing stand in his way. He wrangled his way onto the exploring teams despite his inexperience and his work ethic is astounding. Not only is he naturally gifted but he has worked very hard to get where he is at. And if he succeeds, it will be completely worth everything."

They had entered the building and into an elevator that the admiral accessed with a special card. It dropped three floors and the door opened on a small room entirely surrounded by glass. Through the windows was a busy scene like those found in most medical facilities that Lenore had experienced. A woman in another one of those pristine white coats approached them. She appeared middle-aged but her flaming red hair had no gray in it and her wrinkles were mostly worry lines, to be expected for a doctor on this planet. Though the smile on her face showed that there were laugh lines as well.

"Good morning, Admiral. What have you brought me today?"

"This is Captain Fleming. Captain, this is Dr. Dena, one of the best doctors on our worlds."

"You flatterer," she said, lightly smacking the admiral on the arm. The exchange told Lenore they were obviously well acquainted.

"Please take them to a secure location, Dr. Dena," said Admiral Frisson. "They are from offplanet."

The doctor raised an eyebrow. "Well, if that's not a loaded statement... but to business. I see you need the use of our bone-knitter. And maybe a cerebral scan by the look of that bandage." She spoke into a small device attached to her jacket. "Prepare room seventeen, stat." She nodded at the admiral as she indicated Lenore should follow.

Lenore turned to the admiral. "Thank you for your assistance, Admiral Frisson." She moved her good hand in a gesture similar to the one he had made. He did the same with a twinkle in his eye that told Lenore he appreciated her keen sense of observation.

"The honor is mine. I hope we will meet again soon."

Lenore nodded and she and Allison followed the doctor through a glass door with a large picture of a person coughing overlaid with an X. Dr. Dena swiped a card to open it and they proceeded down a pristine corridor and paused in front of an open door. The doctor swiped the card again and pressed a button, causing a soft glow to fill the doorway.

"That is the disinfectant, getting rid of any trace of disease so you can remove your fields to be treated." To demonstrate, she walked through the glow into the room. Lenore and Allison did the same though Lenore could see that Allison closed her eyes tightly as they passed through. The doctor smiled and indicated that they could turn off their personal fields.

The room was spotless with brightly gleaming instruments, a sink with several cabinets surrounding it, and a medbed that looked as efficient as it was complicated. Allison's low whistle showed her appreciation for the high-tech bed.

"You like it?" asked Dr. Dena. The huge smile on her face showed that she enjoyed showing off the fancy bed.

"This medbed makes ours look like a cot."

Lenore saw her put her hands behind her back and she knew Allison was itching to take a closer look.

"Well, let's get you up here for a thorough check," said the doctor, looking at Lenore while patting the side of the control board.

"Please, no. Just the knitter please. Our medbed may be only first aid level, but it cleared me of any possible hemorrhages and gave me drugs to counter pain and concussion."

The doctor gave Lenore a penetrating look as if she knew exactly why Lenore didn't want to be in a medbed. "Hm. Well, I don't usually let my patients dictate their care, but we can start with the arm." She typed a command into the bed's console and a cabinet on the wall beside it opened to let a large device descend to the level of the bed. It resembled a small coffin about half a meter wide and two meters in length. It split lengthwise to reveal a pink substance on both top and bottom. "As you can see, this will work on most limbs, where we see the majority of broken bones. Now, we need to keep your arm as still as possible, so I do need you to sit up on the bed."

Lenore complied and the doctor efficiently removed the sling and immobilization sheath.

"I haven't seen one of these since I was an intern," she said with a chuckle as she placed it to the side. She maneuvered the device so that it was on Lenore's left side at shoulder height. As gently as possible, she placed Lenore's arm in the pink substance, a warm gel that held her arm firmly as the top came down to completely enclose it. Another tap on the command console and the wall lit up with a display of the bones in her arm. Dr. Dena closely examined the entire picture.

"Hm. Yes. Several breaks along the entire arm and hand. How does someone break only the middle and pinky fingers?"

Allison laughed aloud. "That's what I said." The doctor laughed with her then grew serious.

"This device is very efficient. However, quick regrowth of bone is quite painful. Since I don't know what painkillers you have already had without a blood test, I don't want to give you more. We sometimes have to sedate our patients."

"I will be fine," said Lenore. "I have a high tolerance for pain."

The doctor glanced at Allison who was nodding. "All right, but if it becomes too much, please inform me right away."

A gentle warmth spread along her arm and Lenore thought this would be easy. Then an ache started deep in her arm and the pain slowly increased. The doctor approached her bandaged head with a medical instrument. Lenore leaned away from the doctor.

"Please, hold still or the bone may not repair correctly."

"I told you my head is fine."

Dr. Dena sighed as if she was losing patience with her stubborn patient. "This is merely a tissue regenerator. It will seal the wound correctly and heal it enough so that it won't scar. The medbed would do that if you let me hook you up but since that's not going to happen, this is the next best thing."

Lenore assented and Dr. Dena removed the bandage and went to work. The distraction was welcoming as the pain in her arm was getting stronger.

"So," said the doctor as she held the regenerator near the wound. "Since you are from offplanet, I assume you were the ones who brought in the vaccines that are supposed to get rid of the plague."

Lenore couldn't help a large twitch, and the pain that shot down her arm brought tears to her eyes.

"How do you know about that?"

"Well, I was in the room when the call came to organize assistants for the researcher. Bondly, I think?"

"Bondle," said Allison.

"Right." She changed her grip on the medical instrument. "When a planet goes through a crisis like a decades-long plague, they tend to grow closer. And something like a possible cure is sure to make gossip rounds fairly quickly. If it does work, Bondle will be hailed as a hero and savior of this system." She packed away the regenerator and tossed the bandage in a disintegrator. "As would the people who fought to get him here."

The doctor was leaning against a cabinet, but Lenore wouldn't meet her gaze. She was determined not to give away any more information than she already had. Searching for a change of subject, she patted the bed.

"Our medbed came with the ship so it's over forty years old. What are this one's capabilities?"

"It can diagnose faster than any earlier medbed design and perform a wide variety of functions. All the way from sealing a wound to minor surgeries." Dr. Dena's tone was full of pride.

"Surgery? How complicated can it get?" asked Lenore.

"Well, it can perform simple operations like an appendectomy or repairing a slight tear in a damaged organ. It can't perform heart surgery or any kind of serious alterations in the body. And it can't diagnose anything that isn't in its program. It's not up to the artificial intelligence level yet." She grinned. "I guess there will always be a need for us doctors."

"How much to purchase one like this?"

"Probably as expensive as your ship. Well, I don't know about your ship, but I do know that offworld sales of these beds account for all of our current research revenue."

"Maybe I should buy a regenerator instead," said Lenore with a light laugh.

"Maybe you should." Dr Dena tapped a few keys on the control board. "Fifteen more minutes. Pain tolerable?"

"Yes."

The device attached to the lab coat gave a soft chirp.

"Excuse me, Chief?"

"Go ahead."

"You are needed in five two three stat."

"On my way." Dr Dena turned back to Lenore and Allison. "Excuse me for a moment. I will be back shortly." She shook a finger. "Don't move that arm."

After she left, Allison turned to her mother. "Chief?"

"Apparently we warrant more than simply a doctor." Lenore made light of it but her tightening gut wasn't only due to pain. Why were they being given such special treatment? Bondle was the important figure here. They just delivered the cargo. Granted it was very important cargo, but it still felt uncomfortable. And talk of being hailed as a hero was even more unnerving.

Chapter Forty-three

Diarmin and Quinn had finished the patch job of the breach on the outside and were moving everything back to its place in the cargo bay.

"It's a good thing the other cabin doors were closed or all of your little inventions might have been sucked into space," said Quinn as he dropped another box of items on the workbench.

"Closed doors will be standard procedure from now on, I think," said Diarmin. "Maybe installing a few automatic bulkheads as well."

Both turned at footsteps on the ramp and saw Lenore and Allison.

"Why do you still have that on your arm?" asked Quinn. "I thought they were going to fix it."

"Apparently newly healed bones are fragile and will take twenty-four hours to set fully," said Lenore.

"That's better than six weeks," said Diarmin.

"Absolutely." Lenore hit the button to close the ramp. "How are the repairs going? Is the ship space worthy?"

"Barely. The admiral returned shortly after and offered us use of a ship repair facility up at the station. I was only waiting for you to get back to head up there." Diarmin brushed the dust of his equipment off his hands and held up a small metal globe that began to hum.

At Lenore's raised eyebrow, he explained. "It's a scanner for any plague particles. If any are found, this little wonder device will activate a sterilization field."

After only a minute, the globe gave a pleasant chirp and the red light turned green.

"All clear," said Diarmin. He turned off the personal force field and started for the bridge.

The rest of the family followed, the ladders only slightly awkward for Lenore. As they took their seats, Lenore spoke as she readjusted her board. "Maybe we should leave and repair the ship somewhere else."

"I was thinking the same thing but there are two problems with that," said Diarmin. "First, I wouldn't trust that patch job to hold up through transwarp transitions. Second," he pointed at Quinn, "our son pointed out that we didn't get paid yet." He grinned so nobody would think he was criticizing.

"I think we should consider leaving anyway."

Three heads swiveled to look at Lenore whose eyes were firmly on her console, as if she didn't want to face her family.

"You think it's still dangerous?" asked Allison.

Now she looked up. "Possibly."

"I think we have at least a short window," said Diarmin. "Let's get up to the station and get the ship fixed as soon as possible." He started inputting commands. "We will contact Bondle or whoever to get our money while I am fixing it."

Lenore looked back down and nodded.

It took only a few moments to get clearance to lift off and soon they were headed toward the coordinates for the correct berth on the station. As they approached, Diarmin noticed several official looking ships going in and out of the bay that he was supposed to land at. He double-checked the directions, saw they were correct, so opened a channel.

"Welcome," said the pleasant voice over the comm. "Admiral Frisson told us to expect you. Is all of your crew aboard?"

"Yes," said Diarmin, hesitating at the question, fingers hovering over the keyboard just in case something wasn't quite right.

"Since you were on the planet, you must take your ship through decontamination. The portal to your left is the decon chamber. If you bring your vessel into the bay through that, it will suffice. As long as nobody on board is isolated or in a spacesuit."

"Acknowledged," said Diarmin and flew the ship toward the portal irising open. It was large enough for ships three times the size of their yacht. As he entered, a red light pulsed in front and he stopped the forward movement. The door closed behind them and Diarmin heard the slight intake of breath from Lenore.

"Is this okay?" asked Quinn. "Do I need to close my eyes or anything?"

"Mom and I did this already," said Allison, with a little smug smile at Quinn. "We are fine."

Lenore hid a smile. Being the youngest, Allison didn't get the chance very often to experience something before Quinn. She patted her son on the shoulder. "I'm sure a planet that has been dealing with plague for so long has developed a completely safe procedure," she said. "They would have warned us if we needed to do anything."

A soft glow lit the viewscreen. A warm yellow light filled the chamber and somehow made it through the ship and was gone in less than a minute. The red light in front changed to green and an opening opposite of the one they had come through opened.

Diarmin continued through it and was surprised at the size of the bay. It must take up more than half of the station and was filled with ships and shuttles, all with the military markings.

"This must be the main hub for their sentry fleet," said Quinn. "Is that good or bad?"

"It seems to me that Admiral Frisson is not taking any chances," said Diarmin, more to Lenore than to Quinn. "I have a suspicion that he has already thoroughly checked out and approved the rest of the personnel so there won't be a repeat of hijacked ships."

Lenore said nothing so Diarmin concentrated on landing the ship where directed. It was a scaffolding, set up to accommodate their ship's frame perfectly. Men were standing behind it, evidently trusting the landing skills and the sturdiness of the frame which had to have been put together within the past hour. So not only was this large bay designed to repair ships, it was completely pressurized. This planet definitely had resources.

As Diarmin powered down the ship, a bleep indicated a message. Figuring it was the man in charge of the bay, Diarmin put it on the viewscreen.

"Ah, hello! Good to see you all again." Ven Bondle was standing in what looked like a laboratory, the admiral next to him. Everybody barely got a quick 'hello' back before he kept right on talking. "I tried to get in touch with you before you took off, but I wasn't in time. Then Uncle

Dom, um, er, Admiral Frisson, said I should wait until you docked so as not to distract you.”

Diarmin heard a chuckle from one of his children but their faces remained polite.

“I wanted to tell you that eighty-one percent of the samples were still viable and the ones I have already purposed are showing signs of fighting the disease. Another couple of hours will confirm it, but I wanted you to know that this medicine is a success. We will soon be rid of this plague forever.” The man’s face was pink with excitement and the smile on his face was the widest they had ever seen on him. “I have told everyone the brave story of how you rescued me and went after the pirates. If it weren’t for you, this success wouldn’t have been possible. All of your heroic efforts have paid off!”

“And speaking of paid,” the admiral broke in, patting Bondle on the arm as if he were calming down a child, “I have the rest of your payment here.” He held up a flimsy. “Plus a small bonus, for your ‘heroic efforts.’” He smiled at Bondle. “In addition, my personal repair crew will assist you in getting your ship back to top condition.”

“Admiral, that won’t be nece—” Lenore began.

“Nonsense. You are all heroes and we are happy to do this free of charge.” The admiral tipped his head. “And I said it was my personal, *extremely trustworthy* repair crew.”

As Diarmin had thought, Frisson was determined not to have another incident.

“Thank you, Admiral,” said Lenore. “We would still like to have someone from our crew supervising.”

“I wouldn’t have expected anything less. Crew Chief Savoh will help with anything you need. I will be there soon with your payment.”

Bondle waved enthusiastically as the admiral signed off.

“A bonus?” said Quinn. “Well, that’s a first.”

***

The crew chief proved to be extremely intelligent and proficient. He had already walked around the ship and saw the external damage so by the time they disembarked to meet him, he knew where to start.

"Also, this is Lieutenant Griffiths," said Chief Savoh, indicating a woman behind him. "If any of your crew wishes to visit the station, she will be happy to show you around."

Lenore eyed the woman. With a blaster on her hip, the well-muscled woman gave a salute and Lenore knew she was more bodyguard than tour guide.

"Thank you, Chief, but we will probably stay aboard the ship," she said.

"Very well. Let's get started."

Despite the whirlwind of activity, Lenore started to yawn less than an hour into the repairs.

"Surely this isn't boring," said Diarmin when he stopped briefly for a drink.

"No. The doctor said part of the healing would be extreme fatigue and the meds are wearing off." She gave a weak smile to Diarmin. "No more stimulants or painkillers and my arm aches abominably. Could be worse though."

"Why don't you take a nap? This will take several hours anyway."

"I should help you supervise. There's so much going on, I won't be able to sleep anyway."

"Then just rest for a short while, maybe take another painkiller. I've got things covered here and I can tell the kids what to watch out for."

Lenore was about to protest further but another giant yawn decided her.

"You win. Just for a little bit."

***

Lenore had only intended to relax for a short while, but her body had other ideas. When she awoke, she noticed the pain in her arm was considerably less and her head was clearer than it had been since her concussion. A glance at the chronometer showed she'd been asleep for nearly six hours. She swung her feet to the floor and the stiffness told her that she hadn't moved at all. Reluctantly she admitted to herself that she had really needed the sleep.

She changed out of her shipsuit that she had worn for days, promised herself a good shower when the cast was off, and dressed in a short-sleeved shirt and comfortable slacks. Pulling her hair back into a ponytail was impossible with one hand so she gave it a couple swipes with a brush. She opened the cabin door, smiling at the hand-made 'Do Not Disturb' sign on the door. Sometimes she felt her family coddled her too much, but she appreciated the rest. As she stepped into the lounge, her mouth fell open in surprise at the change.

"Mom! You're awake." Allison came bounding over, all smiles. "Wait until you see the ship. First, we got all new food. Good stuff, too, not those hoity-toity meals from our last, um resupply." As there was a young uniformed man stocking shelves in the galley, Lenore understood Allison's careful wording.

"It's so clean," said Lenore.

"Yeah, they sent a cleaning crew right after they finished patching the hull. I don't think our ship has ever been cleaner."

"The admiral insists on an immaculate ship so that's our standard," said the young man with a grin. He had finished stocking and was wheeling a cart out the door. "Have a good day, ladies."

"Are the repairs finished?" she asked Allison and turned to follow the young man out to check on that progress but Diarmin came through the door, Quinn on his heels.

"They are putting the final touches on everything and shouldn't be long now. Why don't we all get a quick snack while we fill in the sleepyhead on what has happened." His relaxed, cheerful demeanor was nice to see but Lenore was still nervous.

She was about to protest that they needed to oversee everything so they could leave as soon as possible, but her stomach rumbled loudly.

"I guess the ship is restocked so I should replenish my own resources," she joked.

"You guys sit. Alli and I will whip something up," said Quinn.

"Okay where do I start?" said Diarmin.

"The repairs. Are we space worthy yet and did they do as good a job as the cleaning crew?"

"Not only are we space worthy again, but they restocked our weapons with the latest concussion missiles. Their yield-to-weight ratio is improved significantly so we now have double the complement of missiles."

"Isn't that expensive?"

"Probably, but it didn't cost us a thing."

"Nothing is too good for the heroes of Reese," said Allison as she slid a plate in front of Lenore. Quinn put one in front of Diarmin and seated himself.

Lenore took several bites of the little savory pockets while trying to process that comment. "The doctor said that if Bondle was successful, he would be hailed as the savior of Reese."

"And that those who 'fought to get him here' are now heroes," added Quinn. "We have been receiving gifts from so many grateful families all day. The medicines are so effective that plague victims that were almost... gone, are more than halfway to a full recovery. We have trinkets of every size, games, programs and even some foods that are specially packaged and marked 'guaranteed plague-free'. And one company sent us a note that over half their employees had been cured so they all chipped in to donate their primary product: brand-new, top-of-the-line space suits." His grin was one of the biggest Lenore had ever seen.

Lenore looked around. "Where are the gifts?"

"In the first guest bedroom," said Diarmin. "But that will soon overflow to the second soon if they keep coming."

"But it can't go to the third," said Allison with a sly smile.

"Yeah," said Quinn, his grin the widest Lenore had ever seen.

"What?" she asked warily.

"Can we show her, Dad?" asked Allison, bouncing in her chair.

"Of course, let's go."

Allison popped up and headed toward the guest rooms. She waited anxiously in the doorway just long enough for everyone to start to follow. As Lenore rounded the corner, she saw Allison waiting outside with the door open. She grandly gestured inside as if she were entirely responsible for what was in there. Lenore's suspicions were raised but nothing prepared her for the sight as she stood in the doorway.

Taking up half of the room was one of the state-of-the-art medbeds.

"But...how...when...who?" Lenore couldn't form the words, but her family took turns explaining.

Allison started. "The doctor who helped you, who is the Chief Surgeon by the way, said she knew our ship's medical facilities were outdated and that this gift is a drop in the bucket compared to what we did for the planet."

Quinn took over as if they had rehearsed. "There wasn't room where the old bed is, so they redesigned this room as a mini medical bay. Take a look in the cabinets." He squeezed by and opened the first of a set along the far wall. He pulled out several small handheld medical devices and the cabinet over the bed held a bone-knitter exactly like the one they had used on her.

"She left a complete set of instructions and informed us, with a knowing look I might add, that you can control the bed through the ship's main computer or keep it as a separate entity with its own power source and everything." Diarmin smiled. "With the cover down, it can even double as a life pod and keep someone safe and alive even if the ship is holed again."

"This is too much," she said.

"But that's not all," said Allison. "Tell her, Dad."

"Well, this is something that you probably won't like." He took a deep breath. "As soon as repairs are complete, they want us to be a part of the festivities that are honoring Bondle and his wonderful discovery."

"And what does that entail?"

"An official presentation of an award, making us honorary citizens of Reese. Televised throughout the entire system." It was obvious Diarmin was steeling himself for Lenore's reaction.

He was right to.

"Absolutely not. That kind of publicity is something we have to avoid."

"That's what we thought you'd say, but while you were sleeping, the security around this bay has been the finest I have ever seen," said Diarmin.

"And the admiral assured us of our absolute safety. And the reason he waited for the repairs to be complete is so we can leave as soon as it is over," said Quinn. "He suspects something other than pirates but is too polite to say anything."

Very perceptive, like the doctor, thought Lenore. She looked around at the bay and her family. She could tell they really wanted this. And she so wanted to give it to them. They deserved the good side of all the hard work they had put in. Despite that, she was about to refuse again until an idea began to form in the back of her mind. It would take some planning, but she could use the broadcast to get some important information.

"As long as we leave immediately after the broadcast, we can do it," she said then had to silence her children's cheers. "But." She looked at each one in turn for a long moment. "This will only happen if one condition is met."

"What is that?" asked Diarmin.

"That we take a page from our last mission to keep us all safe." They all looked confused for only a moment. Then the memories of the mission with the missing princess caught up to them and they smiled knowingly. This was her clever family.

"Let's call the admiral to set it up. Our way."

Chapter Forty-four

Admiral Frisson politely rapped on the hatch. Diarmin opened it with the rest of his family arrayed behind him.

"It's time," said the admiral. It had only been an hour since they had contacted him with their requests for how they would do the broadcast, but they were ready.

Lenore had one last item, however.

"The security sweeps?"

"Completely clear," the admiral said with a touch of his hat. "I attended to the details myself."

Lenore nodded and they followed the admiral out the side hatch, down the scaffolding and into the waiting shuttle. Within minutes they were in another part of the station and could see Ven Bondle on a simple stage with a podium. After greeting Bondle, they all took seats on the stage. The admiral stepped up to the podium and lights came up.

In front of them was an audience of thousands. Diarmin leaned to whisper in Lenore's ear. "It must be the entire population of the station."

"And perhaps a few citizens who could get a flight up here. But notice the first five rows."

Diarmin had noticed the sea of military uniforms. Someone would have to wade through a lot of military to get at those on stage.

"This is an historic occasion," Admiral Frisson said into the microphone as a spotlight illuminated him only slightly more than the rest of the stage. "The plague's hold on our planet is finally over!"

The applause was thunderous and Diarmin noticed cameras everywhere, most likely transmitting to the entire planet. He tried not to squirm and a glance at Lenore and his children showed a similar lack of comfort.

"Senior Researcher Ven Bondle is responsible not only for the discovery of the organism that will heal our people, but also for creating the perfect treatment to prevent a recurrence as well as another medical marvel to sell." More applause as Bondle gave a shy wave.

"The others on stage are those responsible for bringing this precious medicine to us. They went above and beyond their duties when they retrieved the stolen cargo from pirates and asked for nothing more than transport fee. And the most amazing part is that they are not from Reese, simply good people who are willing to help others." He was silent for more cheers and had to hold his hands up for silence. "This is why we are giving this award to them on the station and not the planet. They may know there is a cure to our plague, but that's no reason to risk coming down with it." Scattered laughter. "And now we will present the awards. First, Ven Bondle."

The applause went on for far too long and Bondle turned beet red as he approached the microphone. A glance at Lenore showed her scanning the audience and Diarmin knew she was watching for some type of attack. As Bondle gave his short speech, Lenore looked at her timepiece then at the admiral. He nodded and was ready as Bondle wound down. Admiral Frisson gave the scientist a wooden plaque with a shiny metal plate on the front.

"You are the savior of our planet. And are in charge of bringing this new drug to market. Or you can retire, the choice is yours."

"Admiral, I won't stop until all our people are free of the plague."

More applause and quite a few yells and catcalls including, as the clapping eased off, one woman asking Bondle if he'd marry her. The admiral again motioned for silence.

"And now we present to the heroic crew, an award that grants all of them honorary citizenship in the entire Reese system."

Yells of 'Speech!' reverberated through the crowd as the admiral handed a plaque to each of them. Lenore, with a significant look at Diarmin, approached the microphone. Her eyes wandered around again and she seemed to be considering what to say as she idly scratched at a spot near her left shoulder.

"Honored people of Reese. I am pleased that my crew and I could do th—" She hesitated only a second and then yelled, "Down!"

Lenore ducked under the podium and Diarmin threw himself on top of Quinn and Allison, the admiral doing likewise with Bondle. A large cylinder hit the stage and a large cloud of smoke caused screams to erupt. Diarmin saw chaos reign briefly until all went silent.

The holographic image of the theater snapped off and the six were left on a silent stage in an empty hangar bay.

They quickly picked themselves up and ran for the door they had come in. They had pretended to enter a shuttle, but instead had gone in one side and out the other to the fake stage. That stage was then holographically projected elsewhere on the station. A trick that they had seen during the duel between a princess and prince.

At the base of the scaffolding, they paused. The admiral spoke first.

"I apologize, Captain. You were right to worry. I thought those pirates would be long gone by now."

"I hope the people in the audience are all right, but I think it was just a very large stun grenade."

"I will check on them after you are safely aboard and Bondle is secure. They were prepared and know what to do. They may even catch the perpetrators."

"I doubt that," said Lenore.

"My officers are very capable."

"Yes, they are, and you have been phenomenal." Lenore appeared undecided for only a heartbeat before she continued. "Admiral, I have never told anyone outside my family what I am about to tell you, but you have earned our trust." She leaned forward to whisper in his ear. Diarmin could see Frisson's eyes grow wide but when Lenore was done, he held out his hand.

"It's has been my honor. Our entire planet owes you its life. We will always be at your service."

Lenore shook his hand and everyone else did in turn. They headed up the ladder as the admiral had a few final words.

"You have permission to leave as soon as you are ready. I will let the tower know. Good luck." He disappeared into the doorway with Bondle in tow as Diarmin closed and sealed the hatch.

Everyone was on the bridge and secured in less than a minute. Diarmin had already done all the preflight so he immediately engaged the antigrav. Lenore didn't bother to send a transmission to the tower since they had discussed beforehand that they had a slim window to get off the station and into transspace if anything happened.

They left the station's protective field and were out into space.

"All systems working perfectly," said Quinn.

"Good. Input this nav plan," said Diarmin as he handed a pad to his son.

"No, Diarmin," said Lenore. "Use this one." She handed her own personal pad to him to pass along to Quinn.

Diarmin glanced at the pad, then paused in handing it over. "What's this?"

"There is something I need to take care of first. I'll explain when we are out of here," she said, indicating him to continue.

Quinn gave both parents an odd look but input Lenore's coordinates.

"Ready," he said.

As soon as they were clear of the station and planet's gravity, Diarmin fired up the engines and headed into transwarp.

"Only ten minutes from the stage to now," said Allison. "We are good."

"Yes, we are," said Lenore. "And we will have to be even better from here on out."

That sobered everyone and the silence was awkward. Quinn broke it first.

"What did you say to the admiral?"

Lenore locked down her board then looked directly at her son. Then to Allison, then Diarmin. Her gaze returned to Quinn. "I said, 'Watch yourself carefully. Those weren't pirates, they were Xa'ti'al.'"

"But—" started Quinn but stopped as Lenore held up her hand.

"Hang on to that thought." She turned her head to Diarmin. "Please get and activate your best privacy device. We need that now."

"Why not yours? It is the highest quality," he said as he unbuckled to go retrieve the device from the cargo bay.

Lenore shook her head. "Not this time." She unbuckled herself as well and motioned to the children. "We will all meet you in the lounge."

As Diarmin headed down the ladder, he could hear Allison's voice.

"Mom, what is going on?"

"Into the lounge, Alli, Quinn. I will catch you up."

Catch them up? On what? Diarmin hurried to the workbenches now back to their regular place. He punched in the code of a locked drawer and pulled out his device that would let them speak freely without any chance of being overheard. *Why use this now, after all the eavesdropping devices have been discovered? Well, the sooner I get to the lounge, the sooner Lenore will reveal what is on her mind.*

As he entered the lounge, he heard his wife's voice.

"When Kurla spoke of my medplant being gone, I wondered how she could possibly know that since the only people, well, alive people, are you guys. So..."

As she trailed off, Diarmin finished for her. "Then your mother destroyed the medplant, point blank with her blaster." He mimed her action and the kids' heads turned to look at him.

"They were tracking you?" asked Quinn.

Lenore nodded. "It's the best explanation for how they were always one step ahead of me."

"But if they can track your medplant after it was removed," said Allison, her face thoughtful, "what about your hearing and subvocal implants?"

Lenore nodded again, her face grim. "My thoughts, exactly. So here is what we are going to do. Quinn, scan every inch of this ship for a tracking device. We were meant to find the ones Kurla planted, but she very well could have planted others."

"I examined the entire outside when it was being worked on," said Diarmin. "And double checked that leak. It was expertly done, sabotage not to destroy but just enough to cause us to drop out of transspace."

Lenore nodded as she noticed the kids' wide eyes. "As was the plan."

"And while he is checking the inside, Diarmin, you are going to assemble a drone to fly to predetermined coordinates. Alli, you will help him program it after you assist me."

"Assist you with what?"

"With programming the new medbed to perform surgery on me."

Chapter 45

Lenore sat in the command chair on the bridge, willing the energy shot to work a little faster to clear away the post-surgery drowsiness. *I've been using too many of those lately. Another side effect of losing the medplant. I won't need them after today, but right now I need to be fully alert.*

"How long until we reach those coordinates, Quinn?"

"Five minutes," he said.

"Are you going to tell us what to expect?" asked Diarmin, who was sitting in her usual seat at the science console.

"And why you picked this spot in particular?" added Allison.

"I am expecting one of three things. The first is nothing will happen, though I don't really think that will be the case. Second, there will be a ship arriving within a few minutes after we do, and they will be prepared to communicate. Third," and she took a slow breath, "that ship will arrive and attack immediately."

Lenore saw everyone tense at that and hastened to reassure them. "We are going to be completely prepared, but I truly believe it will be the second scenario. You might be wondering why I agreed to the award presentation since, even with our careful deception, normally I wouldn't. But, as I was preparing to speak, I gave the Xa'ti'al a sign."

"That weird scratch?" asked Quinn. "It looked like your fingers were crossed. I thought it was kind of odd."

"That was part of it. It's too complicated to explain now but the sign said, 'Meet at my beginning.' If they were watching, which I am convinced they were, they will show up to talk."

Lenore glanced back at her husband. He appeared calmer than she thought he would be. She continued with the explanation. "Now 'beginning' could be taken in several ways. It could mean where I was first recruited into the Xa'ti'al or where I was born, or even my first official mission."

"Which one of those is this planet?" asked Allison.

Lenore gave all three a significant look before she answered.

"None."

Everyone was silent as they considered that. Lenore began transferring pilot control to the science station. Finally, Diarmin spoke.

"You want to see if he is tracking you," he said.

Lenore nodded. Quinn leaned forward, a confused look on his face.

"But why would he tip his hand by coming to a nondescript planet? Wouldn't that show you that he was tracking you instead of going to one of those other places?"

"First of all, the sign said '*my* beginning' which means where I was born. If it had been where I was recruited it would have been 'our' instead of 'my', meaning where I met my mentor." Lenore paused as their eyes goggled at that. She didn't have time for the entire back story now. "And 'the' for my first mission. Thus, they would know I was talking about where I was born. Now my official record says I was born on Gravidon, but I had those altered before I ever met the Xa so it is not my birthplace. I am sure they know those records are false."

"Where were you born?" asked Allison.

"I don't know. I never found out." She ignored Quinn's odd look, was it of sadness? Pity? "But if he comes here, I will act as if this is it and, well, you'll see." Lenore took another breath and she felt the energy meds kicking in fully. "I transferred the pilot controls to your board, Diarmin. We will need you flying the ship, but I need to be in the command chair for this."

"Sixty seconds," said Quinn.

"Alli, raise shields as soon as possible after we come out of transwarp. I don't think the ship will be there yet, but I want to be prepared."

Allison nodded and turned to her board.

As the seconds ticked down, Lenore reached into her shipsuit pocket and pulled out the two tiny implants that she had carried in her body for more than two-thirds of her life. Closing her fist over them, she shoved them back into her pocket and focused on the mission.

"Coming out of transspace in five... four... three... two... and..."

Stars appeared on the screen, one significantly brighter than any others, the sun of this system. Diarmin rotated the ship to see the nearest planet.

"Confirming location," said Quinn. "Kitrun system. We are looking at the fifth planet."

"Diarmin, move us behind its primary moon," said Lenore. She toggled the communication switch. "This is Lenore Kelton requesting an open channel to the Xa'ti'al ship in this system." She punched in the broadcast code, using the Xa's special encryption so others on the planet couldn't read the signal.

They waited for an answer. Nothing.

"Shields are up," said Allison.

"Scans reveal ships around the fourth planet, the usual amount for a settled world," added Quinn.

"Weapons ready," said Diarmin. Lenore realized that was the first time he had spoken since he knew what she was up to. She looked at him to see if he disapproved but his face was blank.

Lenore put the hail on auto replay.

Silence descended on the bridge, broken only by Allison's tapping fingers.

"How long do we wait?" Quinn asked.

"It's only been three minutes. I will give it up to thirty, but I don't think we will need more than ten."

"A ship is dropping out of transwarp somewhere on the other side of that moon," said Quinn, anxiety making his voice louder than necessary.

"Will we have line of sight?" asked Lenore.

"Negative. Looks like it is putting the moon between our ships."

Lenore smiled. It was Daviss. She sent the message one more time, adding a request for visual. It was received instantly.

"Follow my lead everyone. Opening a channel." She tapped the appropriate keys and Daviss's face appeared on the viewscreen. The background was indistinct, and she knew that Daviss had a similar view of only her face.

"Hello, Daviss. I knew you would understand my message, just like I knew you would already have knowledge of my true birth planet."

Daviss's signature smile was firmly in place. "You know we have our ways to get information." He tilted his head. "Does this mean you are coming home?"

"Of course not." Lenore leaned forward. "Kurla told me of her mission. How you were testing me and my family."

Daviss grimaced. Again, the emotion was perfect. Lenore had no way to tell if he was truly annoyed or acting. But she would get it out of him. Today.

"That may be, but it was still no reason to kill her and the others," he replied.

Out of the corner of her eye, she saw Quinn jerk in his chair, but he managed to keep quiet.

"Stop trying to rattle me, Daviss," she said. "You know that's not how I do things. She was perfectly fine last time I saw her."

Daviss's eyes widened an infinitesimal amount, but Lenore caught it. *Damn, he is good.* She almost believed he was surprised.

"Well," said Daviss. "That will take some looking into." His right shoulder moved, indicating a gesture that was out of her line of sight.

He let me see that. He really wants me to think Kurla is dead.

A buzz by her left hand caused Lenore to glance down at her personal pad. Quinn had sent her a private message. There was another ship separating from the first.

"This is your last chance, Lenore. Rejoin the Xa'ti'al."

"Why would I come back after all you have done to me? Before and after? Rejoin a group that sterilizes their agents and experiments on families?"

"The Xa'ti'al wanted to kill you. The test was the only way I could convince them to keep you and your family alive." Now his face showed earnestness.

Lenore laughed. "There is no way you will convince me that you give a damn about whether I live or die, Daviss."

"You are more important than you realize." Daviss leaned forward as if in mimicry to Lenore's pose. "They are done with you now, though. The order has come down to kill you. Please, this is your last chance."

Lenore leaned back, noticing out of the corner of her eye that Quinn was making a small circular motion with his finger. That ship was circling to move behind them. They were running out of time.

Without taking her eyes from Daviss, she typed a note to Diarmin on her pad. "Then pass along this offer to whoever is making these ridiculous decisions. I will stand down with my investigations of the Xa'ti'al's illegal activities, such as the Beryshie Corporation, and you will leave us in peace. We will disappear and have nothing to do with each other from this day forward."

"They will never bargain, you know that," said Daviss. Lenore noticed his eyes flick to the side as if reading a message on his own board. "And they will never stop hunting for you. You can't hide from us forever. There are many of us and only one of you, Lenore."

"Wrong, Daviss. There are four of us. We are better together than any hundred of the Xa. And you just made a terrible mistake by threatening this family."

Lenore closed the communication and signaled to Diarmin to finish the command she had typed to him.

"Get us out of here. I've learned all I need to."

Epilogue

"Is the drone ready?" Lenore asked her husband. They had made two preprogrammed jumps in the past thirty minutes and were preparing to exit transspace and do their third and most important one.

"Yes. Course programmed in." He held out the pod and Lenore fished in her pocket once more. As she pulled out her former implants, she looked at her family's concerned faces.

"Are you sure this will work, Mom?" asked Allison.

"We know he was tracking me. The easiest assumption is by these things. And those." Lenore held out her hand for the bag that Quinn was holding. It contained every item she had ever been given by the Xa'ti'al, all the secret devices and tools that made her an agent.

She tossed them into the pod, one by one. The grapple, the tiny EMP device, the holdout blaster. The specialized gloves were the last item she pulled from the bag. Lenore handed the bag to Quinn and turned the gloves over and over in her hands. They, along with all the rest, had been a part of her for so long that she felt a little hollower, almost incomplete, without them. But as she put the gloves into the drone, she realized that hollower also meant lighter.

"I know I need to get rid of all this, but I will admit, I will miss some of the more useful stuff," she said as she closed the pod on the final remnants of the Xa'ti'al. The physical remnants.

"Not as much as I will," said Diarmin. "I'm the one who has to make the replacements."

Everyone chuckled but sobered as Diarmin placed the drone into a launch tube.

"So," said Quinn. "The idea is that they will track this drone instead of us, and we will finally be able to drop out of sight."

"That's right. Alli's found the perfect job while the ship is undergoing upgrades," said Lenore.

"And we won't have to worry about the Xa trying to kill us," said Allison.

Lenore glanced at Diarmin and saw him glancing back at her.

"What?" asked Quinn. He sighed loudly. "I've said it before, and I will say it again. You know we notice it every time you guys give each other significant looks like that."

Allison nodded vigorously in agreement.

"I didn't explain everything to you. That last conversation with Daviss told me that they are not done with testing. Now they want to pursue us even harder and farther."

"How do you know that?" asked Allison, but Lenore could see Quinn was trying to figure it out on his own.

"They showed up at that planet which is surefire proof that they are tracking me." Both looked impatient at her summary, but she ignored it. "But if they could track me all along, they would have known that we were not really in that room for the awards ceremony. They staged that attack as much as we staged the deception. I do know that Daviss will no longer ask me to return. As soon as they catch up with the drone, they will know that I am on to them and their games. But for now, we have a respite."

"And the downtime will give us time to tell you guys everything about your mother and me," said Diarmin.

And also, thought Lenore, *time to plan how to get rid of the Xa'ti'al threat permanently.*

THE END

Acknowledgments

As with any book, there are so many people to thank; friends and family who have supported me from day one, those that enthusiastically congratulated me on the first book even if they hadn't known me all that long, and yet others who may not read much but believed in me enough to encourage me when I falter.

But most of all I would like to thank my beta readers and editors. Shonna Slayton, who is the strictest editor, will tell me things I may not want to hear but are sorely needed for improvement. She has also given me plenty of publishing advice, even when I have emailed her three times in one day. My mother, Sandra and my newest betareader/editor Jennifer all caught typos and general wording mistakes that a writer tends to overlook on their tenth time through.

Thank you goes to Christian who designed the gorgeous cover. You can find his work at coversbychristian dot com.

And a final 'thank you' for those who told me you liked book one of the Kelton series, giving me the ego boost needed to write another one.

About the Author

K. A. Bledsoe's writing journey began at the age of six with a story about kids growing up on a space station. Even through other jobs like scooping ice cream, shoe salesman, pharmacy tech, band director and parenting, writing has been a constant.

The author currently resides in Arizona and continues to pen stories in all genres despite the distraction of two cats underfoot and the occasional bobcat or roadrunner strolling through the back yard.

Here is a sneak peek at the first chapter of K. A. Bledsoe's new novella, a companion tale to "The Lost Princess" the first in *The Kelton Cases* series.

THE PRINCESS'S COMPANION

The Princess's Companion

The two girls giggled as they turned the corner, hand in hand.

"Look! There goes another." The one in the lead pointed at the ship rising in the distance. The drive kicked in and it shot into the sky and out of sight in moments.

"We're almost there," said the other. Her brown eyes, straight long black hair and aquiline nose resembled the other closely enough to be a sister. "Another couple of blocks and we'll finally see the spaceport!"

"A true adventure!" They locked eyes and giggled again as they continued down the street, unaware that another pair of eyes was watching them.

The next street over was not as welcoming. The girl in the lead was oblivious to the hostile stares but her companion took notice of the poorer surroundings. She let herself be led, but her eyes roved everywhere. Her other hand had slipped beneath her coat to reassure herself that the knife was still easily accessible.

"Damn." The two girls pulled up sharply at the blocked street. "How do we get through?"

"I thought you had this all planned out, Maya."

"I did, Lara, but I can't remember everything. Gimme the map." They sat on the edge of the street while Lara removed her backpack and dug inside.

"Here." She said and handed a roll of paper to Maya. "I'm hungry. What do we have to eat?" She reached for Maya's backpack.

Maya snatched at the map and slapped Lara's hand away. "Silly. Don't you know anything? That food has to last a long time. What good is running away if you eat all your food in one day?"

"Of course, I forgot." Lara smiled while Maya studied the map. Every year right before her birthday, Maya "ran away", determined to have an adventure. Every year Lara went with her, a faithful companion since birth. On their first "runaway" at five years old, they spent the day in the fruit orchards, stuffing themselves. They were found three hours later sick with stomach cramps. When they were nine, they made it into town before they were discovered. At ten, they travelled in the opposite direction into the forest lands but were driven home by a fierce storm. Every year an adventure, it became tradition. This year, three days before her thirteenth birthday, they might finally get to see the spaceport before her parents found them. It was their best escape yet.

"Ah, I see." Maya thrust her finger at the map. "This road was supposed to be open but according to my data," she stood up and fiddled with her wristcomp. "It is now closed for some repairs to the sewers. Ew."

Lara packed away the map and stood beside her friend. "We could always take a cab." She hid her smile at the predictable outburst.

"Never! You know the rules! A real adventure means no cheating. Hey..." Maya frowned at her friend mouthing the mantra along with her. "Hmph. If you knew, why did you ask?"

Lara grinned. "Is there another route to the spaceport?"

"I can get you there."

Both girls gasped and whipped around to see a strange boy standing with his hands in his pockets. Lara's hand grasped the hilt of the hidden knife, but she refrained from pulling it. He looked to be about their age with the same dark coloration and features of a native of this planet. So far, he was making no hostile moves. She could tell Maya was instantly interested.

"You can? How?"

"My father is a baggage handler. He runs the computers that route all the stuff people carry onto the ships." He shrugged. "I can actually get you in the back, close to the touchdown fields, not through the front like a tourist."

"Why would you do that?" asked Lara, ignoring the dig in the ribs by her friend.

"I didn't say I would do it for free." His chin pointed to the backpacks. "Got anything interesting in there?" The girls clutched the bags a bit tighter and looked at each other.

"I'll give you ten credits," said Maya and Lara stifled a groan. The boy's eyebrows twitched slightly but he maintained a serious face. Lara looked closer at the boy's threadbare clothing and worn shoes. She could tell he didn't expect such a high offer, but he went with it. "Make it twenty."

Maya's chin went up and the spark behind her eyes became defiant at his counter. Lara pinched her, trying not to show this boy that Maya was unused to demands from others.

She whispered. "C'mon, Maya. Part of the adventure is the bargaining."

Maya gave her a grin and relaxed. "Twelve credits," she said to the boy.

"Eighteen."

"Fifteen. That's all I can afford."

"Done then." The boy held out his hand to shake. Maya took it while Lara's tightened on the hilt, but nothing happened.

"This way." The boy motioned and they headed down a small side street.

"What's your name?" asked Maya.

The boy looked at her as if surprised at the question. "Dhan."

"Hello Dhan, I'm-" Maya began but Lara tripped and bumped into her.

"Oh, sorry, Mitali." Maya's eyes widened at her comment, but Lara narrowed hers to remind her of their situation. Maya acknowledged the reminder with a rueful grin.

"That's okay, *Lisha*." She turned to Dhan. "We are Mitali and Lisha. It's nice meeting you."

The boy smiled. "If we hurry, we can make it before the next transport."

Dhan led them on a twisty route that crossed many streets, a few alleyways and even through a couple of buildings. Lara tried to keep track of their route but doubted she could retrace their steps when this was all over.

All over. Even though Maya might think this was truly running away to find an adventure, Lara knew it would end with a return home, back to their regular life. They were always found and sometimes Lara suspected that Maya's parents knew all about it and indulged their spirited daughter. But even Lara was excited that they had gotten so far and now they were going to see the spaceport from the inside. Worth all the planning and watching Maya more than usual.

But that was her duty, had been since being bonded when they were both two years old. Lara was extensively trained to safeguard Maya but along with that responsibility came privilege and education, not something she would have had in her regular life before she was chosen. But Maya was a joy to be with, making Lara's job as companion and bodyguard one she never regretted. They were sisters of the soul, closer than most blood siblings.

Maya stumbled and Lara caught her just before she hit the pavement.

"Careful, *Mitali*. Don't want to get any injuries." Lara leaned in to whisper. "Especially not when you are supposed to meet your future husband in three days."

Maya groaned and she let Dhan get a little further ahead. "Why do you think I am so anxious to run away? I don't want to be bonded to a strange old man."

"Old? He's a month older than we are. I am sure that your parents have picked a wonderful boy."

Maya looked away in disgust. "Yeah, whatever. He's still a stranger." She turned back to Lara, a smile twitching her mouth. "*Hm.* You play my double often enough, maybe you could with that too."

Lara took a swing at her best friend. "Stop it!" They both burst into laughter but Dhan hushed them.

"We're here," he said quietly.

They went through a wooden gate and the spaceport loomed in front of them. Well, the back of it anyway. Pictures they had seen showed the regular entrance with beautiful glass windows that stretched from floor to roof and flags of sister planets flying. Here instead were solid concrete walls with a few doors, one or two small windows up on the second and third levels, and even a couple of colossal garbage bins.

Dhan led them to a door slightly behind a wall. It was locked but he punched numbers into the code pad and it opened noiselessly.

"My dad gave me his code in case of emergency." He shot a grin back at the girls. "Fifteen credits seem like an emergency to me,"

Maya grinned back as Lara rolled her eyes, but all went through the door eagerly.

Twisting and turning again down corridors that seemed unused made Lara uncomfortable again. They passed nobody and her instincts started screaming a warning. Dhan glanced back and appeared to sense her discomfort.

"These halls are for the workers to come and go without being seen by the customers." His lips twisted and Lara felt the sting of the underprivileged. "There won't be a shift change for another couple of hours."

Well, that did explain the emptiness of the halls, but she only relaxed slightly. Maya ignored the entire conversation, eyes sparkling in anticipation of seeing the huge starships.

Dhan brought them to another coded door and then they were through. A pile of crates surrounded them, but they could see the sky above easily.

"Ok," whispered Dhan. "Be very quiet as there are cameras and sound pickups stationed throughout the platform but if you edge around this way..." The girls followed until they came to the end of the boxes. They couldn't hold back a gasp. There was the landing and take-off platform just like he promised. It was large enough to house several shuttles, four medium ships and one starliner.

"Beautiful," breathed Maya.

"That one looks like a cargo ship," said Lara. "Two small shuttles and what is that middle ship?"

"Private yacht," said Dhan.

Lara looked at him, eyebrows raised.

He shrugged. "Being around them all my life, I kinda got to know all the types."

"Look! The cargo ship is lifting slightly on its antigravs. Must be getting ready to launch," said Maya.

"Yep, it's moving toward the center of the platform." All Lara's tension was forgotten as she focused on the fascinating scene. All their eyes were riveted on the ship as the antigrav lifted straight up until clear enough to engage the drive.

"This is entirely worth it," said Maya.

"It's so majestic," replied Lara and Maya nodded in agreement. The flare of the drive caused the girls to squint and sigh in satisfaction.

"Ok, let's go," said Lara.

"No, let's watch another," answered Maya.

"We need to leave." Lara's voice dropped to a whisper. "Something is not right. Dhan has led us down a path I can't retrace, and he hasn't even asked you for the money."

"Oh, come on. He's just a kid."

"Call your parents. I'm telling you, this feels wrong somehow."

"What a smart little girl."

The two girls spun around at the male voice behind them. Lara reached for her knife but a blue beam enveloped them both and they dropped to the ground helpless. A man's face came into view to look down at them.

"I did good, didn't I, Borat?" said Dhan.

"You fool. Do you know who this is?" The man sounded angry and spoke into his wristcomp something about "immediate removal." Lara's fear rose several notches. She struggled uselessly against the paralyzing effect of the stun bolt.

"Two girls. It's what they want, isn't it?"

"These aren't just two girls. It's the Princess and her Companion."

***

Made in the USA
Columbia, SC
27 July 2023

20835822R00167